THE BEGINNING
OF HIS EXCELLENT
AND EVENTFUL CAREER

Cameron MacKenzie

MADHAT PRESS
ASHEVILLE, NORTH CAROLINA

MadHat Press
MadHat Incorporated
PO Box 8364, Asheville, NC 28814

The Library of Congress has assigned
this edition a Control Number of
2017963984

ISBN 978-1-941196-61-8 (paperback)

Text by Cameron MacKenzie
Cover image: Pancho Villa's Death Mask, National Museum
of Crime and Punishment, Washington DC, USA;
photograph by Karen Neoh
Cover design by Meredith Carty MacKenzie

www.madhat-press.com

First Printing

THE BEGINNING
OF HIS EXCELLENT
AND EVENTFUL CAREER

A special thanks to Tim Fitts, Marlene Adelstein, Marc Vincenz, Travis Ben Robinson, Steve Lento, Rob Schmitt, and to all of those who made this book possible with their skill, patience and encouragement.

For Dad

Table of Contents

I have no intention of even justifying myself nor defending myself. People should know me as I am and was, so that they can appreciate what I am.

—Francisco Villa to Manuel Bauche Alcalde, 1914

PART I
FREE FROM THE CREASES OF AGE

CHAPTER I

The Fields of Gogojito. For Romualdo Franco. Shooting the Don. A Lioness. Nixtamal. A Young Man's Birthday.

It began in this way, and those who would say otherwise blacken their own names alone. Anything that I am today I am from this moment. You want to hear how I came to be that which I now am, as though through this you will see the other thing. This is inconsequential. It is little more than fortune, and the will of the people. I am the instrument of another hand.

I am not the revolution. Madero is not the revolution, nor is Zapata. It was not for Díaz. It is not for Carranza. The revolution is merely the course of things, like the weather and the stars. Tonight the revolution is happening around us. It is the light of this fire and my horse at the tree. It is the bodies that lie on the field not a mile from this camp. I will tell you what it is.

In the summer of 1894 I lived on the Hacienda Gogojito in the municipality of Canatlán in Durango. I was not yet sixteen years old and I worked in the fields of Don Agustín López Negrete. I cut this man's wheat in the fields of his valley surrounded by the broken mountains which were not his. The summer sun scorches this place and sudden wind-driven rains

3

fall down from the slopes to soak the valley before breaking apart in the desert beyond.

I spent my days with the scythe in my hands. It ripped at the skin and tore off the flesh and I stripped lengths of cotton from the bottoms of my pants to wrap around my bleeding palms. In this way I worked through the grass that reached up to my chest in the haze.

My mother and my two sisters and I lived in a house of mud and bricks at the southwestern edge of the field. I returned home by way of the cattle-paths, their hard dirt yellowed by the sun. As I walked these paths on this day the wind moved before me across the face of the field, bending back the heads of grass and turning their green bellies to the low black clouds which threatened over us at this time.

Entering the house I found my sister Manuela clinging to my mother in the center of the kitchen. My mother stood tall in her (I see it vividly) green dress, her heavy hair up and off her shoulders. She held her chin high and kept her hands on Manuela as she moved behind my mother. Between myself and my mother and standing on the dirt floor in the middle of the house was Don Agustín López Negrete. He wore a suit of white linen, and he held his hat at his side. Down the face of my mother ran tears. She spoke firmly.

"Leave my house, Señor," she said to the Don. "Have you no shame?"

Slipping out the door I found myself running through the field threshed by the wind on paths known to my animal instinct alone, and in this time there were in my mind no thoughts. I was but a child, little more than an animal, a wildling with a father long dead, and the hole where he had been filled to its lips with an anger that was both dim and without words. And my sister Manuela but a child as well. In time I arrived at the door of my cousin, Romualdo Franco.

I pounded upon his door until his squat mother answered, her hair about her face like damp strings. I pushed past her into the room of my cousin where he sat on his bed, removing his shoes.

"My gun," I said.

Romualdo stood. "What has happened?"

"Give me my gun. Now."

"Why?" he asked. "What can I do?"

There are men of sober reflection for whom questions are of utmost importance. Such men would fashion an array of approaches and take delight in the composition of each, and in their perpetual fashioning they would find themselves tending the fields of other men. I pulled myself up to my full height in my cotton clothes and my bare feet and my bloody hands, and I knew that I must do this, indeed and in some way, for him.

"My cousin," I said, "our donkey is sick and must be put down. Please go fetch my pistol so that I may shoot him."

"A donkey?" Romualdo still did not move, his eyes as they were. "Doesn't your mother still have your father's rifle?"

"Our rifle," I told him, "is gone, and has been these many years. It was perhaps childish of me to hide my pistol here, but you see now that I am the man of our house. Please, Romualdo, be a good cousin and fetch me my pistol."

As I ran back through the fields my heart lay into my chest like a hammer. The gun hung heavy in my hand as the mountains rose up black and impossible and the path through the grass unwound and unwound in front of my feet. Stepping out into the yard I found Don Agustín's coach crouching like a bug at the edge of the field, surrounded by armed men. In that moment the Don stepped from the black of the doorway of the house, his white suit glowing like a hole in the day. I raised my arm and fired, striking him three times in the chest.

The Don staggered, and he dropped down into the dirt.

His wide-brimmed hat tumbled away across the yard. When he raised himself up on an elbow his call to his men was hoarse but controlled.

Wrapped in serapes with rifles in their hands they came running, their hats flapping in the wind of the storm that would build and build and would not break and their footfalls were the only sound as I stood from where I had fired and Don Agustín lay where he fell. Five rifle barrels lowered to me and I stood simply on wide feet, the pistol hot in my hand. To my right stood our house its doorway black and empty and behind it the fields and the stones of the mountains and the sky and so.

"Don't kill the boy," said Don Agustín. "Just carry me home."

Two of the men kept their guns on me while the others lifted the Don into the coach. His face was contorted in pain, his hands pale, his fingernails greasy in the light. The horses leapt in their leads and the coach went clattering up the road to the Hacienda Santa Isabel de Berros, a league from Gogojito.

The two men remaining did not kill me. They backed away from me as though I were fire, their eyes full of fear and lust over this thing that I had done. They mounted, and they rode out. And as I stood under the sky in the dirt of the yard with the fields shaking and riotous around me and everything else as it had been such as the doorway remaining open and remaining black like the socket of an eye which had been plucked and crushed and lost I came to know that I was free. With the gun in my waist I saddled and mounted my pony, and I rode for the Sierra de la Silla, opposite Gogojito.

My father died in the field that he worked, and no stone stands to mark that he was the natural son of Don Jesus Villa and born a bastard to a peasant woman in a house of earth and straw. Taking the name of his mother as his own, my father passed this name to me. And so to protect my family against further pursuit after the killing of Don Agustín, I chose to take the name of my father's father and it is a name I still carry. Indeed I consider it now my own. When I imagine in the eye of my mind this grandfather, he is a great man. He is a man of significant appetites and he is unrestrained, moving without check across the lands that once were his. These lands are now mine, insofar as I range over them with dominion. They may indeed be taken from me by the next and yet there is no next there is only I, this name forever mine, as I have remade myself of sterner stuff without shame or indignation. This is the natural course of things, and free from such shades as would be put on it by others.

From the moment I shot Don Agustín I was pursued. Crude sketches of my face dotted the marketplace of every district and so I was forced to ride into the sierra and to make it my home. It is a place free from the hand of man or the track of his animals. Water is scarce and the vegetation is scrub and thorns. Rising as it does from the desert in the north, the mountains open southward into ridges spreading like broken hands.

But in truth the sierra resembles nothing. If you fear it it will prove fearful, and if you hate it so then hateful and if you take it as safety and as succor then it may be these things as well. It was in these mountains that I wandered among the rocks as though wild and went without my reflection for half a year. In due time I shot and ate my horse. I ate cactus. I sucked water from the undersides of stones.

A lioness hunted me throughout the mountains for nearly a month. I felt her eyes on me in the day and her breath on my neck in the otherwise cold of the night as she judged my soul from the depth of her own which moved without language. Throughout the otherwise blankness of the days I would catch a glimpse of her shoulders moving over the rocks, her tail flipping in the shadows, her thighs swinging up the goat-paths, though no goat did I ever find in that place.

One night by the light of a fire I saw the green of her eyes hanging in the darkness beyond the ring of the flame. I walked to the edge of the black of the rest of the world and I asked her plainly what she could want of me, and to this I received no response. And neither did the eyes fade for as long as I watched throughout a sleepless and wind-driven night. With the dawn I came to understand the depth of her power, for where those eyes had been was a drop into faceless rock below.

Was I mad? There exists no gauge in that place for the mind required to awake each day and then into the next. I came down into the plain with the first snow, and I made for San Juan Del Rio. The empty pistol had long been useless but I was desirous of keeping it near me. Despite my wild appearance I was soon recognized by the people there and put in jail for the night, my execution scheduled for the morning next.

In the morning before shooting me, they took me out to grind a barrel of nixtamal. The guard stood by as I sat in the dirt of the yard in clothes the cleanest I had worn in a year. These were the garments given to prisoners who were all subsequently shot. Looking at my legs as they stretched before me on the dirt of the yard I studied the faded and innumerable streaks of the last life's blood of the executed as they intertwined in myriad shades.

"My friend," I said to the guard, a fat and lazy man with long mustaches. "How many innocent men have you seen wear these pants into that yard?"

The guard spat. "None." His hands moved about his rifle without purpose.

"How many," I continued, "do you suppose deserved to be shot like a dog for the righteous killing of an evil man?"

"I make no judgments of those already judged," he said.

The guard was silent for a time and then turned suddenly. "Get back to grinding," he shouted, "and wipe that stupid grin off your face. What is there to laugh about when you will be dead inside the hour?"

I gripped the stone pestle in my hands and I said, "I go to meet the Savior with a pure and open heart because my actions have been justified." I bent once more to the work and ground through the grain with purpose. My guard appeared to calm himself, and his rising color told me that he had become ashamed of his outburst, that he believed himself to be a man of principle. Yet I suspected by his shame that it was principle adopted from principled men, and not otherwise earned.

"I wonder," I said to the work under my hands, "if you feel so justified, my friend. You, whose purpose is to shepherd men into the arms of death so sanctioned by the dons of the state." This had the desired effect, and my guard sputtered and gripped his rifle again.

"You," I continued, "who would not judge, and yet are as much a peasant as myself and are so ready to betray your own people simply because a judge with beautiful horses and land commands you to do so. A judge who no doubt secured such things through the blood of your own family."

The guard bent down quickly, so close that his mustaches brushed against my cheek. His breath smelled of rancid liquor and he said, "It is better to kill vermin like you than allow you to breed," and at this I brained him with the pestle until I felled him like an ox. Indeed I continued to beat him there after he had ceased to move or to make a sound. When at length I raised my head I heard not even the birds around me.

I ran to the low wall and climbed it and headed for the nearby river. Out past the few ramshackle houses of stone and through a low stand of trees I moved and my thoughts likewise moved beneath me, buoyant, and clear. I found a suitable pace and sustained it, moving eastward, and as I did so the day slowed, much as water around objects which are hard and undeniable and I knew that I had slipped the hand of fate. I knew as well as I felt my heart move within me of its own accord that a rhythm older than the god who would make mere echoes of this had risen free of explanation to the face of things.

At length I came to a river and there, standing as though placed by a hand was a wild colt, watering in the shallows. I mounted him, and I rode him upstream. After a few leagues the horse tired and I let it go, and I walked north toward Rio Grande. In time I arrived at the house of a distant cousin, and he took me in without question. He and his young wife made a place for me at their table, and she fed me tortillas and eggs. I ate from their plates like the starving boy I was until at length my cousin's toddler began to pull at my pant leg. The little boy's face was serious, round and soft as a doll. I pulled him onto my knee and there we spoke about ponies and dogs and the moon in the daytime sky. He told me it was his birthday. His eyes were as bright as riverstones.

CHAPTER II

Sariñana. On Ownership. Treetoppers. Refugio Alvarado. On the Nature of Debt. A Wife To Us All.

When I returned to the Sierra de la Silla I did so in peace. Having scraped my existence from the sides of the living rock, I was not only prepared for hardship but familiar with its degrees. I kept my fire small, and my horse watered from isolated and private springs. As I was beginning to make a name for myself with the raids I now conducted on the cattle of the dons I received small parcels of supplies—of tortillas of coffee and of jerky—from the peasants who worked the fields. It was after one such simple meal that I found sleep in a field of high grass near La Soledad, the cattle around me lowing in the dark.

I awoke in the morning to seven carbines leveled at my face, and seven men ordering me to stand. These were peasants, hired guns of Don Felix Sariñana, and to my right on the rocks sat Don Sariñana himself, all soft cheeks and shining chin.

"I surrender," I said smiling, throwing my hands in the air. "You have captured the boy bandit! But gentlemen," I said, "it is so early, and the ride back to town is far. Can we not cook up a few ears of corn before we leave?" At this I gestured across the road to the tall stalks in the opposite field.

Seeing that I was but a boy and not a dangerous bandit (I was barely mustachioed at the time), Sariñana agreed.

The Don took pleasure in directing his men: two to cut the corn and two to fetch wood for the fire and so three remained. Sariñana spread himself out leisurely, his belly rubbing against the rocks. He took out a leather pouch of tobacco and began to roll himself a cigarette.

"Tell me, young man," he said to me. "Why do you take cows that are not yours?"

I leaned back on my hands and I reached behind me, pretending to scratch the small of my back. There in my blankets I found the wooden butt of the pistol with which I always slept.

"Sir," I said to Sariñana, "whose cows do you believe them to be?"

"They are my cows," he said. "I have bred them. I feed and water them and I continue to provide for them."

I looked to his men, their faces as closed as they had been. "Cows drink water and eat grass," I said. "Surely they don't require your oversight to mate and breed."

Sariñana licked his cigarette, unmoved. "I have bought them, young man. I pay for them."

"And yet I have them."

"You do not own them."

"What don't I own?" I said to Sariñana. "If you take anything from me today I can simply take it back again. In this way you own nothing. Tell me what you have that was not simply given to you?" At this point I pulled my revolver from behind my back and held it in Sariñana's face. "What have you ever taken in your life?"

"For God's sake shoot him!" Sariñana called out.

It was like nothing so much as a bee at my ear. Only an instant later did the gunshot cause me to jump, shying away like a dog or a horse. Then I turned in black fury to these men.

These slaves with their empty faces and souls, and as I shot two in quick succession I saw no evidence cross their faces of hate or love or fear. Nothing but acceptance, even of this.

The remaining gunman panicked and turned, kicking up dirt onto the writhing bodies of his fellows where they clutched at their guts and moaned like calves. I made for the cornfield, leaving the Don sputtering with his unlit cigarette, screaming for his men.

The leaves ran along my ears as I moved deeper into the dimness of the rows, and as I ran I heard the shouting of men around me, frightened and desperate to find a crazed killer, a demon boy. I crouched and I ran from them and from this, turning left and then right until their voices faded and faded behind. The sky then opened simple and blue above me, my horse grazing peacefully in the adjacent field. I saw no man cutting stalks and I saw no man collecting wood and neither was I seen by them. Not ten minutes later I was high on a ridge, my belly flat on the warm stones, looking down at the comedy of the men I had left alive.

It was three months later that they sent the acordada of Canatlán after me, but they were unfamiliar with the land and I easily led them astray. I toyed with them until they ran in confusion throughout the canyons and at length I shot three rurales from above as they milled in the rocks. Finally I walked out of a narrow passage and pulled from one horse a man and scalped him alive in full view of his fellows. A few days later they abandoned the search. At the end of this time I took twelve head of cattle into the solitude of the Quebrada del Cañon del Infierno. I killed each by my own hand, dried the meat and lived in this way for some time, believing myself to be outcast by man and by other things as well.

I rode alone for many months through Cienaga de Ortiz to San Andrés and into Chihuahua before doing little more than turning around and riding back again, as though progressing hither and yon across the back of an enormous beast that was in fact the mountain range itself. At night I imagined that I could feel beneath me the unsatisfied rustlings of the thing in the base of the earth turning heavy on its flanks as the stars ran by overhead in a soundless riot.

One morning I found myself shouting in my sleep at the pink clouds above me, my fire long gone to ash. I sat up and looked about but there was only the stone and the wind. I cursed myself and lay back down in the blankets until I heard quite clear, quite over the wind, a whistle—short, insistent, its pitch turning up at the end like the wave of a hand.

I leapt with fresh terror to my pistol and scampered higher into the rock and for nearly an hour I huddled there, listening to my own breath. At length I heard the whistle sound itself three more times, each one just as the first, quick and clear, neither closer nor more insistent. I stood, and I moved to the top of the cliff and looked out down below me, down onto the Pánuco de Aveno, heavy with the canopy of large tlacocote pines. From those trees below me I heard the whistle again.

With the full morning I climbed down from my rocks and made my way into the forest. In the dimness I walked past great and severed limbs that lay strewn about in the dry pinestraw for nearly a hundred yards until at length I saw standing at the base of a great tree a logger, the tools of his trade strewn about him, his eyes turned up into the darkness above. As I approached I realized this logger was but a boy, younger than I, and without mustaches.

"Hallo!" I called, and the little logger jumped, startled at my voice in the gloom of that place. He drew no weapons, but he reached instead for the axe that lay against the trunk of the tree. He offered a quick and nervous whistle in the air. I kept my arms away from my sides, my palms open.

"I mean you no harm," I said. "I am a trader, here to offer dried meats. Are you not hungry in the midst of this dangerous work? I have mesquite jerky to sell."

"What do you want?" said the boy. He now held the axe fully in hand and he leaned back to balance the blade over his shoulder. I continued to smile and repeated my call, though my arms now fell to my sides. My right hand began to creep behind me and onto the butt of the pistol nestled in the small of my back.

"My friend," I said to the lumberjack. I was now no more than ten feet away, well clear of any swipe he could make with the axe. "I am no danger to you." My hand gripped the pistol and I prepared to draw and shoot this boy dead who would take me to be his enemy with neither proof nor cause until I heard a pounding up above us, a thick and sticky sound reverberating down the pillar of the immediate tree.

Both the logger and I looked upward to see the shape of a man descending the trunk with great speed. Bark flew from underneath his calipered feet and showered around us as he leapt twenty feet at a time in a manful descent. He landed between us and quickly stood and pulled his own pistol from the holster at his waist, which he then cocked and leveled at me.

"Be honest," he said to me. He was lean, wide-shouldered. Skin as dark as the trees. "Tell me why I should not kill you and take your meat and have your scalp to sell in the market."

It was in this way that I met my two friends, now dead— Ignacio Parra and Refugio Alvarado.

They were cousins and loggers, chopping down the trees for railroad ties, and they told me as much after I had talked them both into calmness and given them jerky and we were able to sit and speak in the dry midday. They were involved in dangerous work, Refugio's father having died the year before topping trees. After lunch I watched Refugio again ascend a great pine with an animal's grace, aided only by the irons on his shoes and a single pale rope the width of my arm. But the pay was not good. With the cost of the horses necessary to carry the logs, Ignacio and Refugio barely broke even. After having listened all day to a story told plainly and without self-pity, I decided to offer a proposition at the nighttime fire, and did so.

"I am more than a mere trader of meats," I began.

We sat on either side of the fire, the two cousins facing me on a cut log, Refugio tending to a coffeepot that heated on the stones.

"You are a bandit," said Refugio, not looking up from his pot. Ignacio looked with disbelief to his cousin and then to me.

"This is true," I said.

"You are a bandit," said Refugio "and a cattle rustler and a killer of men."

"I have done these things."

"You are known to the people here," Refugio said. He held the pot handle with his kerchief and poured his cup full. "You are known to the rurales as well," he said, "who search our towns and our homes and call you by a handful of names, yet you are a boy. No older than eighteen."

"I am eighteen," I said, allowing myself the three months.

"And you are already an exile."

"This is not the life I have willfully chosen," I said.

"Would you have other men chose your life for you?" At this Refugio looked up to me for the first time. His face was smooth and without tension. He had known, perhaps the entire day, that it would come to this.

"I have been exiled by the powerful and the moneyed," I said to him, though I had never said such a thing. "I have chosen to remain so, as I sense the world is theirs."

"It is," said Refugio.

"Then I refuse to accept it," I said.

"This is not a choice for you to make."

We all remained silent for a time and the fire between us dipped and twisted in the wind. Ignacio shifted his legs underneath himself and was again still. Refugio eyed me and sipped his coffee in a wary silence, and yet in spite of all this I found myself pleased to be in their company. Pleased to be with others at all.

"When my father died," Refugio began from the silence as I sensed he would, "I was angry. Yes. He had been forced to work himself to exhaustion to repay a debt he had taken from a hateful man. I wanted to kill the man that had so burdened my father, forced him into unreasonable servitude until he made the simple mistake that one so burdened would make. Alone, in the top of a tree." From across the fire Ignacio shifted once more.

"I wanted to kill him, yes." Refugio said. "But such a man's death would solve nothing. It was not the man that murdered my father. It was the debt."

"It was not the debt," I said. "Your family is one of character; this I can see, and such a family is nevertheless ground under the wheel, but not because of a debt. They are so ground because of a man who believes such a debt to exist."

Refugio scoffed. He looked out into the dark and he rocked on the log and he said nothing in his apparent contemptuousness. I saw that he was waiting to be told what he already knew.

"A debt of impersonal collection," I said, "of the balancing of the columns in a book—such a debt could only live in the wormed mind of a weaker man. Such a debt is used by those men as the only weapon they may deploy against character, and against natural strength."

Refugio spit and he stood and he turned and he walked out into the night. I stood as well. I walked closer to the flames and I called out into the dark, "There is no debt, Refugio, which cannot be paid by a just and an honorable man. There is only a conniving mind who uses his book to manipulate a position not fated to him by God." Ignacio too now stood and looked stupidly into the dark and then turned back to me.

"And it is God," I said, "who calls for revenge for the debt that has indeed here been incurred."

I waited and I looked out into that dark which had swallowed Refugio and I did not allow myself to ask what another version or iteration of this night would be, for I trusted in that which had been presented to me and which I had then taken without either question or fear. And after some moments Refugio's face reappeared at the edge of the dark. It hung there for a time, its eyes alight with something I had both seen and knew. His face closed the distance between us and came close to my own over the flames. Refugio's hands were loose at his sides, his breathing heavy.

"My father was a peaceful man," he said.

"My friend," I said to him, placing my hand on his shoulder, "these are not peaceful times."

From the moment I met Refugio and Ignacio, these two were no longer loggers but bandits of the valley, and I was pleased to have such fine company with which to ride and steal. In the next morning's daylight we rode into Tejame so Refugio and Ignacio could sell their tools. I remained in the wagon wrapped in blankets like an old woman so as not to be recognized by authorities.

Refugio already owned a pistol, and with the profit from the sale of their logs and their equipment we bought Ignacio one as well. A steady shot Ignacio proved to be and eager, gunning down a man not two nights later in a cramped cantina over a dispute the nature of which now escapes me. Emptying the revolver, however, this image remains: Ignacio's hand held out from him as though it were the hand of another entire as he spent the cylinder into the motionless bulk of the figure already passed before him on the floor.

Refugio and I dragged Ignacio from the place as he stood dazed at what he had done. We celebrated that night at the fire with mescal and rode back into town to fetch a woman off the street and back to our camp in the desert and the stars, and she was as a wife to us all for three days until we returned her to her family, and good to us she was, for in that time we were none of us old.

For three years we did things in a like manner. We took reckless chances mocking death and stole more money than any of us could ever hope to spend. Under the desert floor lies what we did not simply give away. We made drunken plans to buy fine houses and horses and land for when we were to grow fat and pleased on porches overlooking achievement, and yet in truth we found such hoarding distasteful and incorrect, the desperate toil of desperate men that we were not.

I earned a bullet hole in my chest from but a single fracas out of an interminable line of such incidents when, as the heat of words and the smell of violence filled up such raw and narrow places in which these things breed I stood tall in the midst of fire knowing that none were for me. And even with the striking of such a bullet—a bullet that would knock me to the grime of yet another cantina floor, the boots of the men around me scurrying on duties untranslatable and foreign to my eyes—I found no fear in my heart. The confidence that possessed me then was as though a voice without sound in my mind that told me I could not die.

The sky was not clearer then nor was the air of a purer smell but in my memory both these things seem as though they were true and so they are. We three went forth in a world without repercussion, and ringed by the mountains we slept unafraid and dreamless on the valley floor, eating what was grown, drinking as we pleased and taking money and women as dictated by the fires of our lust. It was in this time that I grew to love these men and understood myself, who had been so cursed in this world, to be in the midst of friendship, and at times I nearly wept with relief that fate had opened up its fist, and the skin on the palm of its hand was warm and free from the creases of age.

Chapter III

The Sons of Dons. Sara. A Blind Man. The World As It Is. Drinking Pulque. Unlucky Assassins.

On a fine spring morning Refugio, Ignacio and myself rode into a small town outside Ciudad Jiménez. My clothes were both new and excellent, and at my saddle hung a fresh and well-coiled rope that brushed the tips of my hand and swayed with the trot of the animal beneath me. The town—the shop owners and children and women preparing to take up the day's work—all stopped to bear witness to us. As I passed through them a young woman reached out, and she touched my knee.

They were a small people, short and dark and made up in tired clothes, and the eyes of these peasants were dim but each hand as it was offered to me was calloused and warm. I do not know who they took us for. For lords perhaps. For dons, or the sons of dons.

We were on our way to visit the family of Ignacio. We dismounted at a ranch in Cañada de Cantinamais and were greeted by his mother and little sisters, who welcomed us warmly. The girls wore field bags as their clothes, refashioned with holes for the head and arms, the sides sown back to form puckered sleeves in a rough job of needlework.

Sara was the oldest, a gangly colt of knees and elbows. She walked to me directly, holding a chipped pitcher of water which I quickly drained, as the rising heat of the day had become oppressive.

"Ignacio, my baby," said his mother, and she pushed his new sombrero off his head and grabbed his face in her hands and kissed him sternly on the cheeks before pulling his whole head to her breast. She was a stout brown peasant, squat and worked free of excess flesh. "You are returned to me," she said, "as I have foreseen." Though muffled by the woman's bosom, Ignacio managed to introduce me.

Refugio, already known to the family, was the next to receive this treatment from the mother while the three sisters ringed me with shy smiles. Sara was the first to speak.

"Where are you from, Señor?" she asked me.

This was without question the first time I had been addressed this way. I smoothed my growing mustaches, of which I had recently become vain.

"I am from Mexico," I said, "as are we all."

The other two giggled mindlessly, but Sara held my eyes as she swayed her young shoulders in the air.

"What have you done in poor Mexico," she said, "to earn such finery?"

I rested my hand on the butt of my pistol. "I have made my own way," I said, "as God allows each of us to do."

"As God allows you to do, I suppose," Sara responded. The two other sisters, refusing to suffer us further, had moved their attention to Refugio, but Sara stayed directly in front of my gaze and returned it without shame in the shade of the house in an empty yard that stretched to the green of the grasses and the tearing of the clouds around us. And she had ceased in her swaying.

"I imagine," she went on, "that He allows many things for

you." The voices of my companions carried on with tales of our most recent adventures as she and I stood there as though held together by an unspeaking force. Her eyes were wide set, the whites brilliant against her cheeks. As if I were to fall into a feminine self and find I had never sounded my own depths.

"And then there are things," she said, "which will not be allowed you."

The mother interrupted us like a fussing bird with a flurry of arms and kisses. Her worn hands ushered the girl and I into the house.

Before us all lay the crude service of a dinner, wooden plates on an unpainted table. We had brought provisions in our saddlebags but Ignacio's mother would have none of it. She had cooked a meal of frijoles with tortillas and the smell in the house was of sweet onion and goat cheese and the rank odor of black beans.

Refugio and I poured the whiskey which we had brought and the mother's friend, a blind fat man by the name of Antonio Retana, enjoyed the liquor with us. We all sat at the rough wooden table that ran the length of the low front room. The floor of the house was of pounded dirt, the walls of stone. From the ceiling hung drying herbs and flowers, various skins of small animals.

From the opposite side of the table I mauled the young girl with my gaze, and she held it as though in the cupped palm of her hand. At one point she placed her bare brown foot full in my lap. The nonsensical talk of the collected swirled around us, and after all had eaten the girls removed themselves to the back room. It was then that I began to drink in earnest.

The conversation had turned to an exchange between Refugio and Retana, who had been an acquaintance of Refugio's dead father. Ignacio sat staring across the room, heavy-eyed and silent, having already drunken himself into the dim-wittedness in which he found the most comfort. Perhaps it was a result of his blindness, but Retana exhibited a carefulness of gesture I increasingly began to observe. His black jacket had once been very much the style but was now faded to near green around the shoulders and his white shirts were yellowed, but only with age. Ignacio continued to guzzle the liquor until at length his head fell into his arms and he began to snore.

Refugio began to speak of Retana's family, and he told me that the blind man was a widower, the head of a large collective. He also said that Retana feared for the survival of the children and grandchildren and indeed the entire clan of which he was the patriarch, for there were no prospects in that dry and quiet town.

Retana became uncomfortable with such talk. "We will no longer speak of such things," he said, leaning back away from the table. "This is a time of welcome and celebration, for Susana's son is alive and home and he is safe." He waved his hand for Ignacio's shoulder, but our companion had by this point slid off the table and rested on the bench as though it were a bed. Retana's face darkened as his hand searched the empty air. He returned it to the table.

"My family and its fortunes are my affair alone," he said, "and you should not speak of it as a trial to take on the responsibility of such a family as would depend upon one who is capable."

"Pardon me, Antonio," said Refugio, "but as the head of a household in times such as these—"

"And what are these times?" interrupted Retana. "Are these times in which young men wander the hills and steal from travellers? Are these the times you speak of?" Refugio's eyes showed his surprise but he remained silent. "Do you speak of such times as those when neither country nor God provide the ties to civility required to counter the savagery that is the worst nature of man?" Retana's quiet voice honed itself into urgency as he leaned across the table into the nothingness that he saw.

I pushed back from the table and stood and walked on unsteady legs to the back of the house. The walls of the hallway came close around me, the midday lights leaking in from behind shaded windows. At the closed door at the end of the hall I stopped and I raised my finger. I tapped the wooden door with my fingernail. I tapped again and received no response. I tapped for how long I cannot say until at last it opened and the girl Sara stood before me in her bedclothes, her hair loose and about her shoulders. She placed an open hand on the door jamb and she did not speak. Behind her, in the dark, I saw the shapes of her sisters move by the window shades. I stepped into the room.

It was at this moment that a hand fell on my shoulder. I turned to see Ignacio behind me, a wide and a stupid grin on his face.

"If you have to piss," he said to me, "you need to do it outside."

He pulled me gently back into the hallway. On my face I could feel the air of the closing door, and then he and I were in the hallway alone.

"There's nothing back here for you," Ignacio said. His smile was gone. He studied me slowly through his half-closed eyes. "You were mistaken," he said. He did not turn but instead waited for me to do so and I walked back into the kitchen. I took a seat at the table, he laid back out on the bench.

None of the others had noticed my absence, and Refugio and Retana's discussion continued. Susana stood at the sink and eyed Retana with a look of sadness and of compassion and I resumed my agitated drinking of the whiskey.

"The President has no power here," Retana said to Refugio. "This is no secret. Díaz has taken the land back from the people and he has given it to the moneyed and has removed himself like a god. We count ourselves lucky to work the land, and in the haciendas they while away their hours at backgammon and cards, and in the towns the people cannot afford to buy the food that they would themselves grow."

"But when was it otherwise?" Refugio said. "The state is suitably weak. We were always a people apart."

"And now," Retana's head bobbed with the intensity of his speech, "those who would protect us indulge themselves in childish adventure." Retana sat back. "We are scattered, Refugio. You know nothing of your history."

"I know it well," said Refugio, drinking his cup empty and reaching to refill it even as he spoke.

"And what is it?"

"It is silver."

"Yes and the young are fed to the mines at so young an age as to be broken before their thirtieth year," Retana said. "And who takes the silver?"

"The dons," nodded Refugio. "But now," and here Refugio looked to me as he spoke. "Now, Antonio. We can take it back."

Retana laughed and he threw out his arms. "Back to where? There is no place to take it. Look at the towns. Look at the country. The warhorses are dead. The rifles are stacked in the attics. The streets and the plazas choke up with the indigent."

Ignacio's mother came up behind Retana and put her hand on his shoulder. "Antonio," she said.

Retana calmed at her touch. He straightened himself, and he smoothed his shirts.

"I am telling them of the world," he said.

I slapped down my hands and stood up from the table and, besotted as I was with drink, lurched out of the house and into the glare of the afternoon where the mountains rose before me broken and enormous and black. I grabbed the saddlebags from the back of my horse and pushed my legs back through the dust of the lot and toward the shambling house.

"What is this!" exclaimed Refugio as I poured the contents of the saddlebags on the kitchen table. Reales and pesos of gold and of silver rang on the wood and cartwheeled crazed and heedless about the room.

"I gift this to you, Señor Retana," I said thickly, pushing a handful of it toward him until it spilled into his lap. "For you to buy a shop for your work and a house for your family and horses and whiskey and so."

Retana held up his blind head, and I stepped back toward the doorway, unsure of my footing in the place so suddenly strange. The woman looked to me as I watched Refugio's face curl into disgust and the only sound in the silence was the snoring of Ignacio from underneath the table.

"Yes," said Retana finally, and he nodded not to me nor to us nor to anyone in that small room. "So it is," he said. He swung his head to me and he stretched open his blind eyes. They turned gray and dead in their sockets.

"Your are correct, young man," he said. "With the world as it is." Retana then rose from the disordered table and reached out for Susana, who offered her arm and confusedly walked him through the room and past me and out of the door. In the shadow of the house Retana secured his cap and took his cane from where it leaned against the side of the house, and he began to walk down the path in the glare of the day through the fields quite absolutely alone.

"And how is it, then?" I shouted after him, holding tight to the doorframe. The empty saddlebag still hung from my hand, and the woman who watched him go was but a black sketch in a landscape that threatened to rear up and further up upon itself.

"How is it?"

We rode on to the house of Refugio. His mother tended to us, thin and silent in her hand-fashioned skirts. Her feet whispered about us on our first morning where we sat at the kitchen table drinking cold coffee. As it was the duty of the eldest daughter to brew fresh coffee, she had instead fallen in with her own cousin Ignacio, and they both lay in the back sleeping off their drunk and to hell with the mute mother and to hell with my ridiculous brother and stranger was the will of this girl.

Refugio and I sat at the table sipping our coffee with the mother's skirts whisking behind us when this bawd came from her room, shouting down the hallway and scratching at her hair. Entering the kitchen she was interrupted by Refugio's pointed questions, to which came the reply that if the mute old woman would spend the money necessary for coffee which was fit for drinking then such coffee would be prepared with all customary sweetness, but as this was not the case and so forth. And then the furious whisk of the mother's black skirts.

The girl was followed by Ignacio, his face dull and spent. He fell to a chair with a grunt and the mother placed before us all wooden bowls of steaming oats. We each dug into them over the rising din of the oldest daughter, furious at the old woman for her wild assumptions as to the propriety of oats for breakfast or the propriety of anything at all.

After a time the fat girl settled herself, and she began to coo over Ignacio. When her first ministrations drew no response she brought him a large cup of pulque, and I was forced to turn my head for fear of catching the scent of the previous night's debauches.

I sat facing the west window. The day was high and clean and the sky so depthless a blue as to hint at the pure black which lay in silence at the tip of its vault and to which all of this bent as though it be its imagining or its dream. The crisp morning blew into my face, cool above the crags of the bluff. As I watched, two men on horseback appeared over the ridge.

I stood up, knocking my bowl to the floor. Refugio came

to my side and also saw what was now a regular detachment descending the bluff. They wore crossed gunbelts. The butts of carbines protruded from their saddles.

"Ignacio," I said, "get to the rifles."

Ignacio squinted to eye the killers as they navigated the descent.

"Don't worry, little sisters," he said to us. "I still have time to drink my pulque."

And so it was. He had just finished when the men fell upon us. The firing began at sometime past eight and we sustained it, placing the mother and sister in the back rooms. Firing as we did from the bare windows of the place, with bullets exploding the kitchenware, we made our way to the far side of the main room in order to slip out into the back yard.

This was done with minimal confusion. The buzz of rifle fire surrounded us, and though the air may have been thick with death, our movements at this time slowed into something as though of a rhythm independent. The articulation of our arms, the folds of cotton in the creases of our elbows as our rifles were held once more to the window—these and all else seemed to be only the fulfillment of a will distant and foreign to ourselves. The faces of my companions were in this time relaxed, Ignacio now well revived.

We climbed out the back window and withdrew across the rear of the house to the stable as the men came round, and we now saw the assassins for what they were. Dark and lean, long-mustaches flaring beneath broad-brimmed hats, their faces lost in shadow, the reins held loosely in their hands. And as I saw them I knew that never would a dream of us cross the minds of these men, and I would go forever unmourned in the chambers of their hearts.

But the shape of the yard was fortuitous. It narrowed into a funnel, splitting the ranks of the killers and demanding they channel into the tip of a triangle toward which we moved with speed. On one side, a handful of trees; on the other a large wooden cart. As we withdrew through this to the stable the killers followed, their horses whinnying into the neck of the funnel. In the mounting reverberation of our gunfire these animals stamped and shied, and we shuffled backward through the smoke of our own rifles in nothing more than our long undergarments, our broad hats, our boots and gunbelts. We took aim at the horses of these riders and felled them.

There came from the horses tremendous screams as the bullets punctured their necks and breasts and blood began to pool beneath their hooves. The men fell from the horses and the horses fell upon the men and both suffered equally in the yard. Some men had their thighbones broke, some had their ribcages collapsed by the tremendous weight of the toppling animals and some had their heads stove in directly by the thrashing limbs of the beasts. One man was certainly dragged to his death as his bay, foaming and blind with fear, bolted back around the house and into the desert with the man held into the stirrup by the heel of his boot, twisted in such a manner that there could be no bone connecting his foot to a leg of any sort.

We withdrew further into the darkness of the stables and continued our volleys and the massacre became general in the yard of beasts and men. The blood arced and pooled with the feces of the dead, and the broad-brimmed heads which still moved in the smoke made easy targets for riflemen so skilled as my companions.

At length we determined the only gunfire to be our own. We stood, and we looked to one another in our underwear, and we walked out from the stables. We walked into that pit of the dead, and we picked like ghouls amongst them where they lay so fresh in the brightening sun. We took their pistols, their bullets, their keepsakes. We took their necklaces, we took their rings. A locket containing the name *Maria* written on a scrap of paper. His writing, not hers.

Moving through the wreckage I was surprised to see the fat and incompetent face of Don Felix Sariñana sticking awkwardly from the pile, bloated and pale with his own death. I removed the ears of the corpse and pocketed them.

We three bathed unmolested, dressed and said warm goodbyes, and we rode back into Sierra de Gamon. It was one morning a short time later that we awoke to find ourselves staring at the ends of three rifles belonging to deer hunters who had chanced upon us. When we drew our guns Refugio was shot in the leg, but we killed the hunters easily. We stayed in the mountains and conducted no raids for some three months until his leg had properly healed.

CHAPTER IV

Falsely Accused. On the Behavior of Interest. "A Thousand Such Indignities." Sons of Dogs. Villa and His Mother.

In the fall we came down westward onto the plain with a herd of donkeys for Don Ramón Esquivel. Ramón took the donkeys and paid us well, and he supplied us with fresh clothes and beef and good coffee. The old man's house was well appointed, and we remained there in peace for some five days until I was falsely accused. The daughter of the cook had been placed into a state of confusion by what she referred to as my "advances," though no advances did I make. Regardless of my explanations, Don Ramón and the wife of Don Ramón had me thrown out that night into a rising storm.

I will admit that on the evening in question I had drunk mescal, and that my impressions were therefore wild and without focus. Refugio followed me out into the yard and disarmed me against my will, and Ignacio was out in this storm as well, grabbing me by the shoulders and striking me about the face but it would not do. The wind and the lightening made his eyes appear comic and strange.

And then I awoke. I was soaked and stinking in my ruined clothes, my sombrero gone, my holster empty. I was seated at a small table in the corner of an unfamiliar cantina. After a few moments I found Refugio and Ignacio, standing at the bar and speaking to a man in a long black coat and low-crowned hat. The man was wide-shouldered with a great belly. From where I sat his back was to me, and I could make out only the roundedness of his cheeks.

"Boys," I shouted to them. "What is this place?" Ignacio looked to me briefly then returned to the conversation. My head was aching and wet, and I was pleased to find in front of me a shot glass of liquor, greasy in the light. Tipping this cup back quickly and dribbling only a little on my chest, I set the glass on the table and concentrated on standing. After a moment I made my way over to the bar.

"Refugio," I whispered so as not to disturb his conversation. I gripped the bar tightly. "Refugio," I whispered again. He looked up to me with steady eyes but did not cease speaking to the stranger in the black coat.

"Very well!" I said. I waved my arm around. I also made a decisive plan to locate my pistol and hat and leave this place and mount my horse and make for the outskirts of town and to never see my traitorous friends again. I did none of these things. My torso had begun to sway at odds to my lower half, and I was forced to pitch forward and back in an effort to counterbalance my own weight. Refugio ignored me.

"It was 300 reales if it was one," said Refugio to the man. "If I am to pay a debt, I will pay the original price."

"My friend," said the man. "This debt was incurred some time ago. It is natural that you are unfamiliar with the fluctuations."

"The debt does not fluctuate," Refugio said.

"Second," the man continued, "let me say that I am pleased by your desire to even your accounts."

"It will be put to rest here," said Refugio. "Tonight."

"I can't tell you, young man, how pleased that makes me feel. Your father was a honorable man."

"Do not speak of my father to me."

"Certainly. I knew him, and knew him to be that which I have said. About him I will say no more."

"I want to pay."

"Excellent. This you have said and I do not doubt it. Now." The man leaned forward, his attitude conspiratorial. "The debt is some three years old. There are matters of accounting which I must make plain." The stranger dug his hand into the pocket of his coat and produced a handful of dull coins. These he spread on the bar before him.

"For three years I have held on my books the amount of 300 reales." From the pile he drew three coins with a short forefinger. He lined them up so across the wood. "One, for one hundred, you see."

Refugio stared back at the man.

"I give such debt at no less that 12%, and no more—no more—than 20%. As this was the first, and only I may add, transaction with your father in which I participated, I gave him the hard floor of 12%."

"A year," said Refugio.

"Oh, no, sir; a month. Now at this rate, which is fair, eminently fair, for there are those among us, I don't mind telling you, who will go no lower than 15% and that, I admit to you freely, is unconscionable. Embarrassing. Bad for business. We are engaged, you see, in a necessary utility, as your father understood, and for such naked advantage to be taken by others in this profession is simply destructive. To drive away good men in need in the interest of pure profit? Disgusting. My rate, you see, is quite fair. In any event, after a year—a year in which it pains me to add that I was not contacted by your mother or your family to alert me in any way as to the dire situations in which you had been placed by fate—the amount of interest compounded."

The stranger drew four reales alongside the given three.

"And," he went on, "I am not being quite precise. Numbers, you see. Irresistible. No understanding of the human condition. And yet. I may from my position find it possible to take a loss of my own. In deference to your father."

He gestured to the column of four reales. "If we are to say then, for one year," a shrug of his shoulders, "the laws by which such numbers are bound, then, to mark off the time as it has been lived by us ... all our endeavor, you see, but so many ciphers ..." The man pulled from his pocket eight more reales and dropped them to the bar top. From this pile he then pulled the two more rows of four, building a procession of coin between himself and Refugio. Refugio looked from the coin to the man and then took down his shot and placed the glass on the bar, his face unchanged.

"This is where we are left today," said the stranger. His face was a mask of resignation. "Is it not, somehow, grotesque? Your father, bless his memory, took out a 300-real loan from me some three years ago. This loan has then grown. It is now that which stands before us all in the glare of the present. By God, I will say it. We must be man enough to accept it. 1500 reales." The tall stranger reared back his head and stood for some moments in the silence.

Then he waved his hand across the coin. "Before us is a living account, consuming as does life. But does this coin not also represent your inheritance, Refugio? Listen to me now. This sum, as it lies before you, stands in some sense for the earthly evidence left of a great man now and forever lost. And the equaling of its demand, the demand it—nay, *he*—puts upon you, is this not representative of your passing into the responsibility necessary, the manhood required, to take up the hard-earned wisdom of debt for yourself?"

The stranger straightened himself once more.

"I will tell you what I see here," he said. "I see here nothing less than opportunity. An opportunity for you to own what fate has laid in its wake for you and to pick up the desire of your father where he laid it down at the moment of his own demise. I see an chance to provide an answer, son, to the ghost of his passing."

The stranger was close now, his eyes searching Refugio's face. "What say you, young man?"

Refugio picked up the shot glass that lay next to his elbow and jammed it into the stranger's left eye. The sound was such as the grinding of a mirror into the dirt with the heel of a boot.

The man fell back to the floorboards of the place squealing as a pig would squeal. Ignacio was quickly astride him with pistol drawn and cocked. The lender's hands shook in the air, the shot glass protruding from his eyesocket like some nautical instrument of radical design.

The place broke out into a riot. The tables emptied and chairs overturned as the patrons rushed into the rain and the slog of the street. Refugio grabbed Ignacio before he could pull the trigger and struck his own cousin full across the jaw. Ignacio responded with a wordless cry of surprise, and then cracked the butt of his pistol against the face of Refugio.

"Stop!" I shouted, pointing one finger into the air, demonstrative of my high seriousness. This caused both cousins to come to their senses and turn from one another to the man on the floor, who had by now skittered back against the wall. His black overcoat had become muddy from the filth of the place, and his hair hung about his face in disarray.

The cousins fell on him with violence. Their hands quickly silenced the shaking body beneath them but still the beating continued. Labored breathing echoed in the empty cantina.

The barkeep had located a bolt-action carbine which he

now fired into the ceiling of his own establishment and at this Refugio turned and he stood. Ignacio remained as he was, bent on a knee, and continued to beat the lender until Ignacio was in due course shot in the shoulder. The barkeep without irritation reloaded from a box underneath the bar and slid the bolt home as Ignacio fell to the ground cursing and clutching at his arm, the sleeve of which had already begun to stain darkly. Refugio pointed to the motionless body of the stranger on the floor.

"This man," he said, "deserves his death not for one but for a thousand such indignities perpetrated across the span of his miserable life."

The barkeep did not lower the barrel. "As do we all," he said.

So pleased was I with this response that I let go of the bar and put out my hand to introduce myself to the rifleman, but this decision put at odds at my ability to remain upright, and I found myself sprawled out on the floor. It was from here that I watched Refugio slide his hand into his hip pocket and pull out a handful of his own golden reales. He turned back to the lender and held his hand high out above him. One by one the coins began to fall from his hand into the lender's open and bloody mouth. They rang off his teeth. They stuck on his tongue.

I came to myself in a cave. My clothes steamed wet in the air and a low fire smoldered beside me. Ignacio sat across from me, shirtless, a torn sleeve wrapped around his shoulder. His eyes were dull and furious, and he drank from a bottle he held in his fist. The gray morning opened at the mouth of the cave and the day was overdrawn with cloud. The rain had apparently continued, unabated.

"Where are we, my friend?" I said to Ignacio, who drank once more from the bottle. He spat and said nothing. I pulled myself up just as Refugio came in from the rain carrying sticks and branches which he laid by the fire to dry.

"You are awake," Refugio said to me.

"Where are we?"

Refugio nodded across the fire to his cousin. "He said we should leave you."

"Why would you leave me?"

"He said we should leave you, and then when I brought you with us, he said we should shoot you."

Ignacio rolled his wounded shoulder and winced and continued his drinking as before.

"You did neither," I said to Refugio.

Refugio moved a stick into the fire. "Tell me why I did not," he said.

I sat up in my steaming clothes. "Because I am your friend."

"We are here in a cave because you got drunk at Don Ramon's," Refugio said. "You tried to rape his girl. We may lose him as a principal."

"We will not lose him."

"Now we are in the rain," Refugio went on. "Ignacio is wounded, my leg is aching with buckshot still lodged within it and you snore the day away like a child."

"I did not rape that girl."

"And you have no understanding as to why we would think to leave you, or to simply kill you and be on our way."

"I thought only Ignacio wanted to kill me."

Refugio looked back at the fire, poking at it with a stick.

"This is madness," I said. "Ignacio was shot because he nearly killed an old man."

"A man put in our path by your recklessness."

"Then you have me to thank for it."

Ignacio tried to rise and could not. He cursed me, and spat again.

"Once more, my friend," I said to Ignacio, and "I will be forced to kill you."

38

"I have taken away everyone's weapons," said Refugio evenly, "and will only return them when we have come to an understanding."

At this I became quite agitated. I began to slap the blankets around me for my pistols and of course found none. Rage rose up in my chest, and I turned upon Refugio but he held me in check with his eyes alone. I looked at Ignacio and in that moment felt hopeless, and ashamed to be grouped with him. I pulled at my boots and my jacket.

Refugio sat between Ignacio and myself, continuing to poke at the fire. Finally he said, "I have been thinking about Retana."

"Fat cocksucker," said Ignacio.

"I have been thinking about the rifles stacked in the attics and the towns choking with the poor."

"Pigfucking cowards," said Ignacio.

Refugio stood. He walked over to where Ignacio sat and, without anger, punched him in the nose. Ignacio cried out. His good hand flew to his face but he did not otherwise move. Refugio returned to his seat. "This," Refugio said to me, "is precisely my point. Do you know what they used to call us?"

"Who?" I asked.

"Sons of dogs," Refugio said. "They called us the sons of dogs."

And in that low place with the rain about us Refugio told us that we as Chihuahuans were precisely that: not animals but the children of animals. The Aztecs themselves would have nothing to with us. He told us that it was the silver alone that brought the Spanish into our desert to enslave us. That it was the Spanish who built the haciendas. It was they who chained our people to the mines and the fields, and only the raving madness of the Apache could beat back the Spaniard's greed. The Apache came down upon them with the brutality of a people raging against their inevitable extinction and the Spanish and their children ran back south, and still, we stayed. We stayed and we held the haciendas and the towns and the mines and the fields from those malignant horsemen and their drive into death and there were no prisoners in that war. Whole towns burnt to ash, the plains littered with dead and no money taken and no rites performed. For generations we crouched behind our walls as the horses rode around us and their calls rang in the air until, one morning, we heard them no longer. We opened the gates and the plain stretched out before us and it was long and empty. They were gone. To where, no one can say, and Retana was not even a boy. My father unborn. It was our grandfathers who had withstood them and having done so they had become something altogether separate. Something new. A people borne out of the violence visited upon what had been little more than a ragged collection of slaves. A violence unimaginable to us now. They were melted and remade in that fire until they had come into themselves, and then the Spanish returned. No longer Spanish, you see, these southerners. But look at their skin. Listen to their voices. Hear their names spoken aloud and here they came again, drawn by the silver, by new irrigation, and by the possibility of making those who had survived it all into peons once more.

"It took little more than a generation," said Refugio, "and now look at us. What are we again but the sons of dogs?"

He looked from me to his cousin and back. "I too," he said, "can make a picture to show the nature of things." Refugio put his finger in the dirt before him and he drew there a large square. "Here," he said, "we have the land of a hacienda. How many work this land?"

"Forty," I said.

"Forty men work the land of one man and what do they gain?"

"Fuck all," said Ignacio. Refugio turned to him and Ignacio

put his hand back over his nose.

"Forty men work the land of one man," Refugio said. "They pull forth from the land that which feeds the family of the don and yet these men cannot feed themselves."

Refugio split this square up into sections of ten, his finger light across the ground. As he spoke he broke these sections up again into four. "Who is this man," he said, "who would take the land for himself that would feed forty men? What cruelty must he harbor in his soul? Perhaps he is not a man at all. Perhaps he is something else. Something unnatural."

Refugio looked to the gamingboard before him and he said, "The forty would agree. The forty would agree that they should live as men and not as dogs nor should they live as the sons of dogs. The forty would agree that action must be taken. Any action necessary to put this strange and unnatural thing out." He tapped at the dust with his finger. "Any violence necessary."

He swept the back of his hand across his design and obliterated it back into the dust.

"And through this action," he said, "who can imagine what may emerge? Who can imagine what these slaves may then become?

He looked at the two of us, and then he stood and he walked out to the mouth of the cave. Before him was the open land and the driving rain that fell down there upon it.

"Refugio," I said to him. "My pistols, please."

When we returned to Chihuahua I left for a time to visit my family. My mother received me with her usual affection and I gave her all the money I had. She seemed older now, more slow and thin and yet still mighty in bearing. The heavy hair remained, and pulled high back it was as well though shot through with gray that which had once been as that of a raven. Her arms so thin, and her vibrant clothes—a red jacket, emerald skirts— hung loose and swayed oddly around her as she moved.

At the table that evening with my sisters gone to bed, the plates from dinner put away and between us only the raw wood of the table, my mother spoke.

"My son," she said to me, "where do you get this money?"

"Mama, please," I said, for by that time my name was known in that country as much as any other. But my mother reached across the table with her gray hands for my arm and commanded in that silence to meet her eyes and I did so.

And she told me that I was in the midst of uncivil ways. That I was placing at hazard my soul. That I was bringing disrepute upon her house. She told me that she knew me and knew my nature, and she told me that I was better than my actions and to this she added, "You are better off, are you not, to earn your pay from your own effort, and not from the efforts of others?"

I remained silent, as outrage welled in my belly. As she spoke I asked myself if this speech of hers, if it was just the kind of a speech as one would prepare, would practice, and in doing so mastering with each repetition the turn of the voice, the crack of the vowel the moistness of the eye the sternness of the address? Then yet even if all of these were the case, and even still if such condemnation were but so much paint on the face of the truth and a lie, even if this all were so, this woman was still my mother. Could she not see what I had been and what I now was, and what I was to then become? She was a selfish and superstitious and imponderable old woman who held with her bony hands the very hitch around my neck which would tighten or loosen at a moment of her choosing.

I ground my teeth and while her eyes did not waver in the light of the lamps her jaw quivered, and it quivered not with any deviation of purpose, this I could see, but it quivered with nothing other than sorrow. And it was this that I found impossible.

"You know how it began!" I shouted, quite beyond my control.

Her eyes filled up with pity, and she smiled at me in sadness.

"And I would rather be a bandit, yes." I stood and could hear in my own ears my shouting. "I would rather be a disgrace to myself and a shame," I said, "than to let others mistake us for who we truly are."

My mother withdrew her hands from me, and it was at this point that she began to cry, and her thin shoulders convulsed silently with those tears. She, an old woman, long in memory and fierce in heart recoiling in terror and exhaustion from the face of her only son. I looked about wildly, a danger in my own family's house, and my sisters now stood in the doorway to their room, awakened by the shouting, their hair uncontrolled. I stood, heaving, my ears as though stopped up with drink or with cotton, blood full in my face.

"You are a good brother," said Manuela.

Within a year my mother was dead.

CHAPTER V

Refugio's Plans. On Villa's Trouble With Women. Ignacio the Drunk. The Future. A Riderless Horse.

The peasants eyed us nervously as Ignacio and I unloaded the rifles from the back of the cart. Cheap things they were, but we had nearly two hundred of them, and as the peasants came forward it was easy to discern that they did so not to ask who we were or where we were from but to ask what we intended to do with these guns.

I watched as they came, staggering with drink in the noonday sun. As they did so I stood up in the wagon and I said, "My friends, we are here to arm you."

"Arm us for what?" said an old man. Witless. His face like a prune in the sun.

Before I could continue, Refugio came around to the back of the cart where we stood and he said, "We are arming you for freedom."

This was better than what I had planned to say. The men turned toward him and this same peasant then asked what Refugio meant.

Refugio answered this question with one of his own. "Are you not," said Refugio, "each one of you, in debt?"

They nodded their heads.

"Are you not each one of you worked to the bone?"

And to this they all nodded once more, even though it was in fact the very middle of the day and none of these men seem eager to pick up a shovel or plow.

"And every day," Refugio said, "every week and month, every year without pause you fall further behind. Even as you age, even as your body grows brittle, you fear for your family. You fear that although you work like a dog there will not be enough. And lo, your wife is once more with child. And lo, the crop this year is poor. And lo, the don still demands the same amount, albeit with a compounding interest."

I could see this last bit had confused them. And yet I could also see that Refugio spoke to their hearts and it was not his words at all that moved them. They looked to him where he stood by the cart, dark and young and tall and fine. Refugio's father had never worked a field. Never bent behind a plow nor dropped dead of exhaustion in the heat.

"Why the rifles?" a young man asked.

Refugio looked to the guns and he put his hand on the edge of the cart and he looked at his hand and he smiled. And, like Christ, Refugio once more answered a question with a question.

"What is it," Refugio asked, "that binds you?"

The crowd fairly erupted with answers to this. *The scarcity of food. The heat of the sun. The failing crops. The inferior tools.* All were thrown at Refugio where he stood and he raised his chin and waved his hands over his head to silence them all.

"Are you not men of the land?" he asked.

An aggressive response in the affirmative.

"If you are so, can you not grow enough to feed your families?"

"I work ten acres of beans," said a young man.

"Why do you not plant corn, keep a hog, raise chickens?"

Refugio asked.

"I need all the land for beans."

"Who needs these beans?"

"Who needs these beans," the man said, looking around himself at the stupidity of the question.

"So," Refugio was smiling, "how much does the don pay you?"

With the invocation their antagonist the crowd erupted in hard and bitter angst, shouting and shaking their fists and pushing up closer to us and hemming us in so that in short order both Ignacio and I became afraid.

And here—I stood in awe at the control—here Refugio held them back. He held them like horses. He held them and did not rush forward into the chaos that welled up before us. He stood, and he smiled, and he waited for the crowd to calm itself.

Refugio looked about the men, looked over their heads to gauge I imagine the their number, and he then leapt up into the bed of the cart, standing tall above them. There he asked, in a voice of quiet and reasonable sense: "What makes the don a don?"

No one spoke. Befuddlement. And Refugio could see it. And Refugio then asked if the dons went hungry. He asked if the dons had worked themselves or their families to exhaustion. He asked if the dons were shackled in debt. He asked if the dons were penniless and haunted and consumed with fear. The answers to all of these were as expected, the energy of the crowd building again.

"The dons," Refugio said, "do nothing. They make nothing. They only take," he said. "This is what makes them dons." And the crowd began to grow riotous.

"They take from you more than they give. And what of that difference? Now," he said, leaning out over the boiling men. "*This* is what makes a don a don: this difference. It is a difference that they consume. They can never have enough of it. And as they consume this difference, it eats away at their Christian souls. It eats them away until they are wholly different themselves. The dons have taken the difference inside of themselves until they are in fact little more than difference itself. Different from you. Different from us, the difference inside them seething and black and awful where their heart and soul once had been, and this difference, my friends, is a cancer."

The crowd was up close on us now, trembling on the edge of that which hadn't been said, and Refugio did not say it. He reached down and he picked up a rifle by the stock. He held it before them, held it as though he had no idea what it was. As though to allow each of the men to understand for himself what it meant. And then he tossed it out into the crowd.

They came upon us in a murmurous rush, their arms outstretched.

We camped that night outside the town. I was unable to sleep. I walked about the darkness for a time and when I returned to the fire Ignacio was snoring in his blankets. Refugio remained awake, sitting crosslegged, counting the coins left to us.

"My brother," said Refugio. He had taken to calling me such in the intervening weeks. I had tolerated it.

"My brother," Refugio said, "you should rest."

"I must be honest I cannot rest," I replied, "what with the countryside now swarming with armed and drunken imbeciles."

Refugio smiled even as he counted. He slipped the coins one by one back into the leather sack between his knees.

"It's not us they're after," he said.

I felt the anger rising again in my chest. I was envious. Refugio was a masterful performer and had lured those poor fools into an uprising that would surely leave them massacred and he had done it with both subtlety and grace.

"Do you honestly believe," I said, "that these people are capable of revolt? So much as a gunshot in the town will bring the federals. So much as a single night of wildness, so much as a single day where the fields lie fallow ..."

"Please," said Refugio. To my pleasure I had disrupted his count. He tried to regain it but it was lost to him. He threw the remaining coins into the bag and pulled it closed and he said "My brother, this is the way of things now. This is who we are." Refugio put the bag behind him and he placed his palms on his knees to address me.

"What is it that you believe we are?" he asked. "What more drinking and whoring can you do," he said to me, "that you haven't already done? Do you remember the girl in ... where was it?"

I folded my arms and I said nothing.

"It was Chihuahua, wasn't it?"

"It was Torreon," I said.

"Yes. Ignacio took us."

"I don't remember."

"The Red Rooster," Refugio said, leaning over and slapping me on the knee. "Yes."

"Perhaps," I said.

"That little whore charged you ten times the rate for a second go, and you paid it and were anxious to do it."

"I was in the grips of a passionate disturbance," I said, for in fact it was so.

Refugio laughed at my face. "You are terrible with women, my brother. Every single one. It is enough to make me believe you were a virgin until we met."

"Nonsense," I said.

"If they were unknown to you I could perhaps understand it better."

"When I was no more than nine years old I bedded the wife of my neighbor," I said. "I saw her, and I wanted her, and I took what I wanted."

After I said this I looked at Refugio over the fire. His joyous look had faded and he wore the smile he did when he felt superior to his fellows. Nevertheless I continued, as though pulled on by that obnoxious smile. "I took her hand," I said to him, "and she—blushing like so, her hand at her mouth—she followed behind me in the field until we were well away from the others."

And as I said these things and gave shape to my memories I found that they turned again in total to that which I had until then never spoken. Refugio's insolence had brought me to it and returned me for an instant to that day and its smell and light as though they were on the edge of my senses. As though this night and fire sat within this day and its light bright on the cusp of things. She taking my hand in her own. Singing to me as she walked me out past my parents where they bent and worked. She, waving at them. And the wave returned. The sun high over the black ridge of the mountain.

"You were, then, a man with her," said Refugio. "A sturdy nine-year-old." He was still smiling.

"Yes" I told him. "Yes I was."

"And so," Refugio said, sitting back now. "At your tender age, did you please this woman sufficiently? Were you to her as her husband could never be?"

"Of course," I said. "I provided her great satisfaction," and now his smile was gone, his mouth twisted into a deep and mocking seriousness.

"Francisco," he said, "I want you to tell me what really happened."

"I am telling you."

"You are fashioning it," Refugio said. "And poorly."

Still singing as she unbuttoned my pants. Her hair on either side of my face. The sun winking through it, the wind shifting it like silent chimes. I spoke to her. What did I say?

"If you challenge me again," I said to him, "I will not forgive it."

"My brother," said Refugio, "I see a dark future for you."

"You can go find her yourself and she will testify to the truth of it. The wife of Ramon Ortiz. Alba." The song is gone or was it? Her eyes hard as she leaned into me where I lay on my back in the grass. Her hands small and cold, her flat palm moving up my smooth chest. The calluses catch on my skin. Closing over my throat. Alba holding me down in the summertime field.

"Very well," said Refugio. He turned to his bedding. "But a man who cannot be honest with himself will not be able to see clearly when the situation demands it."

"I am the equal to any situation," I said.

"Not to this one," said Refugio, who then turned from me, and went to sleep.

Her hair and the light and her hands upon me, I wished all of these things away. I indeed pushed them away for they were of another time that was not this one and in this one I was alone in the night without these phantoms. There was no boy here, there was a man. And the man had transmuted the boy and that boy's life into choice that was exercised, and not exercised upon. And so with a clean mind I laid down to sleep. And I did not sleep.

Refugio drove the cart down from Palestina to Campo Hermoso. It was a long drive and without distraction and Ignacio had taken to drinking. I sat in the back of the cart with him and shared his bottle.

"My brother," I said to him, "how many rifles do you think we gave away yesterday?"

Ignacio lay on his back, his head propped on a bundle of the guns, his hat low over his eyes. Ignacio had for many months now been drinking heavily and the weight he had gained hung from him, pale and useless. His face and his body had taken on a greasy appearance, as though he were constantly sweating out the poisons he daily ingested.

To me he said nothing. He sat as though I'd not spoken.

"I'd guess two hundred," I said. "I'd guess we gave away easily two hundred."

Nothing still.

I tried again. "How much do you think they cost apiece?"

"What."

"The rifles."

"I don't know."

"You don't know or don't care?"

"I don't care."

"And why not?"

"Because," Ignacio said, tipping back the bottle, "we are just going to go get more rifles and do the same with them."

"Very well," I said. "And do you think this is the best use of our money?"

Ignacio pushed up the brim of his hat with one finger. "My friend," he said, "what are you suggesting?"

"Nothing."

"Are you suggesting that we take the money ourselves?"

"No."

"Are you suggesting that we kill Refugio and take the money and go whoring?"

I sat up straight. "Absolutely not," I said.

"Please," he said. "You act like you haven't thought about it." And Ignacio pulled his hat back down over his eyes.

We rode on for some time in silence. The road as it stretched behind us was barren and cracked dry in the heat of the day.

Behind us walked our mules and horses and their heads were low in the heat. Ignacio belched.

"I'd do it," he said, taking another swallow from the bottle. "I'd do it in a second. Except I can't stay awake."

"He's your cousin," I said quietly.

He considered this for a moment. "Well," he said finally, "I've got more than one."

Refugio was a friend to us both, and we had indeed fought and killed beside him. Had he not made arrangements with cattlemen around the valley with whom we could trade? And had he not envisioned a new path for us and explained what this path was to be and what steps would be necessary to accomplish it? And because of this had he not become our leader or older brother or father as though one who would tell us when to come and when to go? Yes, he had.

The next day Refugio and I were to take several of the mules and ride over the mountain into Buena Union to sell skins for rifles, criss-crossing the terrain over and back like regular hardscrabble merchants. As the trip only required two, and as Ignacio looked forward to a free day to drink himself into oblivion, Refugio and I were to go alone. It was in this ride to Buena Union that I killed my friend.

The night before this ride I sat by the fire with Refugio, Ignacio snoring out his drunk with his empty bottle as a pillow, and I made up my mind that I would speak to Refugio about the morale of the group. I would speak to him as well about any coming plans as he may have imagined them. My aim was simple and to me it was plain and this was to deduce what our future was, or what future for us he envisioned, and I planned as well to offer my own insight as to the best manner in which such a future may be accomplished. This was my aim.

We were sitting on our bedding before the fire, Refugio

finishing a cigarette and the night was moonless and the stars so high as to be invisible by the light of the flames. In my memory it was indeed as though the dark were a round and living thing about us that held us in an otherwise emptiness as though we were travelling in it and through something hollow and indiscernible.

I looked out into this night and I spoke to Refugio from my heart.

"Do you think I lied to you?" I asked him.

He looked up at me for a moment, his face blank. Smooth skin by the firelight. Clear eyes, his black hair hanging long against his forehead.

"About what?"

"About Alba."

"Who?"

"The girl. In the field."

"Oh." Refugio smiled to himself and his eyes returned to the fire. "Certainly."

"*Certainly* you remember, or *certainly* you believe I was lying?"

"It's nothing," he said.

"It's not nothing," I heard myself say. I heard myself say it for I was speaking to my closest friend without censure, and I felt myself begin to be carried along by something altogether else that to which I admit I surrendered. "Is it *nothing* because you now say it is *nothing*, or is it nothing because it truly is not?"

Refugio was silent. And in that silence I allowed myself an indulgence. I allowed myself to repeat myself, word for word, slowly and carefully.

Refugio dropped his hand between his knees. He looked at his hand there and he sighed, at what I do not know, and then he looked up and he looked at me fully.

"What do you want from me?" he said.

"Truth."

"I don't have any special hold on the truth."

"And yet I was under the impression that you in fact had close traffic with that very thing," I said. "Such that you could sit and smoke and it would arrive to you, and you could then relate its dictates to your cousin and to myself."

Refugio flicked his cigarette into the fire. "This has, perhaps, been a long trip," he said. "You need to remember what we're doing out here. Our goals and our aims."

"I remember you taking control."

"Taking control of what?" Refugio said. He was getting louder. "Of a drunk, and of a wildling with no greater ambition than to murder and to rape and to steal?"

"There is nothing special about you," I said.

"No," he said.

"Then why do you think you can tell us what we are?"

Refugio's face broke out into a smile of frustration. Clean and shining teeth. A truly beautiful man.

"Please," he said. He shook his head. He held up his hand. He was at a loss. He looked from me where I sat to Ignacio where he slept and back.

"Very well," he said. He held that hand out to me, gently, as though it were cupping an egg. "You shall have it," he said. "This is what it is. You, Francisco. You believe you can lead. You give orders and you carry yourself like a man of importance, but to lead, you must be able to see beyond the present. You must be able to envision it. To see for yourself what has yet to be. But you cannot. You have no vision," Refugio said to me, and he shook that empty hand between us. "There is no *future* in you, Francisco."

"How do you know this?"

Refugio dropped his hand and he bent his head to the side,

his eyes full of nothing for me other than pity. "I know you," he said.

And to this there was nothing to say.

And so I waited for Refugio to speak, to say something else. To modulate himself or to apologize. To see me as I was and to take that into some account. To take back all of this he had said, to say he meant none of it and that he had misspoken. That I had made him angry and rash, and that he did in fact love me and saw within me ability and great potential. And I gave him such time. Such time that it felt as though the night around me had turned, inversed in some indefinable way, and had become strange.

How can I speak of it? It was as though the entirety of it—the sky and wind and stones—had all ground down by degrees until it was quite still. And the sounds in the darkness fell away. And my friend by the fire, which is but the repetition of a thousand other fires: this moment multiplied, as though giving rise to itself, this fire the center and this moment lived before and since, out and out in a ring without conclusion, and outside of that dark in which we sat and that hollow space in which the darkness lay only this ring would run, and it would run until the end of that hollowness and further out into whatever it was that held even that in its turn.

In the dawn I stood and stamped out the embers. I roused the two cousins who said little. We saddled the horses and loaded the cart and Refugio and I rode out.

In a pass along a range in the blankness of mid-morning, a mule in my train lost its footing. I turned to watch as the stones rolled underneath its hooves and the animal slid slowly down off the trail. And even as its hooves scraped in agitation on the rocks for purchase its black eyes remained as they were and absent of fear. The animal went on to tumble over the edge and out into the air below us, quite without sound, its pack releasing its baubles and skins as though unfurling some new and horrible shape.

It was at this point that Refugio lost his temper with me.

"My brother," he said.

I removed my rifle from its holster in the saddle by my thigh and leveled it and fired once into his face. For some time, and I do not know how long, I looked at the space in the air where he had been. His face. I sat my horse and looked at his horse where it stood and I looked into the air. The day stretched out for ten thousand miles, ridge upon ridge and the brown plain beyond turned up like a table that would spill its careful contents upon the floor.

At length I dismounted, and I walked to the edge of the trail. I saw where the mule had fallen against the rocks—a torn and shabby mess of black blood and valuables and matted hair. I walked over to Refugio's body where it lay, and I nudged it with my foot. He lay as though sleeping, his arm outstretched with his head upon it, his right leg hitched up. I pulled back my leg and I kicked his body off the ridge, taking no interest in its descent.

I rode back into camp with Refugio's riderless horse hitched to my own and Ignacio stood as I approached and he wiped his hands on his shirt. I remained on my horse and I looked down at Ignacio and I informed him that Refugio would no longer be our companion. And I informed him that violence had befallen his cousin on the trail and that he would likely not see him again. Ignacio put his hands on his hips and looked at the empty horse and then back at me where I sat with my chin held high. He once more wiped his hands on his shirt. Then he spat. Then he turned and threw up his hands.

"The way things have been going," he said, "I figured it'd be one or the other."

I was outraged at this callousness, and I dismounted and

I ran up to him as he walked away from me and the horses wiping the palms of his hands down the front of his shirt in bitter repetition and I spun him around at the shoulder and I could smell the liquor upon him as though he had bathed in it. His face was slack, his eyes blurred. He smacked his wet lips in my face.

"Refugio was a good man," I said.

Ignacio broke into a slow and a heavy laughter. I stood there and I watched him and I realized I was waiting for something. I was waiting for anything that would allow me to kill him. Ignacio leaned forward, and he clapped me on the shoulder.

"Cheer up, friend," he said. "The pie pieces just got that much bigger."

Ignacio then held out his hands. A measurement of the invisibles which we were to soon acquire. This space between his hands as though justification. A picture of everything that could be. And even then I knew it would not be enough.

Chapter VI

The Killer Jesús Flores.
What Ignacio Believed.
Refugio's Killers.
Calming the Horses. The
Breadman.

Ignacio and I arrived in Tejame and took lodging with Don
Perez and took pleasure in his hospitality. We took pleasure as
well from the hospitality of his three daughters and maidservant,
though pure Indian she was, with hair as straight as a railroad
spike. For many days we lived in this way and those days passed
as though they were but a single day and that long and with
sun and moon together enough to drive from my mind any
memory as I would want so driven. But fifteen days later we
were again betrayed.

At the door to our house one morning we found two
mounted men, an officer I did not know and Jesús Flores, the
inspector general of police. Flores was the hard sort of man who
had run provinces such as these in the desert for generations.
He was a simple and vicious man who lived by a code more
akin to animals, to predators who culled their existence from
the fear and the failure of lesser beasts, and his kind are now all
but disappeared.

"Who are you, Señores?" Flores said to us.

Ignacio and I stood shirtless in the morning in our gunbelts, still drunk and unshaven on the porch of a small shack in the rear of the hacienda. The great house and its morning business spread out before us, overflowing oxcarts of apples and melons, cattle driven by hunched over horsemen, men and beasts walking on errands hither and yon. Behind us in disordered beds lay the sisters and the maidservant all sleeping off their respective debauchery. Brown limbs, dark hair and twisted sheets, all quiet and still in that room in which the morning may not come, nor any time at all.

Flores had come for us because we were roadmen, and the pursuit of such men was his chief occupation. He had in the previous month run to ground a dozen such unfortunate souls and he had taken to the grotesque habit of removing the noses of his kills. He strung them on a leather strap which he hung from his saddle and there they were in that morning: little black things, like mushrooms.

Flores was skin and bone. He took no pleasure from life as I could see it and I wager he took no pleasure as well from his evident barbarism. As though even the pursuit of men such as us—even the extinction of our squalid lives—was nothing more to Flores than the fulfillment of his duty to a master long dead and gone. He was immensely dangerous.

"What are you doing here?" he said.

"We are the landlords," Ignacio responded, yawning and scratching at his ribs.

Flores would have none of this. He spoke to his men but he did not turn. "Dismount and search them," he said.

Ignacio gave me a wink. He placed his hands on his jutted hips like a maudlin whore and he said to Flores "Are you afraid to search us yourself, Inspector?"

The three of us drew at the same time, firing at close range. I could say that if I had thought Flores could have killed me, then perhaps it would have been so. That the ability to kill lies chiefly in the belief of oneself as a killer and if one harbors no such thoughts then he is here—that is, he lives and he breathes—to be little more than meat for the killer that will inevitably come. Or perhaps I could say that there is no such design in the world, and it is always merely chance that some bullets find their targets while others do not. I say that I knew Flores would fall, and when he did so his men turned their horses and made for the hills. I cannot say what Ignacio believed.

I can in truth never say what Ignacio believed. He enjoyed drink and women and killing men, and he enjoyed having a companion who allowed him to indulge in these things. His mind was elsewhere always—never on the drink before him or the woman in his bed but the next drink, the next woman, the next man who would cross him with some paltry offense. He was stupid and vain and senselessly violent, but I found in my heart no fear of him. Perhaps we had become too close by that time for me to fear him. Or perhaps I would never have fallen in with him to begin with if I did indeed fear him. Flores, on the other hand, was a man to be feared, and my desire to kill him from the moment I laid my eyes upon him was very strong. I felt I must do so in order to appease this fear that gnawed at me like hunger or thirst. I felt I must prove myself against him, my worth or my being. Ignacio was only a man, and the luminous ring of fear not so different in truth from lust that rang those whom I felt necessary to kill was absent from his person completely. Whatever the case, I was perhaps the one man alive who did not fear Ignacio, and because of this I was the one man who would ride with him. In this way we suited one another's needs.

After shooting Flores, Ignacio and I wasted little time retiring to the sierra, fighting off small and unconvincing bands of riders tasked with retrieving us. We rode up to the Sierra de Ocotlan, near the Sierra de la Silla. From there we climbed up to the Medina farm at the Hacienda de San Bartolo. The land here stretched on for some miles southward like a crazed tabletop and below us sat the great scoops of the valleys tinted at the edges with green. We arrived at the corral in the mid-morning and there we saw the foreman Luis working out some horses. As Luis was an acquaintance we asked him for the news.

Luis was a heavy man, with full cheeks and a stringy beard. He stood before us in the crisp air of that morning and grabbed his hat off his sweat-soaked head.

"The news," he told us, "is that they have killed Refugio Alvarado."

To this we said nothing.

"Those bastards in Malpaises de Ocotlan have killed Refugio," he said, wiping his palm across his dark face. "We plan to ride out later today and hunt them down. Will you ride with us?"

Ignacio and I looked at one another from our mounts, our elbows resting on the horns of our saddles. Ignacio sat up straight and eyed the foreman.

"Is this true? That Refugio is murdered?"

"It is," said Luis.

Ignacio squinted out over the valleys around us. "Well," Ignacio said to me, "what do you think?"

My eyes followed those of Ignacio and I squinted into the distances about us and I said, "I think that it is only just and fair that we run to ground the vicious sons of whores who would take the life of our beloved friend."

We left the Medina farm at midday, Ignacio, Luis, myself and three other men from the ranch. We rode down through the passes and as we did so we sang, and we spoke of our memories of Refugio. It was agreed that he was an excellent horseman and a philosopher as well, a man who loved his land and his people.

We could only nod in agreement with the sentiment expressed most fervently by Luis that the likes of Refugio would not be soon seen again.

We caught the trail of a small group of horsemen that afternoon, their tracks showing no more than four moving on ponies across the foothills and into the valley of the Lago de Chapala. We rode until near midnight, guessing ourselves not but a few hours behind. As the half moon rose we dismounted and slept with out heads on our saddles.

Rising before first light, we rode silently to a ridge and stopped and beheld the bowed face of the great lake below us. In its cast we saw a handful of men moving along the shore. They did so without haste. They were nude, dark and bent against the light of the water that caught the light of the not yet risen sun like a uplit bowl in the midst of an otherwise voided land and at that drop we all sat for some moments, the face of the lake white with the light of the sky. The air moved over the water, moved over and past us and back down the trails from whence we had come.

Ignacio kicked his mount. It dropped down off the ridge, the rump of the animal exploding away from us like a fist, and we all gave chase. The valley before us bucked and jumped and the horses beneath us snorted with the fury of the descent. Perhaps fifty yards from the encampment Luis screamed and the desperate sound of it ran through us like fire. Galloping and screaming the oaths of the wronged we burst in upon their camp firing our pistols without discipline and trampling one man full underhoof as he lay asleep in his blankets. We made a wide circle in the sand and turned back upon the men who were now running to weapons at the saddles of their own animals that shied and whinnied with terror. Luis let loose another high scream and one of the men knelt by his horse and fired, this single shot finding itself deep within Luis's arm. A great surge of blood came forth, blanketing my breeches, and Luis nearly fell from the saddle as we galloped back into the camp and shot down the gunman where he crouched in his nakedness. We quickly dismounted and beat the man heedlessly until his face was as though a piece of tin stove in by a boot. We then calmed ourselves, and we gathered up the other two, leaving the trampled one to lie by the lake in his black and soaking bedsheets.

They were nomads. Drifters without cause or story and they stood before us in the morning, confused in their undergarments. An American. A Chinaman. We tied them and led them off to a stand of pines. They were perhaps a few years older. The American's beard was bushy, the Chinaman's sparse. Both their faces ran deep with creases from the sun and their skin so browned that it seemed as though the American had become a Chinaman or the Chinaman another race altogether, a race the American had joined out in whatever waste they travelled, shunned by all save themselves. All that had saved them from the quick death of their trampled companion was their decision to wake and to walk down to the lake and to bathe. And in that bathing would have fallen from them the trail and its traces and the traces of all else besides. But they did not make it to the water. They were ours.

"What is it you want?" said the American.

"You killed a man along the trail," said Ignacio.

"What'd he look like?"

"Dark. Tall. Mexican. You shot him from his horse outside of Tejame."

The Chinese looked to the other and said nothing. The American crossed his arms.

"What if we did?"

"You should not have killed him."

"What if he deserved it?"

"We all deserve it," I said.

The American scratched at his beard and then spit a mouthful of blood into the dirt. He looked out at the lake and the sun that now rose upon it and revealed it to be water and that alone. And he looked back to me.

"That ain't so," he said.

We led them to the pines and tied them to a tree. We then gathered enough kindling and branches to make a decent fire which was built and fed until it was quite high and hot in the rising day and Ignacio bound them. The two men's feet were wrapped as one, and we tied a series of ropes to this footbinding and ran these ropes over a thick and knotty branch directly over the fire, tying the opposite ends round the saddle horns of two horses. I myself whipped the horses until they pulled these men along the ground by their feet and then lifted them up it and off it completely, swinging them like a pendulum by the branch of the tree until they were held at a suspension not six inches above the flames.

What a man will do in this position. What promises are made and deals offered. After a short time the Chinaman's hair caught fire. At first he did not speak but when he did it was in the tongue of his people and it was wild and harried to us, and we mocked it as he burned, jumping up and down and speaking as though we imagined a monkey would speak, digging at our ribs with our fingers.

The flames spread up slowly across both the men and their scalps and the skin of their faces began to bubble and break in the heat, and they made known to us their suffering as they swayed and twisted at the end of the bindings that creaked on the limb of the tree.

We knew, at this point, that the horses must be spoken to. Must be dealt with quietly, and with consideration. When forced to stand with tension at their shoulders and with a great deal of commotion behind their line of sight, it is not unusual for the animals to become afraid.

On the way back to Sierra de la Silla, Ignacio and I took a low road outside of Canatlan. On that day the thin air gave way to a long heat, and the sky itself stretched out into a whiteness absent of clouds and of color and it became with the heated dust a humming glare into which we rode. We were forced to make crude hoods out of burlap sacks, cutting holes for our eyes and likewise our horses were masked, to their profound consternation.

After a time a figure began to take shape out of the white and the dust. He was small, crooked and stooped. A little man, holding in his hands the lead to a mule whose back was weighed with wooden boxes. Our pace did not increase nor did this figure increase his own, though that road was certainly known for its banditry (no small part of such had been perpetrated by Ignacio and myself). This little man did not so much as turn even once to examine the horsemen that rode up behind him. He walked on, indifferent to what the adventure of riders could impart. After a time we overtook him and he stopped on the road, and we trotted our horses around to face him.

The little man's eyes did not meet our own. He was old, his head wrapped in a faded and filthy rag. His jacket was broken and torn, its color and shape forever lost to the desert in which he walked. We looked from this to the load carried by his mule.

"What's in the boxes?" said Ignacio from behind his hood.

The man blinked in the dust and then raised his head.

"Who's asking?" he said.

Ignacio laughed. "We are scourges of these roads, old man," he said, "and we take whatever we choose."

"You are bandits," exclaimed the little man with such force that dust shook off his shoulders.

"We are re-appropriators," I corrected, drawing an audible sigh from Ignacio. "If this load is yours then you, as an obvious man of the soil, are by natural rights its sole possessor. But if you are in the service of a don of the state,"—the impatient movement of Ignacio's horse—"then such a load as your mule now carries properly belongs to the people, and we are its rightful distributors."

We stood like this for a time, the three of us in the whiteness of the day.

"It's bread," the man finally answered.

"Give us a box," said Ignacio, drawing his revolver.

The old man answered that he could not, as the bread was for the owners of the Hacienda de Santa Isabel.

"Sell us a box," I corrected, and drew my mount between Ignacio and the old man. "Sell us a box for we are hungry and have not eaten for nearly two days."

"Sell us a box or we'll take it anyway," said Ignacio.

The man heard this as he stood in front of such a masquerade as hooded men and hooded horses on a road that was barely such in the middle of a place only called into existence by the three who stood upon it.

"In my affairs," he said, "only I command."

Ignacio shot him twice. With the impact of the bullets the little man was taken clear off his feet. His knees locked straight, his face frozen into a rictus of fury. He landed back down on his boots, and then fell on his side in the road. His mule did not move, its lead taught in the hand of the dead man who lay before it.

I watched Ignacio dismount and walk toward the mule and open a box and take two loaves of bread. He then turned and fired another shot into the head of little man and pushed the body—so light did it seem—off the crown of the road and into the ditch.

"That was unnecessary," I said quietly.

"You can't just leave a body in the middle of a thruway," Ignacio responded, his voice muffled by his mouth full of bread.

"If this continues," I said, "I will be leaving you."

"If what continues?" asked Ignacio, mounting his horse, and I found myself tearing the burlap off my head and flinging it in the dust. Ignacio tilted his head back and roared with delight. He turned his horse and rode on but I remained in the road with the still and silent mule in the sunless glare of the day.

"In the end," Ignacio called out, "you will be unable to get along without me."

It was ten years later when I saw Ignacio again, standing in a pen of Huerta loyalists scheduled for execution the morning next. And when he called to me as I rode past, he called not my name, for the streets were already full of this sound, rising in ecstatic chorus and echoing into themselves off the brick walls of the square and multiplying into the heavens.

"Refugio," he shouted at my back. "Refugio Alvarado."

PART II
THE HEADDRESS

Chapter VII

A Child at Dinner. The Wishes of Señora Soto. Power and Its Display. Sparing the Chief.

By the fall of my 30th year the road had given me nothing. Yearning for a roof and a bed, I rode to my mother's sister's house in Coahuila. I knew little then of my cousin Eleuterio Soto. I knew that he was young—some ten years my junior— and I knew what my mother thought of her sister, whom she believed was younger and fiercer than she. My mother often spoke of her with jealousy, for she understood her sister to possess a freedom greater than her own. Señora Soto also had two daughters, about whom I had heard nothing.

But I knew of her husband, Rodrigo Soto, killed many years before by roadmen, gut-shot in a raid and left to die. They had come for him late one morning at his own family's home, and he knelt in the kitchen with a rifle at his cheek, taking aim through the windows as the horsemen circled the house. By his side on the floor sat his wife with a child at her breast and another in her belly, reloading the rifles as he handed them back. The gunshots and the morning sun and the snorting of the horses, the back of the rifleman forever to us, his cause forever just.

Señora Soto received me warmly and brought me in for a

dinner of stewed chicken. I did not drink the wine, nor did she, nor did the sisters, but Eleuterio without question had his share.

He was a fleshy boy, perhaps twenty. He wore a shirt stained with food, his hair too long and he went about barefooted in the house. When questioned about his work or his pleasure or the state of things in his country, he spoke of his friends and their superficial opinions, and the women gave him the silence that allowed him to believe these ideas were sound. He smiled as he spoke, cheerful with his drink. His sisters sat beside him and said nothing and watched the mother who watched us all. So did the evening progress, with the boy talking and the rest of us saying little as he indulged himself in drink and hypotheticals. At length the monologue turned to Díaz.

"But what else are we to do with Díaz?" Eleuterio said to the table. "The President loves the people and the people love the President. What we should do is this. This is the ideal way to proceed. We should simply join the army. Join the army and take the money. My friend Julio—his brother is in the army and he has more money than he can spend. He doesn't worry about food or clothes, and when he is out on the town the girls flock to him in his uniform. Tell me, what is better than this?"

He looked to me. "Tell me," he said again. As I had not voiced my agreement to his childishness, he had begun to doubt the sincerity of my silence. His face began to darken.

"There is nothing to tell, cousin," I said. "Everything has already occurred to you."

The boy slammed his cup down. "Tell me," he said.

"Enough," said the mother. The boy stood slowly and his eyes were still on me.

"Who is this man?" the boy said.

"He is your cousin and the son of my sister," the mother said.

"He is a liar," said the boy. "I can tell from his face, and he lies because he is afraid."

"What am I afraid of?" I asked the boy.

"Either you are afraid of women and you are lower than they are, or you are afraid of me because I am stronger and younger than you."

"I see no one here stronger than myself," I said, my hands folded in my lap. "I do see some younger. They are young as children are young, and they are fat and ignorant as children are."

The boy growled as though he were a bear, and I watched as he threw his cup against the wall where it shattered and fell. I kept my eyes on him as he did so, and I saw his impotence and his terror and all of it plastered over with this fury he would show to me as though performing for a crowd.

"Eleuterio," the mother said sharply. "Clean up, and go to bed." Eleuterio's heavy face hung there, and he did not turn to her but instead kept his eyes on me. At length he moved from behind the table, and he walked past me and down the hallway. We all heard his door swing closed.

As though on a signal, the sisters rose to clear the table. As they did so I reached for my wine, but the mother waved her hand and the daughters took the glasses and replaced them with two small cups and a bottle of mescal. Soto poured both cups full and placed one before me.

Señora Soto did not move, but in that light it was as though she drew the shadow of the room into her and the darkness made her all the more substantial. Her eyes were like my mother's eyes in shape but not content, their darkness full of a quick and deadly light. Her nose and the slope of her face were all as though a cut in the space that opened around her. When she spoke it was of the thoughts she had honed all evening and there was no longer any pretense to solicitude or subtlety.

"You wish to take him from me," she said.

"I have no such thoughts."

"Then why are you here?"

"For rest."

"Do not lie to me, Francisco," she said. "You will take from me that which is mine." She said, "You will take from me that which I have birthed and raised and brought into manhood, and you would take him for your own and you would change him into what you are."

"And what is that?"

She settled her shoulders and she did not answer.

"Your son is grown," I said. "You have done all that could be done but he is far from manhood, and no housewife can bring him to it. I cannot change him," I said. "I have no such powers. I have no such intention."

"Explain your intention."

"My intention is this," I said. I placed my hand on the table between us. "I am done with the road," I told her. "I intend to work. I will ride to Parral and there I will open a small butcher shop. I will build a clientele. I will spend my days on a porch overlooking a river and trees."

"What is he to you?"

"I need an assistant."

Señora Soto raised her chin to me. "This is not who you are," she said.

"You do not know me."

"I have heard enough of you. Everyone, Francisco, has heard quite enough of you, and I see you before me now and this is all I require to make this judgment."

"What have you heard?"

"I have heard of your banditry and your rape and your violence."

"Tales," I said. "These are exaggerated by the people."

"Why would the people exaggerate?"

The two daughters now came from the kitchen and they each took a chair on either side of their mother.

"The people desire that men should do this," I said.

"The people desire that men should rape and kill?" said the mother.

"Yes."

"And why is this?"

"The people themselves desire to rape and kill," I said.

"No," said the mother. "The men desire to rape and kill. The men desire, and the men take what they desire, and as you are a man you can do little but the same."

She was silent for a moment and watched me. I betrayed nothing.

"I have two daughters," said Señora Soto. "Tell me what would you do with them were they not protected by another man such as Eleuterio? Or if you were not constrained by blood or by culture? They are soft and innocent things," she said. "Are they not?"

I did not look to either sister even as their black eyes all rolled up to me like crows. "They are quite beautiful," I said.

"Of course they are. And their beauty is a power over you, and you desire to take it from them because you cannot abide a power other than your own. You know in your heart what it is that we are."

"And what is that?"

"We are fearless. We fear nothing in the world for we are of it. We only fear that which is alien to it, and that is man. But only a man may kill another man, and so we draw you to us, and to keep you we birth the man who would destroy what he does not understand, and you will never understand us."

"Perhaps that is true."

"There is no wonderment there, Francisco. The child of my sister you may be, but a man you are before it. As such you will live out the fate of all men, and you will destroy the life around you to deny your own weakness until your weakness is all that you have.

"I am not weak," I said.

"Then take one of my daughters and leave me my son. You say you will live a quiet life. This is a story you've heard and found it pleasing, and now you wish to repeat it for as long as it serves you. You will take one of my daughters and show her what it is to be in this world that man has made for himself. You will show her what it is."

"And you cannot show her?"

"I am but a housewife. As you see."

I looked to the girls. And I will tell you what it was that I wanted to see. I wanted to see them as thin and as sharp as this mother before me. As tense and as backward drawn like bows and as dangerous and I watched these impressions form within me and I made no questions upon them. I watched these ideas and I held them up to the daughters.

What I saw there were shadows. I saw creatures of cloth and bone. I saw the girl-children of this woman, and I sensed in their reticence the outcome of a life in the echo of this my mother's sister. And I did not fear them.

"I will take the son," I said.

"You shall have him," she responded. "And he will serve you poorly and you will learn a lesson there that you refuse to accept here. You will bring calamity upon him and upon his house. Were I a man I would kill you. As a woman I curse you."

Señora Soto stood, and with her stood her two daughters. She moved back into the further darkness of the house, leaving me the two cups of mescal. I regarded them for some time in the otherwise quiet of the house, both poured both untouched. They were handmade, and as such demonstrated the irregularities of natural work, but such inconsistencies only lent to their appeal.

I reached out, and I moved one before the other, then back, then the other as well. Like a game in the street. The two serving but one purpose and for whom? For we must indeed say so. Or say that it is a purpose and only one at that. I drank them both down, and went to bed.

In the morning Señora Soto loaded up Elueterio's pony with food and with clothes and unnecessaries such as any mother would burden her son, and she kissed him on both cheeks and she waved to us as we left out the yard and rode up into the hills. It was some time later that I turned to look back down at the house and the woman who remained there, small and firm in the hard daylight. I waved out my hand, and I received no response.

Eleuterio and I rode up through the mountains, speaking little. We kept our track sparse and our fires low. My cousin would from time to time tell me to fetch him water or saddle his horse. In response to this I would give him only my empty face which would cause him to fly into a rage. He would stomp and break his own possessions and curse me, and in one such fit of pique at the campfire he went so far as to raise his hand. As he did so I reached up to his wrist and grasped his arm and held it there in the air above us both. I slid the boy's own knife from his belt and held the point of it against his cheek and pushed just enough to draw blood. Then I held the point of the blade to his nose.

"Tonight," I said to him, "I may cut the backs of your knees while you sleep and leave you for the wolves."

After this, Eleuterio spoke to me chiefly in the form of questions. He did not look me in the eyes and he made way for me to pass when I chose to do so and at this all I was pleased. Our time in the mountains thusly proceeded without strain, until we were set upon by an acordata out of the south. I was still wanted in that district and the reward on my head had only grown, and so I chose to use this pursuit to educate my charge. Eleuterio had a childish mind. Despite his professed allegiance to Díaz he was not a lover of the state but only a lover of power and had never seen power exercised by a force other than Díaz. I therefore decided that I would demonstrate power as operated by another hand.

As men of the land, we both knew the acordata was near us before our pursuers found our track. We then began to make our presence evident, tossing smoked cigarettes on the trail, smoking up our morning fire, breaking limbs as we trailed through thickets and brush. As we reeled the acordata ever closer we began to arc widely to the left, circling them slowly. Eleuterio's mood was much improved. He enjoyed this game with men who would, if they only could, kill us and pose our bodies in the marketplace for pennies. At length we determined there were five men, and we led them in an ever-abbreviating tour of the hillsides, winding their animals in tighter circles until their horses became confused by the myriad smells that hung after in the air.

At length their leader quit the trail and took them down into a dry arroyo to camp. The next morning came on clean and sharp and Eleuterio and I stationed ourselves in the rocks above.

It does no good, when dealing with a child, to respond in a childish manner. This only meets his foolishness with foolishness of your own, and it demonstrates that leadership is little more than the application of force. Nor, of course, is it helpful to ignore the behavior. You must understand that the child is trying to destroy you.

Better to let the child know that you could destroy him as easily as you destroy others, but that it your choice to do otherwise. This will cause the child to understand that his rage is encapsulated within your own, which is greater in scope and ambition. As Eleuterio was a child and therefore anxious to destroy and respectful of those who could and did, I guessed (and this correctly), that the proper display of force would bind him that much closer to me. And so Eleuterio was giddy as we took aim with our rifles at the men below us as they moved about their morning cookfire. These were men of the town, older men and as such were short and stout, moving with a slowness that betrayed a difficult night on the hard ground, bending gingerly to stir the pot of beans where it lay on the hot stones. They drank coffee. They spoke amongst themselves. They did not look up, even after our first shot.

Eleuterio and I took to leisurely wounding the men below as they ran about their makeshift camp. Measuring for both wind and distance our aim proved strong, and we landed clean shots in their shoulders and thighs, their bellies and backs.

We rode down in the afternoon to a quiet camp, the bodies lying about the place, the blood skittered across the stones as though by the feet of mice. No single wound proved itself fatal, and to a man they had bled out on the sand of the dry creek bed.

We found the chief unarmed, cowering luridly in his tent, his head full in his hands. I placed this chief up behind me and we left the clearing at a half-trot, riding up out of the arroyo and into the brush and back out into the heat of the afternoon. After some time he spoke.

"Are you going to kill me?" the chief asked, his hands on my hips.

"As soon as we arrive at a suitable spot."

"Why did you not shoot me as you found me?"

"The camp was isolated," I said. "Your men will not be found perhaps for some months. I would like to leave you in the open. If any come searching for you they will know of your fate."

"They will send more," he said.

"Tell me something."

"I will tell you nothing."

"Tell me how you gathered men to come for me. What did you promise them?"

The chief remained silent. I said, "I imagine you promised them nothing but suffering. I imagine you threatened them and their families."

The chief was a young man, a broad forehead, thin limbs and a rich mustache, elevated to this position most likely by family and not inclination. His uniform was of the highest quality, though dusted by the trail and sagging on his frame as though broken by the failure of his leadership.

He said, "I serve out the orders I am given."

"Of course you do. A man of principle and honor." At this I pulled up my horse. "Eleuterio, this is good."

We dismounted. The skin of the young chief had turned to the color of ditchwater and his gait was awkward and stiff as I led him to the edge of the road. His eyes were unfocused, wandering off and away in the distance. Eleuterio and I drew our pistols.

"I want his pants," said my cousin. "And his boots."

The chief turned back to face us. He looked upon the young and chubby and eager Eleuterio as though he were seeing the boy for the first time. The chief's mouth opened to form the words that he would speak but he said nothing.

"You don't want the pants," I said. "He's going to shit them as soon as he's dead." At this the chief's legs gave out, and he fell to his knees in the brush.

"The jacket then," Eleuterio said. He raised his pistol to the face of the chief. "And the ears as well."

At this point, in full view of Eleuterio and myself, the chief began to cry. It was a demonstration that froze us both. He cried and he struggled to free himself of his jacket and the corners of his mouth were turned downward like those of a furious child. He coughed on his tears and he shook quite beyond his control and went on to make a great deal of commotion otherwise until at last he was able to speak.

"I can tell you what it is that they want," he said to us. I looked over to my cousin who even then was squeezing the trigger of the pistol in his hand. I threw my arm against his and the shot popped up in the dust three feet behind the chief, who started at the sound and then fell on his side in the dust, weeping. Eleuterio cursed, and I waved at him with the muzzle of my pistol, gesturing him back to the horses.

The chief told me of unrest in Nuevo León. Every few months the men of Díaz were forced to suppress there a peasant revolt and the federal forces were beginning to strain under the pressure. The crackdowns had become increasingly bloody. I asked the chief if there was love in his heart for Díaz and he said there was none. At this point Eleuterio came walking back from the horses.

"Can we shoot him now?"

"We will not shoot him," I said, and Eleuterio cursed again and stamped in the dirt like the child he was and walked back.

"We will use him," I said, looking at the chief with who knows what he saw in my eyes. And we did. The chief returned to his post and he served his masters dutifully and rose in rank and all the while was of great use to me, keeping me informed of all the federal goings-on in Monterrey, until I returned to that city as its lord and master.

Chapter VIII

The City of Parral. A Guitar. Bleeding the Butcher. The Wooing of Conchita Aurelio del Valle. A Washerwoman. Boris the Painter.

Eleuterio and I gathered some 300 head of cattle from the surrounding countryside and drove them into Parral. We set up our shop, and I took charge. He returned for his mother and sisters and saw them settled in town. The first winter was cold. The second mild.

The city of Parral lies in peace beneath a benevolent sky. Each cobblestone situates itself in harmony with the others surrounding, and each tree leans over its respective path as though offering its shade to those in need. I would often take my midday rest in the shadow of the cathedral along the banks of the river, and I would watch there with a glass of wine the children that played along its banks, as liquor was absent from my diet at this time. It is here in this beauty and quiet that I tried in vain to live a just and innocent life.

Eleuterio had grown into some semblance of a man, and for this his mother and sisters thanked me with food, with baskets of prepared meals and bottles of wine and other such materials dropped on my porch without a hello or goodbye.

I did not know if Eleuterio would take to the sedentary life of a town. He seemed a cruel and thoughtless boy, but in truth he was too unformed to prefer one mode to another. Once he took a breath of the city he became a man of it, no longer rough but buttery, full of the humor and frivolousness that affect city men. He began to spend less time at the shop and more time drinking, thinking and talking. And then, disastrously, he fell in love.

What compounded his error was that the girl's father was Don Aurelio del Valle. Lord of the town and all surrounding, Don Aurelio had made his fortune in the silver mines, staffing them with the peasants of the desert as well as the Tarahumara, sending those pagan souls by the bushel into the pits from which they often did not emerge.

Rejected by Díaz and avoided even by the bloody barons of Chihuahua, Aurelio had settled with age into his own fiefdom and operated it as such, throwing widows from out their homes, letting orphans run wild in the streets, destroying men who dared oppose him. He was a wicked man and his sons were still worse, wandering the streets as though they owned them, and perhaps they did.

Eleuterio was by now a character incapable of high crimes, a plain and naïve and silly young man who had become ensnared in the charms of the young Conchita Aurelio de Valle. She was indeed beautiful, pleasing in both form and color, and she worked away the days at her father's dry-goods store. Every week Eleuterio would arrive for necessities, and she would wander the aisles and climb ladders and dig vigorously (too vigorously, by my estimation, or perhaps just vigorously enough to satisfy the desired ends) in sacks to procure his items. For his part, Eleuterio made certain there were many sacks in which to dig and many ladders to climb.

My cousin had also found a guitar. I do not know where he found it. His mother, when she would speak to me, would speak of little else. She and I would stand in the square under the cottonwoods as Eleuterio with his instrument took his post by the door of the girl's shop.

"You've seen what he's up to," his mother would say.

"I have, Señora."

"Confess to me now that you gave it to him."

"I did no such thing."

Señora Soto's head would shake slowly from side to side. "His father had a low opinion of guitar players. Warbling in the street and begging for coins. It's obscene."

"Without question."

"His father would not abide by them."

"Of course not."

"His father believed they were little better than prostitutes."

"Let's not judge prostitutes so harshly."

She would turn her eyes to me and then back to the porch where her son strummed his guitar and say to me, quietly, "You are a scabrous and a hateful man."

Eleuterio was a poor player, cobbling bits together from tunes he had heard elsewhere, perhaps lying drunk on the floor of a cantina or half awake on the sodden cot of a whore. The lyrics lurched from laments for dispossessed lands to half-forgotten loves to the manipulations of knives in dark alleyways. Regardless of the meandering paths, the chorus always brought home the goal of his quest: the love of Conchita Aurelio del Valle.

"*But despite all of these troubles*"—Eleuterio would begin, free from the constraints of any obvious melodic direction—"*and the troubles of the world in which mine are lost*"—his notes gaining in volume what escaped them in timbre—"*my love for the Señorita del Valle lives on!*"

It is, perhaps, more lovely in the Spanish. Or perhaps not. The absence of the young Conchita's presence on the porch said more than enough. Each day for close to three months (the three hot months of the summer when sensible people would move out of the sun) Eleuterio's interminable yodeling wound its way through the central plaza of the city as an affront, I began to believe, to the dignity and manner of the place.

And on he went. The daily visitations, the daily exercise of fat fingers over recalcitrant strings. It may be said, charitably, that my cousin was beginning to learn the instrument. It may be said as well that after a time his voice found a range more natural to its limitations. Nevertheless, as is the course of such things, the object of such efforts remained at a remove.

The life of a town butcher is not without pleasures. The hours are undemanding, the customers civil, and he eats quite well. There were forces at work, however, which had begun to conspire against my success. Pigs were simple enough to slaughter in the yard behind my market—I could, perhaps, offer as many as two pigs a week—but for beef I was obliged to do my work in the Parral slaughterhouse.

It should be no surprise who owned the slaughterhouse and who therefore employed those who would impede my progress. Don Aurelio had a grand stake in this place, as he did all else in the town of Parral. It became impossible to earn any profit there from a simple exchange of goods and services. I owned the store and owned the cattle but the slaughterhouse was manned by Aurelio's minions, exacting their onerous fees. Here I was, each day with beef that I had slaughtered with my own hands, unable to bring it to market thanks to the escalatingly opaque bureaucracy of the meathouse.

The foreman could never find my papers. They were in the improper order. The animal I slaughtered did not match the description I provided. The number of animals was incorrect. Those things which were to be understood were misunderstood, and those things addressed in vagaries suddenly erupted into decisive mistakes. There were taxes and fees and plans to establish credit, which, on the whole, would cost me more than the beef in the first place. There was no shortage of reasons as to why I was unable, day after day, to leave with the beef I had butchered.

At this point, two conniving lieutenants of Don Aurelio would reliably appear: Terras, thin and dry; Osello, oily and fat. Like a fairy tale, these two would poof into appearance at my side and urge me to keep heart. "We are your friends," they would tell me. "Let us handle this transaction with the officers of this house with whom we are most familiar. Hand the meat over to us and we will see to it that the books are put aright."

And if I were to refuse?

"Do as you may," would come the response. "But the times are difficult for a butcher without meat."

I took their deal, time and again. And in but an hour or two, here into my shop they would slither, accompanied by the slabs of meat wrapped in sackcloth and perched on the backs of short peasants in gut-stained shirts.

Terras: "Allow us to gift you this meat to you as a kind and generous favor."

Osello: "A gift, Terras?"

Terras: "Of course, Osello."

Osello: "But what wondrous charity!"

Terras: "We do and will continue to support our local merchants in any way possible."

On cue, they would turn to me.

"If only, dear butcher, we may ask a little recompense for our generosity. We now find ourselves in your debt twice over, and ask for but a single repayment."

It was in this way that I, the butcher, was bled. And so I raised the prices. I sold the best cuts back to the slaughterhouse at a loss because the cost was too dear for the people of that town. I spent less. I began to shrink. I began to fade.

How was an honest man to make his living in the shadow of such thieves? Could I but butcher these two fools and splay their carcasses in front of my shop as testament and warning. These were the dark connotations my thinking had begun to take on at this time.

I took in the afternoons on the back porch of the shop. As I found the heat terrific and working indoors impossible I would retire to a chair in the shade to sleep and it was in this way on one such afternoon that I was awoken by Eleuterio's ongoing woo.

To my surprise I was not offended. I thought about being offended, in the way that the mind moves at half-sleep from the origin of the thought to the distance from it that sleep would afford, but as the song went forward I found myself wandering on the journey Eleuterio described in song. Past horses and drunken fathers and abandoned mothers and sunsets and impossible romance and all of it pushed onward by the subtle phrases of the guitar.

I dropped my feet from the rail and rose. I walked through the shop and from across the empty square I caught sight of my portly cousin wandering underneath the trees, his eyes closed tight in song. And once again to my surprise at the far side of the square the young Conchita Aurelio de Valle stood, stood in the flesh and blood in her doorway, her hands clasped primly behind her back. As Eleuterio walked through the shadows I watched the girl lean this way and that to keep sight of him through the trees and the shadows of the trees and at length she walked down the steps and into the shade. She moved to him in the thick heat of that day with her hands still clasped behind her, and to my eyes her face was empty of intent, looking up at my cousin as one would a creature curious and harmless and interesting. With his eyes still shut tight, Eleuterio had arrived at his chorus.

"*But despite all of these troubles,*" he began strongly, "*and the troubles of the world in which mine are lost,*" he continued, "*my love for the Señorita del Valle lives on!*"

The girl extended her small hand, and as it came to rest on the arm of my cousin he did not turn even as his song died in his throat. His fingers had frozen on the neck of the guitar and his hand hung in the air and the song was gone to that place where all songs go when they are not sung. Eleuterio then took the guitar from off his belly. He held it by the neck at his side and he looked down at the girl who slipped her hand off his arm and looked at him plainly in the face.

I am a romantic. The romantic in me believes that when my cousin turned and saw this young girl, I believe that he saw there more than a girl. I believe that he saw the answer to the question he had asked every day since he had seen her behind the counter of that shop, and it was an answer that pertained to many other things as well, such as the world and fate and the nature of age, and that all of these elements revealed themselves to him at that moment as righteous and benevolent and aligned with his desires.

And so the girl that was more than a girl raised both her hands and laid them lightly on the rounded handles of flesh which bulged from Eleuterio's tightly-belted pants. He placed his guitar against a cottonwood behind him and he slipped his hand behind the neck of the girl and she relaxed into his arm. At this point I turned back into the house, allowing them their privacy.

He had her in the basement of her store upon the sacks of rice. As was her custom. Eleuterio, simple as he was, believed he was the only broad-backed man of Parral to enjoy such pleasures as could be found in Conchita Aurelio's ricesacks, for an answer to an interminable question she may have been but she was a young girl as well. As such she was careless. And she was passionate, and tempestuous and changeable in that passion. And I knew she loved to love and loved no one at all. This I knew, for I knew of such girls, and I knew that my cousin did not, and that is why, in the following weeks, in which my cousin proposed, I was thankful that she lingered in her acceptance.

It was in the consideration of these things, as I swept off the steps to my shop one evening, that an old woman walked up from the riverbank with a large woven basket jammed hard into her hip. The night was vacant and dull, the square silent save for the insects that clicked and chirped back up in the trees like little boxes of metal and bone. As I swept I heard the woman approach, heard her feet in the dust. Before I could look up— and in truth I desired little to acknowledge her at all—she spoke.

"Who are you?" she asked me.

She wore rags wound up on her head, and she stank of the still and the stagnant water. The basket stained and empty. Her voice worn and yet buoyed by an anger or disgust I could not place. I turned my back to her and continued with my work, and she asked the question again.

"I am the butcher," I said to her over my shoulder. She laughed with a laugh that said to me that my answer was a dodge and a lie.

I stopped sweeping and I turned. I looked at her. Her eyes were wide and white in the falling light, her bare feet on the dirt no different than a crow's.

"Get away from here," I said to her. "My shop is closed."

The old woman bent at the waist to find my eyes which I would not give. And I would not give them because I knew her for what she was, and that was a spirit and a malignant one, a devil on legs that had come out of the water for me regardless of how she appeared, and I felt fear in my heart at her presence. Who can say the nature of this fear? I can say that it gripped me and that I could not deny it. I ground the handle of the broom in my hands and I spied the harmless old wretch out the corner of my eyes as she stood back up, and rested on her back foot.

"Someone has taken you," the old woman said. "Someone has taken you and put in his place another. Who looks and speaks and walks as did the first."

I worked my bottom lip with my teeth. "I do not know you," I said. "Nor do you know me, nor have you ever." I know that this was true. I also knew it to be a lie, for in a time that was larger than this I knew she had there been alongside me. I cannot say. I knew it as I knew my mother's voice. I felt it as one may feel in the moments before one's death that death has indeed come, and all of the life so lived has been done so to seek and attain this moment in all its pathos and mendacity. The town stretched out around us frozen and dead, as though she and I were caught in a moment in which no others moved nor ever even had. As though the world had moved on from this moment and into others even as we stood.

She took a step toward me, the basket out at her side. She leaned her weight now upon that bare foot and she said to me "All of the change you wish to make will be part of the nothing which changes here."

"I wish to make no change," I told her.

"But you have changed. Or have tried." And it was then I was sure that she saw my fear, for it had become impossible for me to hide any longer, and at it she laughed the broken laugh of the crone she was when she saw she had sounded my depths and found the bottom without perhaps even intention. Did she even know what she was? The power that lay within her that she had in her derangement grasped and held and then become? I have never feared a man, nor could I, for no man could know me, for I am beyond men as men would be. I am a new man, newly made by my will, and none may touch me where I lie in my rectitude and strength.

"I have changed," I said.

Her laughter subsided into a crooked smile that opened and lingered across her desiccated face. A handful of dim teeth hung from her gums. "Do you miss yourself?"

"I am right here," I told her.

A laugh from her again. Then she did this. Something pathetic and practiced. She held out a bent finger like a figure at a carnival, like a character in a play on a stage under torches; such was the affect of this performance, the intention of it and the superficiality of it, the veneer of threat that only served in its execution to signal the presence of the threat itself, somehow tied to it, indicative of it.

"You were never here," she said. "And those whom you love will suffer for it. Your children," she said. "And your children's children." She paused for a moment, as though thinking this threat through. "I will come for them as well," she added simply.

She turned from me with this nonsense, and she walked with the basket still lodged at her hip of bone into the darkness of the square and toward the church which she did not enter. She was mad. And I was mad for thinking her to be anything other than a broken washerwoman long thrown out of whatever house would have had her and fated to wander the riverbanks and scavenge scraps from the flotsam. Sweat lay like a cold sheet down my back. I watched her go, moving beside that church and into the alley that ran at its flank and into the shadow that hung there. And was then gone within it.

Conchita Aurelia's dry-goods store was open and cool, and as I entered it the young girl straightened her shoulders to me as she stood alone behind the wide counter. She was thinner than I expected, her face too narrow, and she wore her hair down and about her cheeks to conceal it. A gray and simple blouse, a skirt of faded yellow. I placed my order and I watched her as she filled it. As she scooped and weighed and walked to a side table and slid the powders into three jars which she brought over to the countertop and tightened before me. I looked at her hands as she did so, and then slid two American coins across to her. She made no move to take them.

"Don't you know what they are?" I asked.

"Pay with real money," she said.

"You've never seen these before, have you?"

"Real money," she said again.

"This is real money. More real and backed by more gold than Díaz has ever held in all of his banks."

She took the jars off the counter and walked back to the table. Her fist on her waist. "Pay or get out," she said.

"You are so easily upset. You don't know what they are. Are you embarrassed?"

Her face was unchanged.

"I am from Durango," I said. "Have you ever been to Durango?"

"No."

"And yet you are familiar to me." I tapped my finger on the countertop. "I have seen you before."

"I am here every day."

"No. I have seen your likeness. I have seen you in a painting."

"I have no painting," she said.

"Yes. You have been captured in a painting with a remarkable similarity."

Her eyes dropped to the coins before her and then to the shelves behind her and then back to me."

"Where did you see this painting?" she asked.

"It hangs in the stairwell of the sugar merchant, Ramon De la Cruz."

"I do not know Ramon De la Cruz."

"The painting is of his third daughter. In it she wears a ridiculous dress."

"So the painting is not of me."

"It is labeled as the daughter of the merchant, and yet it is not."

Conchita Aurelio stood back to her full height and I saw that she was quite tall. Taller than me. She squared her shoulders once more in a gesture in which she most likely found confidence and placed her palms on the counter between us.

"How would you explain it?" she said.

"It would seem to be a mystery."

"More than seem."

"And then it came to me."

The girl leaned back, and her face knotted up in concern. "What did it feel like?" she asked.

"What did what feel like?"

"When it came to you," she said. "The answer. What did it feel like?"

"It felt like a bolt," I said.

"From the blue."

"From the clear blue sky."

"Revelations do not come as bolts," she said. "This is childish. You are a childish man and I have no time for childish men. Now take your ridiculous coins and get out."

"But you have not heard my solution!"

"You mean your revelation?" she said. "About the mystery of your own imagining about a painting that does not exist."

"But it does."

She turned to look behind her. To the shelves and the sacks and the cans of tomatoes. She turned back.

"Go on," she said. "And no childishness."

And so I told the girl about the merchant De la Cruz and his third daughter. How she was so plain and homely and without fire and beauty, and how her wealthy father pitied her and the spinsterish life into which she would grow. I told her that as he walked through his house it occurred to him that what this girl required was proof and evidence of her beauty which would serve to feed a stronger vision of herself and inspire her confidence and push her on to do all of which she was capable. And so he called for a painter of great talent from the capital city.

"Here comes this painter," I said. "We do not know his name. Let us say it is Boris."

"Is he Russian?" she asked.

"No."

"Boris is a strange name for a Mexican."

"What name would you prefer?"

"Diego."

"Diego is a common name," I said.

"It is a Mexican name."

"His name is Boris," I said, and the little whore smiled. "Boris arrives into town and he pays his visit to the house of the merchant de la Cruz and he meets with the daughter and afterward the painter becomes despondent."

"Because she is so plain," she said.

"Of course."

"But what do we mean by *plain?*"

"Unremarkable," I said, and now she smiled again. "This painter leaves the house and he wanders through town and as he does so he experiences overwhelming despair. There is nothing in this girl which would inspire a painting. There is nothing to explore within her, no mystery no puzzle no question no joy. And so he has no passion for this work. He cannot begin it. He cannot complete it. The work is impossible."

"He will lose his money."

"You see the depth of his dilemma."

"I do," she said. She bit her lip. It was a heavy lip. I studied the skin of it as it turned white beneath her teeth. She turned her eyes up to the ceiling. "I can imagine," she said, "in the moment in which he is resolving to pack up and return to Chihuahua in shame—"

"Yes."

"A woman passes him by, on a horse."

"Yes."

"A woman on a dark horse," she said, "her hat low on her face. She passes him by, and the painter's eye sees her, and it knows what it sees, and the painter knows this to be extraordinary."

"Yes," I said.

"The painter begins to follow her. He learns where she stables her horse, learns when she leaves each morning for the market, learns her path as she walks past the square, the fountain, the stables. He studies her face and her movements and in doing so he is relieved. His spirits renewed, Diego approaches the canvas."

"Boris."

"Boris approaches the canvas."

"The painting is saved," I said.

She watched me for a few moments. She weighed the silence between us.

"It could be better," she said.

"What could be?"

"Boris should paint the poor plain girl," she said. "In doing so he should find within her the spark of the other woman whom he admires and he should learn that such a spark is the spark of all women. In making this discovery he should fall in love with the girl."

"No!"

"Yes."

"But she is so plain!"

"I know nothing of her other than this vague and unflattering description you have provided. I am unmoved by her plight. If this be a story it should be a story of love."

"That is precisely what it is!"

She slid the three jars across the counter to me. "Take them," she said, "and return to pay me when you have real money. I am very busy this afternoon."

At this she turned and she walked back into the rows of shelves. I watched her do so. And as she did so, and at the moment before she turned the corner to disappear from my sight, she turned back to me, just her head. So slightly. She caught my eye. She turned back.

I climbed over the counter. I climbed the counter and walked down the aisle and at its turn I saw here where she wandered and she turned again at the sound of my approach. Her eyes grew wide.

"What are you doing," she said.

I grabbed the girl by the arm, high up near the shoulder, and there I felt the flesh yield like a fruit as she cried out and I shoved the flat palm of my hand far back between her teeth until it nearly touched the thin film of skin that lines the bones of the jaw. The girl pushed back against me, her hips squirming as I pulled her further into the rows.

"You are a prideful little bitch," I told her. "You are base and vile," I said and she bit down on my hand in acknowledgement of it. "And I would not wed my cousin to a whore." Her long legs kicked and splayed and intertwined with my own and as they did so it became all the more obvious to us both that those legs were inconsequential in relation to my own, and pathetic, and helpless. I found the stairs to the basement and wrapped my arm tight around her waist, so tight that she caught her breath, high, in the back of her throat as would a child when frighted, instinctual and unconscious and beyond her control. I began to descend, my face in that cooling air like an iron lifted straight from the forge.

CHAPTER IX

The Beating of
Eleuterio. A Defacement.
Veils and Dry Dresses.
The City Beneath Us.
Eleuterio's Dreams.

The brothers Aurelio accosted Eleuterio on the square the next day. The four of them grabbed my soft cousin as he walked across the plaza toward our shop—the two twins, a smaller one not barely five feet, and the monster Choro, dark and foreboding and stupid as a mule. It was Choro who took Eleuterio up in his enormous hands and lifted him clear off the ground and threw him with violence against a split-rail fence. Ringed as it was with shops such as my own, the square became quickly filled with witnesses, while by the river the mothers shushed the children in their splashing.

The twins grabbed my cousin's fleshy arms and pulled them tight round his back and knocked his green felt hat to the ground. The smallest brother then stepped forward in his elegant boots (so small and tooled as though for a child) and slowly and with great deliberation brought the black heel of one boot down upon the crown of my cousin's hat, crushing and grinding it into the dirt.

"Outrageous!" Eleuterio shouted. The little man pulled the guitar from his hands.

"Nothing is more outrageous," he said to my cousin, "than your own actions."

"I court Conchita," said my cousin, "with honor and with—"

Here he was cut short by a slap to the face.

"I do so," Eleuterio began again, which earned him a tremendous kick to the groin by the monster Choro. The blow would've felled my cousin if not for the twins who still held him at the wrists.

"With honor—" continued Eleuterio, and Choro clubbed him in the eye. The smack of it fell flat on the yard.

"And with a clear heart," Eleuterio continued, which earned a patiently delivered blow to the other eye.

"For I love Conchita Aurelio!" my cousin said loudly enough to be heard across the square.

"You say you love her," said the little man, "and yet you treat her like meat."

Then the small brother took up the battered guitar upon which my cousin had performed and he swung it against my cousin's head with great force, breaking and splintering the thing until it hung awkward on its neck like a dead chicken. This brought my Eleuterio to his knees.

The little man then reached into his waistband and produced a revolver, which he cocked and placed against my cousin's forehead. It was at this moment that I clapped my hand around the throat of this man, slipping a larding needle clean through both of his nostrils. This caused him some distress, and he began to squeal like a pig and arch his back against me. It was in this state that I dragged him away from Eleuterio, and I turned him to face his brothers.

"Release him," I said to the two idiot twins who held Eleuterio's arms. They did so.

"Back away and keep your hands visible," I said, "or I

will deface your brother." The brothers all stepped away, and Eleuterio fell to his knees.

"You are to let this man be," I said. "He is to walk these streets unmolested."

The twins nodded their agreement. Choro made no move, his eyes black with hate.

I withdrew the needle from the small man's nose and with it came a bright arc of blood, over which he clapped his hand, and he began to moan. I shoved him away from me, while at the same time drawing my own pistol from my waist and leveling it at the brothers where they stood. I walked to my cousin and pulled him to his feet. Making our way out of the circle of men, I made a point to walk closest to the hulking Choro. Taking careful aim, I brought the heel of my boot down with force upon his ankle, cracking it like a dead dry branch.

Such was the beginning of the end of my peacefulness in Parral.

The women arrived with the cover of darkness. Eleuterio's mother and sisters rustled up the stairs and into my house in their veils and dry dresses. They came with beans and stewed vegetables and my cousin's women cared for him as he lay on my bed in the back of the house. I sat in the kitchen with my eyes out the door, keeping a lookout for movement in the nighttime, listening for the sounds of vengeful men approaching us all in the dark. As such I took no notice of the mother as she took a seat across the table from me.

As she cleared her throat I turned to her. I then stood and walked to the counter and returned with a cup of water for her and took my seat across the table.

"You will avenge this," she said, her face abstracted in the light. The veil of crepe was thrown back over her hair as though a headdress.

100

"You will avenge him," she said to me. "You will avenge our family."

"I have every intention of doing so," I said. "Eleuterio and myself."

"Eleuterio is a broken man," his mother said. She did not look at the floor nor the door nor anywhere else in the room. "He is lovesick. His father—" she began.

I held up my hand. "I see on that bed the son of his father."

She looked at my hand and then once more at me, as though to gauge not the veracity of what I had said but my own belief in my utterance, and in truth that belief was flickering, contingent.

"You will see that he does what is necessary."

"I will."

She said nothing for a time. The night and the earth slowed in that silence, in a manner with which I was familiar. It was as though she could will it so. There was in that room then the profoundest silence, and in it Señora Soto said "You did this."

I raised my chin. "What did I do?"

"The girl child was assaulted yesterday. She was brutalized in the basement of her own shop. She lies in her father's house and she has not awoken." She settled her shoulders. "This was not my son."

I waved my hand. "Who is to say how many men that little whore entertains each day."

She nodded at my hand where it hung in the air. "You have been bitten," she said.

I looked at the marks and then held my palm up to her. "The brothers," I said. "From whom I saved your boy."

"You have brought ruin to my boy," she said. "And now you must avenge this ruin as only you are capable. Because you are capable of nothing else."

I sat as I was and for many moments I searched my heart.

In that searching I found that I had no anger within it to meet her own.

"I have lived well here," I finally said.

"You have a house."

"Yes."

"And you have an occupation."

"I make my living."

"And you have nothing underneath it all to hold it as one," she said. "These are but fragmentary incidents for you and are neither solid nor real."

"Perhaps I am more than you see here."

"Perhaps you are a scourge," Señora Soto replied. "You know what you are but you do not listen to your own voice. And you have no business here. Years ago I cursed you," she said. "It was a senseless curse because one already hangs above you and is distributed among those close to you like fog and like smoke. I blame myself alone that I have allowed my family to be so close. It was an allowance I made out of unreasonable hope that the world itself seemed to force upon me. Now I wish only to be quit of you. Time will show me if I am."

She rose, and she returned to the bedroom where her son lay tended by his sisters. The two younger women bent at the knee between the convalescing body of Eleuterio Soto, the small rigid figure of the mother intervening between them both as though a prime third. She bent closely to the prone face of her son. She did not kiss him, nor did she issue the order to quit the room and the house along with it even as it was done. The women gathered their implements, their cures and their food, and they moved soundlessly out the door and back out into the night.

I watched them go and I sat as I had, and I said to myself that I was still waiting for the sounds of men from the river with knives in their belts. Or I waited for the snuffle of a horse tied to a tree at the edge of the light. I said to myself that I waited for others. For others to come to me and in their coming they would call me forth, would demand my act. I would be summoned by them backward into who I had been and that summoning would be beyond me and therefore correct, and I would rightfully take my place, retake my place. I would have cause. And the desire would lie in the cause. Would grow from it like a seed from shit. And in that waiting I saw my lie. The lie for which Señora Soto rightly faulted me and I saw the danger inherent within it. I saw that in my waiting for others the desire does not grow from the cause but the reverse, and so it had always been, and so then I was. And had always been. Others would wait for me. Waited for me. I would be the summoner, am the summoner and not the summoned and never again. And so I walked into my bedroom and I pulled up the floorboards and from under them I retrieved my gunbelts, revolvers and rifles. I lifted Eleuterio from his bed and situated him with a knife and rifle and ammunition and we mounted two ponies for the ride out to the Hacienda Aurelio del Valle.

We rode through the square in that dead night, the scene artificial. That which was before us was but feebly papered over to resemble the square of Parral as I had known it for that which I had known was empty and free from whatever animation it had hitherto possessed. The hooves rang flat on the cobbled streets, the weight of the bandoliers like two arms crossed over my chest.

The town fell away and the night took us in. We went south. No wind was to follow us into the rising walls of the valley and the air smelled not of tree nor fire nor riverwater. Eleuterio remained silent on the pony behind me.

The track in the high moonlight was pale against the black of the rocks and our two ponies snorted as we climbed. We rose higher toward the moon as the track unfolded through the stones as though the track walked on its own two legs and one turn led to another.

Eleuterio finally spoke. "Why did Conchita's brothers attack me, cousin?"

"They are her brothers," I said. "They are protective of her."

"Don't they know that I love her?"

"They wouldn't believe it," I said to him. "And besides," I said, "you had already taken her."

He was silent for some time. We rode on in that silence until quietly, like a child his voice high and thin and full of amazement of the depth of the world he said, "How did you know?"

"Cousin. I do not believe she was the girl for you."

"No," Eleuterio shook his head. "No. We have spoken about our life together. We will settle in town. I will take a job at the mine. We will have as many children as we can."

We rode up the left crest of the valley. The moon lay on its back out in the sky as though to tempt men over the sides of their track and into the air in which it sat further and further away and it was obvious and unbearable to look upon. Gripped by something nameless, my hands ran over my body to feel my revolvers, feel the rifle slung around my shoulders.

We held up not a half mile above the hacienda, its windows black in the night. Crouching against a wall of slate with our horses hobbled beside us Eleuterio and I looked back down behind us upon the town which lay sprawled across the floor of the valley.

"As many children as we can," Eleuterio said again to remind himself of the talk and the promises that lay within it and to solidify those promises in his mind. "You admit that she is beautiful," he said to me, to solidify that truth as well.

"She is," I said.

"And my mother, I know my mother will come to love her as well." Eleuterio turned to me. "You saved me," he said.

"Of course."

"You are helping me demonstrate myself to Don Aurelio."

"I am."

"We will meet with him," my cousin said, nodding. "And we will speak with him about the violence of his sons and their mistakes." Eleuterio's face was firm. "These were mistakes," he said. "They must be acknowledged and tried and perhaps even forgiven before they can be dismissed by me," he said. "And the Don will then see me and will know that I am worthy of his daughter."

"He will."

"I will tell him of my time in front of her shop," Eleuterio said. "And I will tell him that I do not need a job in his mine. I will tell him that I have prospects in this town otherwise."

"Yes."

"For I would not take her from here." Eleuterio looked out over the valley. "And she and I will live on the square. We would prosper quickly. We would prosper and pay him back two-fold," he said, looking out at the lights of the town below us in the dark.

Eleuterio motioned toward the northeastern leg of the uneasy expanse as it lay beneath us across the floor of the earth. "We live over here. It is a fine house, is it not?" This is what he asked me.

"It is a good house," I said.

"It is," he agreed. "Your house is a fine one too," he added. We sat in silence, watching the lights wink in the distance below us. "We are fortunate to have them," he said. Oh I wished he would've stopped speaking but he continued on to say that we were fortunate men. Men who were violent by nature but had fallen into the fortune of the town and of love.

"You know me," he said. "You know I was a fool. And a murderer."

"You killed for your own protection."

"I enjoyed what I did. Shooting men and watching them die as I did. It was an evil thing, this violence. If not for you I would have pursued it. But you, cousin," he said to me. "You have taken me in and shown me the possibility of a better life," he said. "You have allowed me be a better man."

The sound itself did not surprise me, even as the air around us split in two like a tree halved by an axe. Eleuterio leapt up above me, his hands flying out with a grunt of surprise. His fingers, even in his gloves (this I remember, this I can still see) were bent into claws as if to tear down the black around us and expose us there to the blast of the thing behind the stars, the thing that waits for us all behind the back of the moon.

CHAPTER X

In the Stalls of Don Aurelio. The Mystery of Capital. The Skinning of Villa's Feet. Prey For Larger Animals.

I awoke with a snap. I was seated, my hands tied at my back, my chest damp with sweat and blood. I smelled hay and shit and the movement of horses and knew at once that I sat in a stable.

"Where is my cousin?" I demanded. For this I received a strike on my head from the butt of a rifle.

Blinking through sweat, I saw that I sat at the back of a stall, facing the doors. Before me stood two of the brothers— the small one, delicate almost, his features those of a child that had weathered and never yet turned into a man. Another stood beside him, unfamiliar to me. The little man wore an enormous bandage over his nose, and this pleased me. The other was bootless, short and muscular. He wore the cotton shirt and pants of a peasant, and his hands were clasped behind his back. He looked at me as though I belonged in that stall.

Between them both sat a large man in a plain wooden chair, his brown face like a carving made by primitives with dull and simple tools. His white shirt hung open at his chest and from his neck winked a single thin necklace of silver. The mood of the Don was sanguine.

"Choro," he said, his eyes above me. "Put down the rifle."

Shuffling. The clink of the metal barrel against the stone wall.

I spit my own blood into the hay and twisted my neck to see the enormous brother. He stood right at the edge of my vision, his eyes furious. He wore a rough brace of planks on either side of his booted leg, the entirety wrapped about with yellow ropes.

"You are the butcher," said Don Aurelio. "You run a mediocre shop in the plaza. You sell meat, which you buy back from me due to your own stupidity and neglect. You are the cousin of a barbarous simpleton, and the owner of a fine rifle which I will gift to my granddaughter so that she may hunt pheasants on my land."

The little brother shook with silent laughter.

"I run a fine shop," I responded.

"The condition of your shop is immaterial," Don Aurelio said. His little eyes opened wide to accentuate his speech. "It would be disingenuous to consider it your property in any event. As it is on loan from the bank of Parral we could not say it is your shop, fine or not, can we?" He cocked his head to one side and waited. "It has ceased to be your shop," he said. "It is now mine."

"You plan to kill me," I said. "You plan to take that which is mine."

The Don snorted. His heavy skull ground out a circle in its socket and then fell still. The two brothers on either side of him stood entirely still, as though they were stone protectorates of an obscene orientalism.

"Your inability to fulfill such a contract as has been drawn before you and signed by you in the witness of your fellows brings you into default," the Don said. "I have adjusted the date of repayment on your loan and I find you late by," at this the Don paused and withdrew from his hip a spangled pocketwatch.

The face popped open with a click. "One hour and seventeen minutes." He clapped the face shut and assembled himself as before. "As I currently have no payment from you, I accept your shop."

"Which is my home," I said.

Don Aurelio snorted. He placed his large hands with great deliberation on his knees. He leaned forward. His jowls sagged before me like a hound and his voice was little more than a whisper in the stall.

"You have no home," he said. "You have no property. No name, no license, no mark upon the land toward which you may signal your dominance and possession. You exist," he said, "by my dispensation alone." He leaned back once more into the chair. "As does Parral," he said, sighing, and he smoothed his necklace against his chest. "As do its inhabitants."

"You have killed my cousin," I said. "Where is his body?"

Don Aurelio gave me an odd look. He returned, by patient degrees, to the shape of broad and golden idol he affected from the outset. The face of the Don sat in the gloom as though no expression had ever passed across it. He watched me breathe. The shadows of the midday sun lay on the floor of the place. The shuffling of the horses.

The Don moved one hand from his belly to gesture outside my field of vision and the eyes of the muscular brother brightened in his hatchet face. I suddenly had the impression that I had just now awoken, that we had not spoken at all, that a century and its proprieties had passed in my absence.

"I have burned your cousin's house to the ground," said the Don. From behind me came tottering the giant Choro once more, holding in his fist a long black sack swinging in the shadows. This he brought to the waiting hand of Don Aurelio and as the sack turned I came to know that it was not a sack at all which the Don held out from his seatedness to spin

109

slowly in the squalid place but the collected hair of no less than three heads, their eyes turned inward as though investigating the innerworkings of their skulls stopped in midstroke. The bottoms of their necks were stained black.

"And I've taken the heads of his women," said the Don.

The features of Señora Soto and the sisters rotated slowly in the still air of that place.

"His body," I said again.

"The body of the rapist will be drawn through the streets by his own horse and then burned in the Plaza de Parral. The remnants will be strewn about the northern edges of the municipality, as warning."

He handed by the hair the triple heads to the silent brother. The chest of the Don rose and fell with his breathing.

I could feel the air of the place against my eyeballs. "I am a fearsome man," I said. "I have killed men and ordered men killed." My brain felt set to boil in its case, and I began to struggle against my bonds.

"Whatever you have been," said the Don, "you are principally a debtor. As such you are outcast." He rose, and with his rising the little brother came forward from the shadows and from behind me came the sickening double skip of the single-booted Choro. "Habits such as yours," said the Don, "habits of indulgence and of sloth—these must be struck from out the people lest they catch hold and spread. Such a disease unchecked would leave this town body insolvent."

The two brothers now each grabbed one of my legs and pulled them out straight into the room, stripping off the boots and throwing them out into the stable behind and exposing my bare feet to the air. The silent brother came forward in his white cotton and from his waistband produced a large Bowie knife, the blade in the place like a dim and self-perpetuating light. He knelt before me.

"You are unprincipled," came the voice of Don Aurelio. "But there is something further irreducible and black in your constitution. In you is neither the will to embrace the mystery before you nor the power to rise up against it. As such I drive you out. May you wander the desert, butcher, possessing nothing save your thirst."

The silent brother took careful aim at my heel with the belly of the blade, and he skinned alive the sole of my outstretched and wriggling foot.

I was deposited in the hours before daybreak by the monster Choro on the far side of Mount Parral. I went away from the mountain and into the desert, dragging myself across the stones. Cactus. The creosote. The cracked earth and sand. There was no shade to be had, and there was no water to be had.

At the end of that day I made a hat of grass from a brackish seep near a collection of man-sized stones. By night my dreams were clamorous and without shape. On the second day I drank of my own evacuations. The days continued in this place that stretched to the ends of things and movement brought with it no correlating advancement.

After having rolled into the well of a shallow basin I attempted a fire and did not succeed. In the furthermost reaches of this basin however lay a pool of water which I bent down toward and lapped at like a dog until it was gone. I dug at the sand with my raw fingers until clear liquid began to finally seep from the ground dampening the sand, and I tore the clothes from my body and pressed them into the dampness until they held that dampness themselves and I then wrung this into my mouth. It tasted not like water but my mortality rendered liquid, drained back into me as sure as my own urine. At length I was able under a rushing sky to dig a crude shelter into the side of the basin. I lay awake there as night came on, my body seizing violently. I did not sleep.

Crawling out of the basin in the early morning I headed east with the rock and the sand underneath me as before, my skinned feet seeping and raw. The skin flapped from the undersides of my toes like the dried wings of beetles and I moved as though a sick and rotten animal and indeed I was and my mind went without sophisticated thoughts at this time. As I crawled I remember only that I watched as the earth beneath me lay perpetually covered in a shadow of my own making in which I could myself find no shelter.

Were I to give my salvation preamble, were I to give it explanation or excuse, all of it would fall lifeless. As well it should. Life is greater than its explanation for in life occur horrors beyond mere imagining as well as otherwise, as well as moments of such serendipity as would lie on the other side of belief. This is so because that which is this thing that I would here call life and that which would set it and place it and move it as it moves stands outside of that which we are capable of believing. We would in fact in our comprehension but occupy such a narrow spectrum of events that the majority move past us without our slightest recognition. And yet other times such events brush up against our lives, and in those eccentric moments we can only understand such impossibilities through reference to things we have seen before. Have heard, or sensed in dreams. Here is our imagination, giving shape to things otherwise shapeless and yet undeniable, and so when I saw the fleet of white tents lapping in the wind of the desert I thought that I saw ships. Tall ships. Galleons.

Gigantic, they stood scalloping in the midday not a quarter mile off like fat-bellied sails. I believed them to be a total mirage. Or I believed them to be vessels from an other world passing me by or perhaps searching for me in that waste in order to pack me aboard and take me to whatever infernal reality awaited me next. And so I believed I was dead. As I was dead I decided that I would then hail them on my feet, and so I pulled myself up to standing, and it was in this way that I walked into the camp of vacationing Englishmen.

CHAPTER XI

Red-Cheeked Women. On the Nature of the Mexican. On Fate and Ephemera. The High Jinks. Hanging in the Tree.

In truth I collapsed before the tents. In truth I cried like a child as men brought me into the shade and set my shaking body on a low pallet, and there I stayed for many days. Cooling balms were placed on my face and hands. The soles of my dead black feet were salved and wound with long bandages. Water tore down my throat and I raved against it.

After some time—it was days perhaps—I regained my senses. Two women, large and red-cheeked, watched over me and fed me and washed me. I slept without dreams, or rather the dreams that did come were such that my mind in sensing that it could heal disallowed such dreams to stick and to lodge, and so I remembered blessedly nothing. In time my feet began to heal, and other things did as well.

One morning after how long I could not say I was told by one of my nurses in passable Spanish that I should assemble myself to meet the collective, as they were waiting patiently for my story. They had provided me with a full suit of white—pants, shirt, jacket and vest—and I raised myself up to sitting and nearly broke down anew when I saw what had been provided.

The thin black socks, the sturdy shoes, the wide-brimmed straw hat. I was shaved by these women (warm water! my cheeks fresh as the skin of a babe!), and my mustaches clipped into a style perhaps too thin for my liking but as I was so grateful to them and confused otherwise by my surroundings I could not manage to protest. Sitting on the edge of my pallet I pulled on the clothes with my nurses' assistance but, before I could stand, the larger of the two women bent down to me, and she lifted me up like a baby in her arms. She was full-cheeked, skin untouched by the sun of that place or even any other. She smelled of powder and jasmine and she walked out of the tent and carried me into the company of my hosts.

I was laid gently in an empty chair in the center of some fifty well-dressed and similarly pink-faced people. And so I sat. A saucer, a cup, a spoon. Tea was poured from a silver pot, the spout as delicate and curving as the neck of a swan. And so, teacup in hand in a white linen suit with broad-brimmed hat, I composed my face for my hosts. To my left was a circular table on which stood plates of assorted sweets.

"A scone," said the man across from me, noticing my interest.

"Ascone," I repeated. He held my eyes. The man was upsettingly thin, reclining in a cream-colored suit with chocolate vest and high collar, legs crossed and shoeless in this desert of broken stones. Although his finery hung from him as though he be a wraith in a man's clothes he did not seem in the least uncomfortable. Somehow in his element in this unlivable place. His beard, heavy and unkempt, seemed outsized as well. His eyes were of a remarkable blue.

"They taste only fractionally better than they look," he said.

"I apologize but I simply must ask," said a large woman at his side in an extravagant hat. "You see, I've been waiting patiently for so long." She turned to the circle of others that surrounded me who nodded and murmured their agreement with her, and I could see the woman was excited by the recognition, and excited as well by her shame.

She continued. "I have made—we all have—so many wild assumptions as to your," here she paused, and I allowed her the time to search for the word. "Situation," she offered.

"Señorita," I began, "you are confused as to how it is that I came to wander the desert without food or water."

"Yes." Her eyebrows arched significantly.

"How it is I came to be without horse or clothes."

"Most certainly," she nodded her head, and her headgear bobbed along with the heads of the group.

"Why was I forsaken in the wastes by both God and man?"

"But not by the English!" shouted a man too loudly at my side, young and blond. His exclamation silenced the others, who turned to him with annoyance. A few cleared their throats. For a time there was only the tinkling of china, the wind lapping against the canvas. I watched them all as the moment crested and passed.

"I found myself in such circumstances," I finally said, "after a disagreement over the price of meat."

"Ha!" snorted the bearded one, slapping his hand on his knee. "This is the thing about these Mexicans. Fatalism and brevity. Very black, yes, but not also quite primitive? Quite potent?"

"Perhaps," said a small man sitting close by the bearded one. "But also a curious degree of self-possession."

"Such a collision of attributes," the bearded man went on, "stands in evidence of, as I've been trying to explain to you, the divided nature of the Mexican heritage. The cruel rectitude of their innermost being as softened by a decadent civility."

The small man sighed and sat back. "Yes, David," he said to the other, "but mustn't you then also believe in the primacy of the *decadent,* as you've put it, half of such a soul?"

"I must do nothing other than that which compels me," the bearded man continued, his rising fury difficult for me to place. "And belief compels me the least. And as to primacy," he was now near to shaking with his own vehemence, "yes, by God, primacy I do assert and it is the very primacy of the sand-blasted animal ignorance of the black soul of this damned Mexican."

I did not grab the man. I blinked. I put my teacup to my lips. I sipped.

The small man's eyes cut to me and then back. He said, "You have a poor understanding, David, of the human condition. And you always have."

"You are a eunuch and a coward," the bearded man replied.

The smaller man placed his saucer and cup on the table and re-crossed his legs. "David," he said, "you would have him do what, exactly? Rend his garments and live in the hills? You would have him abandon his civilization? His history insofar as such a people recognize that one exists?"

"His history, Paul, is the gods. The gods and their deeds and their triumphs."

"These are your fantasies, David."

"You couldn't possibly guess at my fantasies."

"I imagine they involve sacrifice, virgins, a great deal of drumming."

"A Mexican," said the thin man, "is a wild thing, is it not?"

"David."

"He is a superstitious being, dogged by fate and haunted by the hands of his gods."

"A generalization."

"And yet if a native such as this," the bearded man extended a long finger toward me, his eyes on the other, "were to have the courage to take responsibility of his own dark gods," he was now nearly shouting, "of his own *black god!* To in fact do battle with the forces of his constitution much as Jacob and the angel and, yes, if he were in fact to bend that heavenly messenger and break him and prostrate the divine figure on desert floor," he said, stamping his bare foot on the ground, "what may a Mexican then find in the splayed hand of his god?"

"A rope," said the small man. "With which to hang himself."

"Does he not find a sword?

"No."

"Yes! And if this savage is born to the sword then what at the end have I?"

"You're missing the point."

"No, I don't think I am. I think I have the point exactly." And then the bearded man leaned to the side and, pulling back his open hand, struck his own woman full across her face.

This caused a general uproar. The large woman stood and threw her cupful of tea into the bearded man's face and he propelled himself out his chair, aiming his bony shoulder at the wide woman's waist and, standing, lifted her clear off her feet as she beat at him vigorously. Woman secured, the bearded man kicked aside a chair and walked with her toward a billowing tent, across the rocks in his bare feet, her hat now fallen and blowing out into the desert and her hair then as you may imagine.

The crowd, mumbling to themselves and adjusting jackets, gradually dispersed. As I could not yet walk with any confidence I remained, as did the small and gray man. Reaching once more for his cup and saucer, he sighed, and he looked out into the plain.

"You are British," I said.

The man took a sip from the cup. "I'm afraid so," he said. And we sat for some time in silence.

They were a collection of artists, of writers and painters and singers. Some claimed expertise in dance and others in photography. Many had no expertise at all but had money and time and the desire to spend it on those who did. The small man told me they assembled yearly in Taos and came south into this desert, and here they stayed for some months to draw and drink and perform.

"So you come to the desert to escape," I said.

"Did you not escape into the desert?" he asked me.

"I was captured. I was tortured by an evil man."

He smoothed his pant legs with his hands and spoke tentatively, as though to himself. "Will you have your revenge?"

"I will," I told him. "I will kill him and his wicked sons."

"Have you killed before?"

"Yes."

"And what did you learn from this?"

"There is nothing to learn," I said. "Fate requires the deaths of men."

"So you have been the vehicle of fate."

"Yes."

The small man sipped and placed the cup it back in the saucer. "What is this evil you speak of? Is it not the killing of men?"

"A man does not die but by the hand of fate," I said, "and those who would seize that fate and bring it about are good and able men."

"You speak like an imbecile." The small man was smiling, his eyes twinkling with enjoyment as he spoke. "Was it not fate for you to suffer?"

"No."

We said nothing for a time as the wind pushed over the plain. The sunset lit the back of the mountains as though they were drawn on a pane of glass. "You cannot imagine true evil," the small man finally said. "Nor can you imagine what good truly is."

"My imagining is my own affair," I told him.

"Yes," the man said. "Yes, I suppose it is." He looked over at me and his smile was gone. "But good and evil are ghosts. Those who live by them chase ephemera."

"Ephemera."

"Yes, precisely."

"And what do you chase?" I asked him.

The small man recrossed his legs. He picked up his saucer and his cup and he circled his cup in the air before him and he looked into it as he did so, as though reading there what was shown to him or occupying his mind in the mindless and insensate motion of the liquid. "I chase nothing, young man," he finally said. "I am the prey."

"This is a difficult fate," I responded.

"If there is fate," he said standing, "I would say it is the only one."

That night I was witness to the high jinks. A pinch-faced woman with high-piled hair held my elbow as I stepped gingerly to my seat, and as I held her near boneless hand between my own I took in the scene: ringed and expanding rows of chairs under the night sky facing a low stage. At its sides stood torches that pitched in the wind blowing from off the waste.

Around me sat the varied faces of the crowd, all untouched by work or time, and yet each one stretched to a fine intensity, as though shaking ever so slightly under the weight of something other than the evident and the true and each one resembled another. In the midst of the faces, suddenly and without preamble, came dancers. They came down between the chairs in white masks and velveteen black shawls, moving through us with exaggerations and we all turned to them, some banging tambourines and some playing pipes and one picking a lute, and after them came a juggler, and now one walking on his hands. These all moved between us to the stage and mounted it and stretched across it, pausing in jamb-boned poses for the muted applause of the crowd.

As the performers stood frozen, up the steps came the bearded man. He wore a flat black jacket and pants, black vest and tie, a white shirt. His face was heavily rouged, his eyes wide as a puppet's. He stepped upon a small riser to the far right of the stage and stood a head above the players, his legs stock-straight, his hands clasped tightly behind his back. His hair flipped about his painted face in the wind.

The crowd silenced themselves, and a thrice-whistled note from a flute marked the closing of one time and the opening of this, the other.

"He do the fall in different voices," announced the bearded man. One of the masked figures broke his pose and fell flat on the stage with a slap. The other players gripped one another in a mocking fear. They pointed, crouched and held themselves, their masked faces buried in one another's shawls. They then began leak toward the fallen figure, crawling toward him on their knees until they circled him in total, and then they began to move round the figure in a slow circle, the wind catching at their garments as the circle began to pulse upward and down and circling once more.

"Here there is no sound of the earth," said the bearded man, "or otherwise the land or the water beneath it. Hands in the dust and no water beneath it." As he spoke, the circle of moonfaces sped once more on their cycles under the black and starless sky and only these flat faces caught and held the light of the torches, and now they halted in their steps.

"What was it you used to call me?" said the bearded man. At once the players fell upon their own circle, collapsing toward its center and the figure that had lain in its mouth.

"Stetson!" the bearded man shouted, and from the pit of bodies began to rise again a central figure identical to all the rest save for his hand, which gripped high above him what appeared to be a playing card.

"Handsome and young as you," the bearded man said.

The hands of the others began to rise up the flanks of this figure. They came up his waist, then his chest and he still held his card aloft, mask still focused sightlessly on it above him as the hands came on. Fingers pulled at his abdomen, his chest and his shoulders until he was overwhelmed in the teeming black hands of the collective. His high-held hand and its card now began to sink, and just at the instant before it too became overwhelmed this card was taken by another hand. This hand now, indistinguishable from the first, came rising out of the mass. Shoulders, face and chest turned toward us in a posture identical to the original, to the first.

"The Lady of Situations," said the bearded man.

"What do you make of it," whispered a voice to my left.

I turned to see the small man seated next to me. A coarse knitted scarf swaddled his neck.

"It is a mockery," I said.

"Certainly," he said. "But of what?"

"Eyes are burning," said the man on the stage. "And bodies are burning and minds are burning." The forms were now fully upright and interweaving amongst themselves. We could hear their dampened footfalls in the otherwise silence, their movements interspersed and without direction. "And pale forms float past the Isle of Dogs."

From the mass, two figures slid out, two on their backs, their heads downstage, their legs upraised. Behind them came two others who grabbed their ankles, and suddenly the four of them leapt as one, pinwheeling off the stage and down the center aisle, each holding the ankles of the other as though a giant wheel, each leaping through the legs of their partners, rolling down and amongst us. "I can connect nothing with nothing," said the bearded man.

I turned to speak to the small man, but beside me now sat a prunish woman with elaborate hair. She put a gloved finger to her lips and scowled. She turned back to the stage.

"Amongst the rock one cannot stop or think," said the bearded man, "and there is no water." The thunder came again out on the desert (had it come once before?) and only now did the rain begin to fall. As the circle on the stage widened and constricted in rhythm the forms became wet and slick, the garments sticking oddly to their gesticulating bodies.

"If there were the sound of water only," said the man, the coloring of his face beginning to run down into his beard.

"But what of the city over the mountains?" he shouted, and the wind-driven rain blew the torches out flat. The crowd began to murmur. "In this hole in the mountains!" he said. The dancers had begun to slip in their stockinged feet and fall upon the rain-slick stage. A mask slipped off and rolled out down the aisle and into to the dirt. "Shall I at least set my lands in order?"

A great gust now blew out the back of the stage in total, blasting the draperies and the paper maché into the unfathomable black behind it and the players were now absent from the stage as it began to tip and to rock with the force of the sudden gale and the abandoned chairs smacked and overturned as though beaten flat by a hand and still the bearded man stood on the riser in the rain, shouting words that were drowned out by the enclosing thunder. He raised up his hands, and with his hair flat plastered against his thin face he addressed the sky as though it could be addressed and implored of it something insensible.

In the morning the rain of the night was gone and the things of the night had gone with it. I took my leave of these people on a brown pony with a rifle and pistol and turned west, back toward the sierra.

Perhaps a quarter mile below me milled the herd of antelope. As the wind moved across them I watched down the sight of the rifle as their white heads lifted and their bodies stilled and stopped as they took in the news the wind brought them. Then, as though an invisible and silent and collective decision passed over them en masse, each small body released itself into motion once more.

My antelope staggered, dropped as though oppressed by a heavenward weight. Fearful now, it brought itself up to standing and drove madly into its own herd even as the sound of the rifleshot arrived overhead. And the herd flipped eastward as one body entire and fled as the antelope buckled under the mark of the bullet, watching as its brothers flowed away from it and did so forever, a repetition at the end of which lay nothing but it's own death. And do we not know the nature of the collective in which we move until the end of things, when it leaves us and we must watch it as it leaves, watch it as it inscribes in space the shape that it is, and that we once were within it?

I rode down from the bluff for perhaps a quarter hour until I came upon the carcass of the animal, and I went about its dressing.

I turned north at nightfall to ride along the edge of the greater range through the evening and into the morning, and the narrowing cant of the valley ringed me round with greater features of stone. I fell into a gap in the mountains and went east once more. I spent the evening with no fire, curled into a low and empty cave.

Before daybreak I rode over the ridge and down into the opposite valley, and the great hacienda lay on its southeastern edge, its orchards stretched out across the valley floor. A compound of buildings circled the great house, the red-tiled roofs bright in the sun. All was silent. The odor of wet apple trees hung in the bowl of the valley and I descended into it.

No dog did I hear nor bird, nor any shouting of children nor distraught mothers, and no laughter either did I hear. I rode further through the orchards, and into the yard.

In a tall oak to my left hung the bodies of three men. Still. Blackened like diseased features of the tree itself, their features burned away. I turned down this row and cut deeper into the trees, riding under their feet. Further in hung two bodies more, an enormous one with its leg broken and twisted in an unnatural state. And also there in the air hung the body of the Don. It sat in the tree like a metronome stopped in midstroke, a black and twisted bolus stuffed in his mouth. The wind shifted, and the bitter smoke from their clothes swirled about me and saturated the air.

I rode on further. I rode past these things and deeper into the world that would hold them and I saw no girl in the trees. In this place of death the only death would be that of man, a man and his sons, their bodies left like tokens or signals or signs of a force that spoke in this manner and no other. None other than this performance. I saw no woman. No mother or sister or female child. As though the violence upon men was to be impressed into the day and left there as the message itself. The presence of death. And of the women there would be no message. No evidence of struggle or suffering as though it had never been, as though they themselves had never been other than in the mind of those who would so die, those who would mark time and place with the body that is indicative of their suffering and extinction. And what of those who were not so marked? Those who going so unrecognized would be in death as lost or unborn, undead, ground down to dust. I took my pistol from my holster and I cocked it and I held it to my head.

Behind the house came the bark of a single dog, short and impatient. I dropped the gun and turned my horse and I ran. I ran once more past the Don and his retinue, his children, his boys. Gaining the ridge I did not look down into that valley, and I have in truth never returned to it.

PART III
HOW IT BEGAN

CHAPTER XII

The Mines at Santa Eulalia. Lucio Escárcega. Land Redistribution. Rodolfo Fierro. Armchair Despots.

I was a beggar. I walked into the town of Santa Eulalia and labored in the mines there for a peso a day until I bruised my foot on a stone and caught gangrene. I sold my horse and saddle for treatment from an alcoholic doctor who did nothing to aid me, and then one day he was gone.

Unable to pay for lodgings I retired each night to the lime pits, lighting matches to burn away refuse. Every morning I rose at six with the work whistles and went down into the mine on my rotting limb. I collapsed in that dark from exhaustion and the stress of my wounds and was taken out by foremen who could not abide another dead peasant and they left me on the mountainside to die. Tarahumaran women took pity on me. They collected me and took me to their hovel underneath the train station and tended to me with herbs and the hot water compress until I was cured. I could give them nothing and did so, but to them I owe my life.

I stole horses. I sold them. I slept on street corners. I lived in the mountains. I set upon solitary travellers and took from them, and in time other men even more wretched than myself asked to join with me in my wanderings. In all truth Díaz had driven many such men to a life not dissimilar from my own and we banded together in those places of wind and rock in ways so that we became as though brothers of a hateful family with none of us happy, or content.

The talk at each night's fire concerned how we had come here and who was to blame. We spoke often of politics, and on the night I met the devil himself, the night that the devil walked out of the darkness to us as I never sensed he would, I was sitting beside the high-born Lucio Escárcega. Strange that the devil would choose this moment to approach me, or perhaps not. Perhaps it was his time, here, at my lowest. Time to show his face or the face that he would wear with me. Another man amongst men outcast and alone and I did not suspect him at first. I did not suspect that he resided so close to me for if there be devil there be others with whom I cannot abide and so no devil can there be. And yet. I will tell it to you as it occurred, how, as I sat with Lucio, who was bent on revisiting, for how many times in how many nights, the issues of land reform.

"This is what we do," Lucio said to us as we sat round him listening. "We take it from the landowners, by violence if necessary. We divide it. We give it to the poor. This is the simple cause and the justification for a war."

I remember that it had been a difficult day. Another sign, perhaps. I had lost my favorite horse that afternoon from a broken leg. We were picking our way across a fall of scree on the way back to camp when I heard the sickening crack of the foreleg. The horse screamed as he fell forward to his knees. He was a good bay and he trusted me as I leaned down to him where he lay. I drew my revolver and placed it to his head as his eye rolled up into mine.

"The farmers," Lucio said. "They have little more than pitchforks and machetes. All illiterate. Some are little more than half-civilized Indians, and yet they are the untapped army that will overthrow Díaz. They must be tamed and they must be rewarded with that which they value most and that is land." Lucio was a tall and rangy man too young for his white hair which gave him a gravity and seriousness perhaps not completely earned. I was unsure why he had come to us in the mountains, well-born as he was, but I sensed in him some romance toward the squalid life in which we were engaged at this time. Nevertheless he was the only one of the group capable of intelligent conversation and so I suffered him, but on this night I was tired of suffering.

The story he told, the story he told over and again is of course a story that I had heard before, and one told better by those closer to the soil. But as Lucio was well-respsected by the men, and as I was and desired to continue to be the leader of this band, I had to acknowledge both him and it. Reluctantly.

"The peasants," I said, "are not an army."

Lucio turned to me. "I did not say they were an army. I said they will become the army."

"The peasants know only how to farm and how to drink and they are not fighters."

"The peasants grow up with horses," Lucio said. "They grow up with guns. And they grow up with hatred."

Some of this was true and some was not but I allowed it all, so tired was I on this night. I asked the simple questions. The ones I knew he had no concrete answers for. "And who will bring this rebellion about? Who will gather them?"

"The issue of land will bring about whatever change necessary."

"You misjudge the enemy," I said.

"As they are Mexican they cannot help but see the truth."

"Tell me," I said, "what a Mexican is. Is it skin or name? Is it residence? Are the Chinese washerwomen Mexican? Are the

German Mennonites Mexican? Or no. The Mexicans are from Mexico City. The Spanish and the sons of the Spanish. Or are they Indian? Or are Mexicans simply the poor? Are we only those who have nothing? Tell me how I am to judge a man, and tell me how much land he deserves by dint of his destitution, and his birth."

And it was at this point a man, awkward with drink, wandered into the circle of the fire. He was a stranger to us. His dress was haphazard—wide chaps and a sombrero. His features were sharp, dark and smooth. Kicking aside another man to make room the stranger sat down heavily, nearly tipping back onto the dirt.

"Heritage is irrelevant," answered Lucio, taking no notice of the stranger. "Díaz wouldn't entertain such questions."

"Díaz is a pigfucker," shouted the stranger from his place on the ground. "As are all mestizos." The stranger let loose a gurgling belch.

Lucio ignored him. "Díaz," he said, "has led this country like a king for generations. This is what the people understand. If we are to lead the same people we must learn from his example."

"Díaz can lick the shit out of Villa's asshole," shouted the stranger. The men seated around him began to stand, murmuring as they slapped the dust off their legs and wandered away. Some walked over to another fire, some walked back out into the dark.

"Friend," Lucio said, turning to the stranger. "You should count yourself lucky I don't shoot you."

"No, no," I said. "I will not close my fire to the *honest* people of Mexico. Is it not," I said to Lucio, "for these very men that you would have us go to war? Let's ask you, friend," I said to the stranger. "What you do you think about the redistribution of land to the peasants?"

"What is that?" he asked.

"We take the land from the dons and we give it to the poor."

The man sat back and blinked. "I think," he said, "that every landowning don should be gutted in the public square. He should be pulled into four quarters by half-broke horses."

"Yes." Lucio waved the back of his hand and turned to me and said, "But who is going to work these fields if not the sharecropping peasants who have been working them from the beginning?"

"And," continued the stranger, "after the body of the don has been torn apart, the men of the town will be forced at gunpoint to grab his remains. They will set about one another in battle, the sundered limbs their only weapons. They will be driven to beat one another with the corpse of the don." The stranger belched again. "The last man standing gets the land."

Lucio turned back to the stranger. He watched him and took him in. "You are offensive sir," Lucio finally said, "and out of place."

"Says who?" The drunk leaned back on his hands.

Lucio looked to me. I said nothing.

Lucio then said slowly "I don't think you're from here, friend. I don't think you understand us. Nor do I think you know what it means to work the rough northern soil."

"What are you saying to me?"

"I'm saying that Díaz, to whom you refer as a *pigfucking mestizo,* may have more in common with you or your blood than you are willing to admit."

"Are you saying I'm a half-breed? Is that what you're saying to me?"

"I'm saying that you are obviously not a man of Chihuahua," Lucio said—not without some sweetness—"and that we appreciate your service."

The man spit toward Lucio and stood awkwardly, nearly tripping over the log behind him. He staggered off into the darkness.

"Idiot," said Lucio.

"Lucio," I said, smiling, "are you truly willing to turn over land and supplies to a man such as that? What do you suppose he would do with it?"

"Nothing," said Lucio, looking after the man into the dark. "He would let the land lie fallow and drink himself to death or be removed from the premises for slothfulness."

Lucio and I sat for a time at the fire. The embers played among the logs, glowing and pulsing and fading once more. And after a time I told Lucio that I knew what the stranger would do, for I did. I knew it as sure as I knew what Lucio himself believed, and the knowledge of it struck me with force because it was the knowledge of another Mexico of which Lucio could not speak and in truth I had heard no one speak of it for some years. I told Lucio that such a man would kill his neighbor. Would take his land. Such a man would then kill another neighbor and take his land in turn. And another, and so.

"Ridiculous," Lucio said. "Who would work the land?

The logs glowed before us and I saw it plainly. The terrible truth of the thing as it was. "Such a man would enslave the women and the children of his murdered compatriots. He would shackle them to the plows. He would take what he desired from them and would drive them back down into the soil as food for the crops that they themselves would grow and harvest. And it would begin again."

"Pancho, you speak as though this is the dark ages."

It was at this moment that into the half-light of the fire came the man once more. Over his shoulder loomed the long and steady face of a horse. He led it by the reins and his other hand held loosely a wide, dim knife.

"Explain yourself," said Lucio, rising. "What are you doing with my horse? Did you hear me? I said how did you get my horse?"

The man brought the long snout of the animal close to his own face, rubbing his cheek against the horse's nose.

"I'm no half-breed," said the stranger, and he brought the blade of the knife to the horse's cheek.

"What are you doing?" Lucio took a step forward.

The man's long hand continued to caress the snout, and the animal snorted its approval and pleasure at these attentions. Its large, soft eyes smoldered in the light of the fire.

"Stop it," Lucio said, and now began to walk around to the man. The long face of the horse drooped further still in its stupor and relaxation.

"Half-breed," said the dark man again. His drunken mouth broke slowly into a wide grimace, leering and obscene. Then the stranger reared back with his big-handled Bowie knife and plunged the thick blade deep into the half-lidded bubble-black eye of the animal.

The sound of the horse was terrific. The stranger was knocked to the ground as the thing rose and reared up above us all in the dark, the great bones of its forelegs articulating over the fire. Lucio screamed as though he himself had been stabbed, and I leapt from my seat so as not to be trampled by the animal that landed and galloped full through the flames and across the logs and out into the night, the knifehandle bobbing grotesquely from the side of its head.

Lucio, his own knife now drawn, advanced on the prone figure of the man who lay splayed in the dirt. I walked sideways around the fire, anxious to see a death. The sound of a cocking pistol halted Lucio immediately, and the stranger began to laugh.

"Go on, college boy," the stranger said, and he sat up with a pistol already in his hand. "Go fetch your baby."

The animal could still be heard shrieking out there in the night and Lucio, his face pale as a corpse, turned and ran out toward it.

This was Rodolfo Fierro, a former railway worker who knew the routes and payloads of every worthwhile haul in the area. I took him in immediately, and not two weeks later did Fierro organize and lead a magnificent robbery of a train coming out of Torreon. We took silver from the mailcar destined for the federals and then entered the cars themselves to relieve the passengers of their materials, walking down the aisles with our bandanas over our noses like real and proper bandits. Before we could finish in the passenger cars, a gunshot from behind the train startled us, and we rode back up to camp with loot so heavy it slowed the horses.

It was not until later that night that we learned the cause of that mysterious gunshot, as Lucio Escarcega's horse walked into camp with its murdered rider sagging in the stirrups. The bullet hole in Escarcega's back stood as evidence of an ambush, mysterious and obscure.

"It is a shame," said Rodolfo Fierro as we all stood around that quiet horse, "such a pure-bred man of vision was cut down in his prime by a nameless coward." To this we all agreed, and as we dragged the body down from the animal the horse stood by admirably, the skin over its punctured eye mottled and sunk.

The months passed in the mountains and we brought more men to us. The rate and size of our robberies increased thanks to our new access to the payloads carried by rail. I began again to traffic in cattle, plucking choice animals from herds both wild and otherwise. I sold the cows throughout the area, thereby forging and strengthening ties with the local operators.

It was in this way that I learned a certain Don Velasco was selling good animals for whatever money he could find. Through intermediaries I discovered Velasco was taking this money to finance a revolt, buying rifles for peasants to attack the local authorities. His uprising—one of many in those liminal years—

occurred on schedule, and some seven local officers were killed before the authorities put down the rebellion. Two hundred barefooted peons fell to the federals' guns. I was both fascinated and appalled, and endeavored to speak with Don Velasco at my earliest opportunity.

The details of this meeting are inconsequential. I found Velasco slight and unimpressive—a man who pulled on such strings as he saw for little more than a salve to his own seething vanity. I saw that his motives were superficial and his maneuvers obvious. He was a man who had no deeper understanding of things.

"Better to turn the filthy dogs against Díaz myself," he told me, "than wait for them to turn on me."

However, one single piece of information from Velasco interested me, and that was the name of Don Abraham González, a prominent businessman in Chihuahua City who covertly worked in similar methods.

"Another armchair despot?" I asked Velasco.

"If nothing else," Velasco said to me, his mouth forever on the verge of a smile that never came, "he will buy the cows."

Business, then. At this I was relieved.

CHAPTER XIII

The Cloak and the Match. A Husband's Proxy. Without Name and Face. The People of San Andrés. A Bite on the Hand.

I had made arrangements for a nighttime meeting with González on the edge of town to discuss the procurement of a large herd of cattle to help finance his endeavors. Fierro and I had staked out the meeting place and from our concealment watched the carriage arrive, the cloaked figure of González emerge, wait in the dark of the street for a time, and then return to the carriage. I then left Fierro and rode to González's house to lie in wait for him there.

In a short time I heard the arrival of the carriage and from my vantage saw the coach come to a halt. The cloaked figure emerged once again and moved across the courtyard. As González gained his door I stepped from the darkness and struck a match and held it in my cupped hand. The cloaked head turned to me, revealing not the wide and jowly face of a comfortable don but instead a face of high cheekbones, thin lips.

"Where is González?" I hissed.

"Señora González," said the woman, "is here."

In her eyes I saw no fear. I saw curiosity, and annoyance. "And whom might you be?" she said.

"You know damn well who I am. Where is Don González?"

"Please, Señor Villa," said the woman, and she put her hand into the folds of her cape. I dropped the match and grabbed my pistol and cocked it and pointed it at her nose. Out from her cape González's hand emerged holding, then tinkling for my observation, her house keys.

"Let us both go inside and speak civilly," she said. She turned from me and unlocked the door, then stepped into the unlit hallway, throwing her cape on the back of a chair.

"Please put away the weapon, Señor Villa," came her voice from the darkness, "as I am indeed quite harmless."

"Why do you want stolen cattle?" I asked her. I was standing arms folded in her kitchen as she busied herself with a pot of tea. "And further," I said, "why should I deal with a woman who speaks without the proxy of her husband? I can imagine no business we could have between us this evening."

"Señor Villa," she said, "I want cattle because I have land in the country, and the market prices for livestock are excessive. I believe that cows on our hacienda will be better kept, for we have the clearest water, Señor Villa, and the sweetest grass." She was looking at me with a mocking smile. "You are aware, Señor Villa, that the sweetest grass produces the best milk."

"Do not waste my time."

"I want the cattle for money for guns," she said. "And in this, as in everything else, I have my husband's proxy."

I watched her as she turned again to busy herself with the teapot and the fire. Tapping my finger on the butcher's block that stood in the center of the kitchen I looked around the wide and empty room. The doors to the back garden were open. The smell of the night hung in the house.

"Where are your servants?" I asked her.

"We no longer keep them," she said as she walked over

with two steaming cups and saucers. "We find it troubling to be waited on by those who would slit our throats in our sleep."

"Why didn't they?" I asked her.

"Slit our throats?"

"Yes."

She sipped from her cup, her eyes steady over the rim. "They feared us," she said. "As well they should."

Her attitude made me anxious to return to the main question. "Why do you tell me this?" I waved my hand about. "Why should I care that you want cows or milk or guns? I have seen what the rich and the idle do with peasants."

Señora González placed her cup on the dish, and she stood back from the block between us, smoothing her skirts with her hands.

"Don Velasco is a fool," she said quietly. "Not all are as ill-prepared, or as naïve, as Velasco."

"Ill-prepared for what?"

"For revolution, Señor Villa."

"Ha!" I slapped my palm on the block. "Yes! I see it clearly," I said. "Let me make this plain to you. You and those like you are greater perpetuators of evil than a thousand Díazs, a thousand dictators and despots because at least they are honest in their exploitation. You, on the other hand, will always use the poor for your advantage and amusement."

"And who am I?"

"You are money. You are power."

"There is something greater than power, Francisco," she said.

I started to laugh. She did not laugh, and this only increased the advance of something that hung silent on the edges of my mood. Something white and burning. A fear.

"You take me for a fool," I said, looking into the darkness of the garden.

"There is something greater than power and that is an idea," she continued.

"You are poisonous," I said.

"There are those, Francisco—and these are few—there are those that refuse the world as it is."

"Madness," I said, suddenly furious at her posture, her ignorance, the danger of her. "Let me tell you how it is."

"How is it?"

"The fate of a man drags that man behind it like a mule. These people," I waved my hand again. "You would give them weapons and a lie. A lie with which they rail against their fate as it has been delivered upon them by the rich. By *you*, Señora." My hand was slapping the butcher's block as I spoke, and it stung from the force of it.

I stopped. I gathered myself against that whiteness that had begun to eat into my mind and push me to the edge of my control. After a moment I said, "We must be content with this world. We must not make up another. There is no other."

Señora González stood looking at me for some many moments. She took again the cup from the saucer and put it to her lips. "Are you *content*, Francisco?"

"Stop calling me that."

"What is your fate?"

"You know nothing about me," I said and it was true.

"What is there about you to know?" she said. "What are you other than defeat and anger and humiliation?"

"I am twice the Mexican you are."

"Because you come from the land."

"That's right."

"Tell me this, then. Tell me why Velasco failed."

"Because he is as ignorant of the world as you are," I said.

"But what is this world, Francisco?"

"It is right in front of us," I nearly shouted. "It is the room.

The house. The night. The men I have stationed at the end of your block who would burn this place to the ground at but a single signal from me."

"Was it this that defeated Velasco?"

"Peasants were defeated by a superior force that was armed and trained."

"We need more," she said, raising her chin. "You cannot believe that there are no more."

"You are irresponsible," I told her, "and murderous. And hungry for war."

Señora González took a step back. She composed her face, and as she did so she placed her hands on the block with deliberation. She leaned forward and she said "I am hungry for this country to become what it was meant to be." She said, "If war is what brings this about then yes," she said, "I am hungry for war. But the war is not yet born." Her eyes searched out mine. "The war tonight is as shapeless," she said, "as a man without faith."

"There is nothing worth belief."

Her green eyes did not blink. "There is you," she said.

As she spoke I gripped the edge of the block in my hands and felt as though the ground itself were tipping beneath me. I squinted at this woman, hair pulled back high and away from her face, her chin haughty, her voice even in the empty room.

"You say that I know little of you but this is not the case," she said. "I know that as a child you ran in the hills and stole from the rich and that you gave this money to the less fortunate, did you not?"

I did not answer her.

"I know that you gave away rifles to the peons in the deserts in the north. I know that you worked in Parral until you found, as have so many, such work to be impossible in accordance with dignity, and with self-respect. You believe yourself to be alone,

Francisco. You believe that none have seen you. That none ever will. You believe that this is the case. But this is not the case. What is the case," she said, "is that your life has been bending toward a state of affairs as yet unnamed. Your life is the preface, the preparation. It has been clearing the way for not only the inexistent, but for the new."

"I am complete," I told her. My ears were stoppered with the pounding of my own blood. "I am in total, as you see."

"You say so," she said. "But I know that you believe that you are not yet who you should be. That you have for your entire life been sculpting before you an image that was little more than a vanity and a mirage, but I am here to tell you something else. I am here to tell you that the image is now complete, Francisco. And you know it as you know the hands that made it. You must be free to allow yourself to become what you most desire to be."

"It is a lie," I said. "A phantom. It does not exist."

"It can exist if you believe as I do. If you allow yourself to see what your fate has always been."

"It is not enough."

"There are more," she said. "The people want to believe," she said. "They want to believe in that which they sense lies before them but for which they have no name. The future of the people today has no shape. It has no face." She leaned back and away from me. She took me in, and as she did so it was a though the room itself bent its light and its sound and its time around her. As though the night fed through the doors and into her, as though all of it focused into a single instant of such intensity that it even came into a knowledge of itself as night through her presence, her stance in that room.

She said, "I don't need cows, Francisco. I don't need guns."

"What do you need?" I asked.

"Everything," she said.

This is how it began.

I rode south with my men to Monterrey, recruiting men and women to the cause as we went. Such recruitment was open and simple as Díaz has so thoroughly betrayed the people that the only sensible response was the join in arms against him. The people were waiting to be told what we said and even as we were saying it they knew it to be true, for it was. We went up into the Sierra Azul and took fifteen hardened half-Indians and came down into San Andrés with a full force of some 300. With the starving and quiet people from Santa Isabel and Ciénaga de Ortiz we entered San Andrés before daylight and caught unawares the federals stationed there and knifed them in their beds.

By afternoon we had control of the town entire and the following day I was forced to shoot three of my own men for looting. I did so in front of the townsfolk assembled in the square. I stood before the people of that place in the heat of the day as the bodies of my own men lay awkward before me in the dirt and I promised the people of San Andrés that no further harm would come to them. Ever again.

We rode east. We rode until the sun went down and we rode on still through the cold and murk of the darkness that was on that night all but complete. At some point a new recruit named Feliciano Domínguez rode up alongside me. He was young and small with sparse mustaches, anxious and intelligent. But perhaps less intelligent than he believed.

He told me that his uncle, a man named Pedro Domínguez, had been recently appointed judge in Chihuahua, and that this judge had promised to never relent in his pursuit of factions rebellious to the government of Díaz.

"He is at his home now," the young man told me, "and it is not far from our path. I believe that it is dangerous for him to be a judge. I do regret it, for he is a strong and brave man, but he must be killed for the good of our cause."

Leaving the battalion at camp I took eight men south to the Rancho de Encino and we rode down upon the hacienda of Judge Pedro Domínguez in the mid-morning. As I ran my men across the plain toward the ranch in the bright of the day the judge and his men situated themselves about the place in a hasty defense. The judge himself shot out two horses from my squad as they advanced, but we beat them back into the house proper and dismounted and kicked in his doors. As we advanced into his kitchen the judge stood and shot the man beside me dead under the eye.

The old man dropped his rifle and fled out the rear of the house, his black jacket opening about him in the wind. It was my own bullet that caught him before he reached the first fence but the judge did not turn. He kept on, leaping another fence and landing hard on his knees. I ran upon him and grabbed him by the arm and as the judge turned he bit me on the hand. I watched him as he did so, and slowly pulled from the old man's holster his own pistol and put it to the side of his head. It was then that the old man spoke.

"Bandits," said the judge. "Filthy, thieving bandits." I cocked back the hammer and fired.

When all of the judge's men were killed I ordered a hole dug for the judge where he fell and as the ground was easily turned this was done. I then looked to the house in time to see Feliciano Domínguez walking out into the yard, carrying over his shoulder a bulging brown sack.

This is a story that is told widely. I have heard it told at campfires and in cantinas. I have heard it sung at weddings and funerals and I have been told this story by those who claimed to be there when they were not. I am only waiting to be told the story by a man who claims to be Pancho Villa himself, and I have little doubt that even this will come to pass.

Some say that as Feliciano Domínguez exited the house that

I spoke to him, saying "Show me what is in your sack, brother."
In this telling Domínguez opened the sack to reveal plates of
silver and coins and candlesticks of ivory. I then looked to the
mound of newly dug earth under which the judge lay slain and
I said to Domínguez, "We have not come to steal, my friend.
We are agents of the revolution, who serve at the will of the
people." Feliciano Domínguez then apologized to me, and we
took the sack to the local church. There we gave those riches to
the parish priest for the construction of a school much needed
in that impoverished district. Domínguez was then shot as a
looter, and a traitor to the cause.

Others say that when I saw Feliciano Domínguez exiting
the judge's house with a full and heavy sack and said to him
"Show me what is in your sack, brother," that Domínguez
refused, saying, "These are the rightful spoils of our danger and
adventure." I then told him in confidence that we should bury
the sack and return for it in a week's time to split the loot. In
this story, not two days later I ordered Domínguez on point for
a dangerous raid in which he was killed. Later I returned alone,
dug up the bounty, and kept it for myself.

And then some say that as Feliciano Domínguez stepped
out of the judge's hacienda with a sack in his hands that I said
nothing but simply pulled my revolver, and shot him dead.

And then some say that Feliciano Domínguez had no sack.

I say that the revolution is not a series of events. I say that
battles are not fought in return for battles which have been
fought before. In the time of the revolution the betrayals
are perpetual and the injustices flatten out into a mural of
humiliation forever in need of bloody correction and all the
facts have been lost. Pancho Villa is a boy running through a
field, a commander of a thousand cavalry, a corpse propped up
in the market for tourists. In the revolution the low talk in the
back rooms is never hushed. The campfires on this plain never

go out. The horses are riding forever in a permanent present. I say that the judge and his nephew are dead. I say that I am alive.

Chapter XIV

Three Mescal. Singing of Mexico. Colt Will Be Pleased. The Role of the Sphinx. A Foreign Diplomat.

See the night as it unfolds. The sun sets over three men as their horses pick across the desert. As the darkness comes on the sky pales and deepens and the brush before them opens into the path toward the village to the south.

The larger man wears a khaki suit and knee-breeches and a bolo tie. The lean man at his side a short black jacket and scarf of blue silk. The third among them is tall and thin beneath a ragged linen suit and his skin smooth and dark. On his head a battered straw fedora. They all dismount in the broken square and tie their animals and their boots ring on the makeshift steps as they move into the cantina. Sawdust lies scalloped on raw wood planks. Haphazard tables. No piano, no cards. Dark men wrapped in serapes. The rattle of glasses, the movement of the bartender.

"Three mescal," says the man in knee-breeches, sliding coins on the bar.

"No mescal," answers the barman.

"Closest to it."

The barman nods and pulls up from underneath the bar a

bottle of high yellow liquid.

"You'll not ask for more," says Knee-breeches and the barman pours full three glasses. A voice sings from a dim corner of the place, then stops.

At a table the three sit and drink in silence and stare at the open door and the dark of the oncoming night. The drink smells of paint.

And then, of course, a peasant. Ragged and unsteady, he approaches the three men and he pulls out the empty and remaining chair and he sits.

He looks at them all with milky eyes, one to each.

"You," he says to the man in knee-breeches, "are the American."

The large man breathes in and holds that breath and lets it out and says nothing. The thin man pulls at his scarf and looks to his friend and then turns to the peasant and composes his face.

"Yes," the peasant says, "I know Americans. I've been to El Paso." The peasant puts his fist to his mouth and puffs his cheeks in a belch.

The man in knee-breeches places the butt of his revolver on the table and points it squarely at the peasant and with no particular ceremony cocks the hammer with a large thumb.

"Put it away, Bill," says the man in the scarf.

"The barrel of this gun," says the large man, "would make a perfect fit right up this dirty fucker's asshole."

The expression of the peasant turns by degrees. He becomes sorrowful, and he slumps into his chair. "No questions then," he mumbles, and he remains there long enough for the two Americans to believe he may have fallen asleep. They turn from him, and back to their liquor.

"And here I was thinking I might have to kill somebody," the scarfed man says loudly. He smiles, and he looks about the place. He looks to the other two at the table.

Without preamble the peasant suddenly rights himself. As though shaken awoke from a dream.

"Let me tell you something," he says.

"Say it," says Knee-breeches, putting down his glass. "Say it and get the fuck out of here."

"Yes!" The peasant throws out his hands. "You are here," he says, "for the revolution. You are here for the people." He places his palms on his thighs and bows his head. He continues speaking loudly as though to his shoes.

"You are starting a fire here in deadfall." The peasant says this to the floor.

"In what?"

"Deadfall," the peasant says again. "Deadfall strews the bottom of this land."

"Oh, Christ."

"Bill, make him stop."

"And you will not put out this fire," continues the peasant with intensity, "for this fire is Mexico."

"Fierro, do something."

"Díaz was no fool," the peasant shouts at the floorboards. "Mexico loosed will eat itself."

The man in the white suit stands with speed and not without some grace, not without an aspect of performance that registers with the men on a level deeper than they grasp in the moment. He grabs the peasant by his serape and throws the man from his chair and onto the floor. Standing in one motion with the peasant's serape still in hand, the man in the suit slides a sudden knife underneath the peasant's outstretched chin. The peasant's cry of surprise falls off short, strangled in his own throat.

"Put him down, Fierro." The man in the scarf begins to stand but does not complete this act, squatting, then, over his chair. "Put him down and kick him out."

The man in the white suit does not move.

"Fierro!"

Rodolfo Fierro turns, and he walks to the door of the place dragging behind him with one hand the silent figure of the peasant. Fierro throws him out into the dirt of the yard, and returns to the table.

The three once more, before their drinks. The song from the smallness around them resumes:

> *Los ojos de Los Ríos*
> *llorar por los hijos varones*
> *perdido en las orillas distantes*
> *horrores imprevistos*
> *Golpeado y le entregaron*

"What's he singing about?"

Fierro sips at his glass. "Mexico."

"Jesus Christ."

Outside the night rises up high and clean over the desert. The moon shines on the sand and salt. The night opens once, and then opens again.

Fierro sits up and places his empty glass mouth-down on the table and he says, "You should not pull out a gun at a table unless you intend to use it."

Knee-breeches watches him. He squares his shoulders to the table. "I intended to use it," he says.

Fierro shrugs. He crosses his legs, and he begins to pick at the wooden table. After a few moments he looks up into the wide red face of Knee-breeches, its little pig nose, its black eyes shaking with hate.

"I would have shot him immediately," Fierro says.

"I'm not you."

"No."

Fierro uncrosses his legs and turns. Small scratches crisscross the shoulders of his white jacket. Yellow rings of sweat glow faintly from underneath his arms. Dried blood stains his shirt in miniscule trails like the tracks of mice.

"Tell me, Bill," he says. "Have you ever shot a man from this distance?" Fierro motions to the space between them with his hands in the air.

Knee-breeches crosses his arms and bites his two lips and says nothing.

"If you have," Fierro continues, "then answer me this question. Which direction does a man fall, forward or backward?"

Kneebreeches grips the table in large hands and leans forward, his eyes stuck like black rocks in his face.

"Get," he says, "fucked."

"Honestly, if you've shot a man from this distance you surely would know," Fierro replies. "Unless you never have. And you are a liar."

Out comes the revolver, again its butt placed on the table. Knee-breeches cocks it and slides his finger across the trigger. And he says to Rodolfo Fierro, "There's something about you. If I could've killed you in Texas I would have. I want you to know that."

"He falls backward," says Fierro. "Naturally."

"Bullshit."

"I can only say what I have seen. A man falls backward."

"A bullet from a Colt ain't strong enough to knock a man back."

"Bill," says the man in the scarf.

"Shut up."

"I don't know what else to tell you, my friend," Fierro says, "other than that you are mistaken. Or misinformed." Fierro rolls his shoulders and looks again out at the bar. "Or inexperienced."

"Bill," says the blue-scarfed man as he bends close to the table. "We're at least three days out from Villa."

"This pigfucker ain't got three days by me."

Fierro smiles and he nods at the American. The teeth under his moustaches are yellowed and broken.

The American extends his arm until the barrel of the revolver is nearly touching Fierro's face, and at this Fierro stands.

"My friend," he says, "you are empty." He sweeps his hat off his head and bows. "Allow me." Fierro turns and he walks to the bar.

"You brought it up, you fucking maniac," Knee-breeches mumbles, and he releases the hammer and slips his pistol back into the holster. He looks about the gloom of the place forsaken by whatever god had ever once been there or perhaps never was. After a moment, and this moment is a long one, Knee-breeches comes to realize that the men who had lain about that cantina sprawled and drunken were now absent. Indeed the entirety of the cantina seemed as though deserted. And the song had stopped as well.

Fierro returns with two cups of the filthy liquor. He places one down at his own seat and hands one to the blue-scarfed American.

"Where's mine," Knee-breeches says.

Fierro drinks his own cup down in a long and silent sip, then pulls his revolver and fires into the chest of the larger man.

The shock runs through the big man's body like a continuation of the sound itself, and Kneebreeches lurches from his seat, overturning the table and reaching awkwardly for his own revolver, his hands suddenly unable to clench or grab. With a mind both numb and burning, Kneebreeches begins to focus, with great intensity, on his breathing.

"Ah!" he says.

Fierro gestures at this all with his revolver held high and, like a fencer before his opponent, bends deeply at the knee, sliding one foot behind the other.

"Forward or back?" says Fierro. "Twenty pesos to the winner."

Knee-breeches lurches toward his killer and then turns away. One hand claps to his chest as the blood only now begins to run down his vest in earnest.

"Backward!" Fierro reports. "Samuel Colt will be much pleased."

The sensibility drains out of the larger man's eyes. His ragged breathing slows and slows until it reaches its stop, and then the great body pitches forward onto the sawdusted floor. It lies still.

Fierro's arms drop to his sides. He sighs. He re-holsters his weapon, reaches into his jacket and pulls from it a long red wallet from which he produces two paper notes. These he throws on top of the body.

"It's your fat that's unbalanced you," he says. Then he rears back his boot and strikes Knee-breeches's thick dead face, caving in the nose.

The man in the blue scarf remains seated before this all in horror. Sits before it as though a child with broken toys. As though his sheer indignation would alter the course of the events. And then he is standing. He screams at the body of his companion as it lies like a great beached walrus on the filthy floor of the empty cantina. He fumbles out his own weapon and swings it in his terror about in the place, cursing the white-suited man and Pancho Villa and the entire lurid country of Mexico, and as he gradually calms, he finds himself pointing the barrel of his revolver around an empty room.

This is what I know of it. As you can see, it is a story. A story perhaps with even some truth, because that truth is one that speaks to the nature of its protagonist who is such only in the service of another, that other being myself. I am here a name alone, and one that stretches across this country and into that other one and appeals to those who would there live, the only approach to me guarded by this character in white—an assassin, a madman who may devour the travellers who would traffic with him with the impartiality of the Sphinx. Pancho Villa is here a salvation never to be achieved. He is the future incarnate, and the present aches to be with him. I approve.

But what I know as well is that outside of that cantina on that night of the tale did stretch all that is outside the tale, all that is dark and untranslatable and therefore part and parcel to the whole. The wide plain and the sand and the salt. And the wind moved over it and all that is absent of intent, while in this moved those who were otherwise and therefore made it all so, without exception. My Rodolfo Fierro continued south.

Nine days later it is said that he approached a foreign diplomat in the streets of El Fuerte just after ten in the morning. Fierro demanded this man's weapon and received it without quarrel. He examined the piece, and then lowered the small pistol into the diplomat's pudgy face. With the preponderance of movement resulting from many days in the company of strong drink Fierro pulled the trigger not once but three times, each attempt stymied by a hidden mechanism on the pistol with which he was unfamiliar. The diplomat—shaking with fear, the weapon still aimed so closely at his head that he could see the swirling grooves along the inside of the barrel—demonstrated for Fierro the proper operation of the safety. Fierro, amused, pocketed the small piece, tapped his breast where it lay, and looked down at the diplomat where he stood.

"You are a sweet man," he said to him. "Go home."

CHAPTER XV

A Strong and Capable
Race. Coronela and
Terezio. "What Do You
Know of Limantour?"
The Telegrapher of
Anáhuac. The Way the
Women Wear Their Hair.

The wintertime sun lay low across the square of Ciénaga de Ortiz where some fifty men stood before me. They held in their hands whips and axes and more than one gripped the handle of a three-pronged pitchfork that rose above the heads of the assembled. They were young and old, their bodies stung by the sun and the wind in that high place where they had been born and indeed passed the entirety of their lives.

Up from the plain and into the Sierra Azul we had ridden and with every town came new recruits. They lined the streets and asked that we take them into our fold, and we did, and we spoke to them of pay and food, of rifles and horses. We spoke to them of killing rurales, marauders and roadmen. We spoke to them of uprooting the dons from the valleys where they grew fat on the labor of honest men like themselves. We told them that each soldier would get what was fair to him and at this they rejoiced.

By Ciénaga de Ortiz we had some 400 to our side. We had come to this place to take more, as well as to procure rifles and ammunition sent there from Chihuahua by Señora González, its location remote and difficult to infiltrate. Rodolfo Fierro rode with us, and on this morning I watched as he walked back and forth before the men assembled in the square, judging their fitness and ability. Where I stood I conferred with González's agent, who had arrived in the night before with the crates of weapons.

A woman, old and with a face like a tanned hide. Her frame was long and tall and she wore a man's clothes, her grayed hair piled up underneath her wide-brimmed hat. A long black holster hung nearly to her knee and her hands were knobby with years and use.

She took a crowbar to the two large crates before us and showed me therein the rifles and belts of ammunition, three feet deep and coiled like snakes. A third crate held boots and jackets and blankets, and as the old woman pushed aside the wooden top she reached down into the clothes and fished up a smaller box. This she pried open with her own hands, the metal nails sliding out the thin wood with a sigh. Inside sat five holsters, nestled in hay. Each was leather, long and black as the one that hung from her own thigh. I took one and popped free the clasp and slid out the weapon.

The pistol was a strange contraption, compact and layered as though it be more a machine, built as though imagined and worked into life by other machines. The long thin barrel seemed an afterthought or mistake. The provenance of another construction.

"German," said the old woman.

I gestured with the thing to the holster at her hip and she nodded.

"Twice as fast as a Colt," she said. "The penetration is

incomparable. Ten rounds. Magnificent." I hefted it again in my hand. The thing felt total, a single piece, a stone carving, the balance impeccable.

"The Germans are a strong and capable race," said the old woman. "Unencumbered."

"Unencumbered by what?" I asked. I brought the pistol closer to my face and I saw etched into the side the outline of a woolly lion walking before a low and flaming sun.

From across the square came an immense commotion as the men broke and came toward the crates to collect their supplies. The agent and I stepped to the side.

"Coronela," came a call from the group. We both turned and we saw one of the men cutting away from his fellows and walking directly to us. He was disheveled, and limped heavily to his left. He wore a cloth hat, pants held with a faded and a yellow belt. Simple leather shoes.

"My Coronela," he called again. At his approach I slipped the pistol into my waistband.

He shuffled up to us and pulled himself to his full height in front of the woman.

"I am Terezio," he said.

"What of it?" she replied.

"Terezio of Dolores."

"Terezio," said the old woman, no inflection to the word at all. And then, "Terezio Ayala," she said, and her face creased in sudden joy and recognition. The two clasped hands and shook warmly.

"Yes, Terezio," she said. "Of course." The old woman turned to me. "No better horseman in the north of Mexico than this. I've seen him ride down natives in the blackest midnight and kill the chief with a single shot." The old woman was still pumping the peasant's hand with vigor, and yet the face of Terezio was pained, hesitant. His bad leg hung out rigid to the side of his body, stiff as the dry branch of a tree.

"Now," the old woman said to me, "you will see the sort of soldier we once had. The sort of man who rode for us once and will ride for us again."

"My Coronela," said Terezio. "Please. This is what I want to say. I want to say that I indeed rode with you at Dolores."

"And at Temosachic," she said, "and against the landowning bastards of Limantour. We killed their regulators to a man, did we not, Terezio? And they thought twice about coming for the peasants again."

"Yes," the man said, "yes, and I want to say that these times were the most magnificent of my life."

"Of course."

"But at Temosachic I was badly wounded, my Coronela. If you remember."

"Wounded in what way?"

"I was shot in the leg," Terezio said, and gestured to his rigid limb with his free hand for the old woman still held the other tightly. She held that hand and she had ceased to shake it, and the smile drained away from her face.

"I was wounded badly," Terezio said again. "And I came home to find my family in disarray and my lands in desperate need of work." At this I caught the scent of liquor on the man's breath, and the peasant Terezio turned from the old woman to me, now seeming to plead his case with us both.

"I have come to ask you a favor, my Coronela," he said. "I have come to ask that you let me take that which you offer to those who would join you as one who has joined you before and asked for nothing in that time. I ask that you let me take these weapons and supplies back to my family, and allow me to stay in this town as defense against any federal involvement here. I can alert you to the comings and goings of troops. I can keep you abreast of their movements and intentions. I ask you this because I can no longer ride a horse without pain, as my leg is as you see."

The old woman's eyes had narrowed as he spoke and she still held the hand of the peasant in her grip. And she said "If I remember, Terezio, you had no family. You had no land of your own."

The peasant licked his lips and he opened them to speak. He tipped his ear to his shoulder. "Allow me to take the boots," he said. "A rifle. I need no ammunition."

"What good is a rifle without bullets?" asked the old woman.

"Allow me to take the boots."

The old woman watched him for a moment and then she turned to me.

"What do you think," she asked.

"You're asking me?"

"I am asking," she said, "what you believe to be the proper course of action."

I looked over to the volunteers of the town where they stood around the crates and I looked at Rodolfo Fierro who looked back at me with his face implacable and black and indeed all of them, enlisted and volunteered stood still, their eyes on the three of us.

I folded my arms. I said to the woman, "This man has served you."

"He fought bravely against the dons some many years ago."

"And he did so with honor."

"Yes."

"In that case," I said, "I believe we should give him boots and a serape and let him return and live out the remainder of his days in peace."

The haggard face of the peasant Terezio broke into a joyous smile and again I caught the scent of the liquor. Terezio began to shake the old woman's hand again, to jog it from where it had been held but the old woman's arm did not move, and her eyes were still on me.

"You believe," the old woman said, "that this man would no longer be of any use to you."

"I don't see how he could."

"You believe," the old woman said, "that we should free this man of his obligation to the people."

"I have fought for the people," said Terezio. "I have fought for the people and have sacrificed myself for them again and again, before many of these boys were even born." He then turned to me with a vicious look. "Where were you in Dolores?" he said. "What do you know of Limantour?"

"You believe," the old woman went on as though Terezio had not spoken, indeed as if he were no longer there, "that we should set the example, here in front of all the men of this town, that there are those who are treated by some other set of laws, unattainable to others. You believe that we tell these men that they are of less worth to us in this time than others. You believe we should tell them this now, and here."

I opened my mouth and closed it. The peasant looked back and forth between the two of us. The woman stood waiting for my answer and I could feel the eyes and the silence of the men around me.

She still held the peasant's hand even as Terezio struggled against it and she said to me, "You believe that you understand but you do not. We are in the midst of a great violence," she said. "Our enemies will kill us to a single man and they will let our bodies rot on the field. Terezio, here, is a man of talent."

"I can no longer ride, Coronela."

"Shut up. But beyond his talent, Terezio represents something of equal importance. He represents, here in this moment, an exception. He represents deviation. He represents defiance."

Terezio's free hand shot to the handle of the pistol where it stuck from my belt, and he turned the gun on the old woman.

"I am not defying you, Coronela," Terezio said, his voice rising up beyond his control. The old woman's eyes were now locked with those of Terezio, the nose of the barrel not a foot from her chest. And then she said, "Here is the result of a moment's indecision."

Terezio swung the pistol at me and pulled the trigger. The hammer fell with a cold click on an empty chamber.

The old woman pulled hard on Terezio's hand and lurched him forward even as she brought her knee clear up to her chest and brought her boot down with great force on the peasant's lame and rigid leg.

Terezio screamed. He crumpled to the ground and his simple hat fell into the dirt. He stuck the gun into the air and pulled the trigger again, the clicks faint and small in the square. Rodolfo Fierro was at his side immediately, kneeling, drawing a knife from his waist and slipping it across the peasant's throat.

The square entire was silent as blood spilled down Terezio Ayala's neck and onto his shirts and onto the dirt. He coughed just twice, and as he shook in death his rigid leg rose high up into the air. For some moments it held there, like a final salute.

The old woman bent down to the body and took the pistol and stood and held the grip out to me.

"Terezio Ayala," she said, "was a man of honor. I do not know this man."

None in the crowd spoke, and the recruits turned back to the crates and situated themselves with rifles, and with bandoliers. I watched this for a time, and then I returned to the small box which held the four remaining Mauser pistols. I dug in the hay until I found the cardboard boxes of ammunition. I loaded up the weapon and slipped it back into the holster and fixed this then on my hip. The old woman stood by, hands clasped behind her, watching the new recruits. The sun had fallen to the edge of the day.

"You would have yourself my teacher," I said to the woman. "And you would impart your lessons over the bodies of other men."

She did not look at me when she spoke but she watched the men as they moved before her. "Lessons are worth what is paid to learn them," she said. "The best ones cost what you see here."

"Who are you?" I asked her.

"If you continue in this way you will die very soon," she said. "And if you die this will go on without you. These men that you see here. The thing for which they ride and in which they believe. What you have set in motion here cannot be so easily unset. You should ask yourself," she said, "if you are its equal." The woman did not stay the night. Shortly after sunset she mounted her horse, and she rode back down the mountain alone and unencumbered in the gathering dark.

East of La Junta the land is low and brown and bereft of life. Chaparral litters the plain and through this place run nothing more than lizards or scorpions or the snakes that would feed upon them. And through this place as well run the trains. The rails run over the ground like a metal nerve across the southern stretching void and in the midst of it stands the town of Colonia Anáhuac: a telegraph office, hotel, dry goods store, cantina.

The telegrapher of Anáhuac was a small man with glasses and thinning hair. I can tell you only what I know of him, and that I know from observation alone. I know that his jacket hung on a peg by the washbasin. I know that the room in which he spent his days was narrow but full of light. I know that each day he bent in his office to the transmissions from Chihuahua to Hermosillo or from Hermosillo to Chihuahua. I know that he watched the schedule of the trains.

Three times a day they pulled in, each one larger than the town entire, easing into the depot like a great and sighing ship. At rest they threw their hot shadow on the clapboard buildings and there in that town they would take in water, relay their monies, and drop off mail. They would then continue on. The telegrapher worked in the midst of them, was intertwined with them and their business, reported to others their comings and goings. Such was the nature of his work.

On that morning the train came out of the east. Standing on the horizon as though it were a mirage, its call distorted across the space of the desert. The engine grew larger on the track even as it began to slow in its velocity, approaching the town with a speed not so different from the striding of a man, steadily never arriving until it did arrive, the locomotive easing into the midst of the buildings, its black sides wet with whistlewater.

Into the office of the telegrapher burst four men, their boots loud on the floor. Each man wore a pale and stained sombrero, a jacket filthy from weeks on the trail, kneeboots. They grabbed the operator and they threw him from his chair and one of these men bent low over him and began to beat him in the head. The train outside the door continued its long and loud and inexhaustible sigh.

The telegrapher held up his hands. He curled his legs into his chest but he did not scream or cry out even as the fists knocked his glasses across the floor and pounded down upon his cheeks and lips, his teeth tearing the insides of his mouth with the force of the blows. And then a gunshot, deafening in the room.

"Stop," I said.

The telegrapher was dragged back up into his chair. His fingers held like a cage over his face. I saw him there as he was and I saw my men, and I told the telegrapher that he might lower his hands, and after some moments indeed he did so. What he saw was three of his attackers standing up against the wall at gunpoint and held there by Rodolfo Fierro. And he saw on the floor the fourth of that group, coughing out his breath, his shirt torn open by buckshot.

And he saw me and this is what I saw: a small and the defenseless man beaten and cowering in the chair in which he did his daily work. I saw this and I saw that the eyes of my troops were like the eyes of dogs that smelled weakness and fear. I walked up to their comrade who lay on the floor. A young man. I did not recognize him and knew not how he had come to us. His hands held his chest. A bright string of red blood had appeared at the edge of his mouth. He was young but old enough to know what he was. I put my boot on his face and I pulled the Mauser from the holster. I bent to one knee, and I shot him in the head.

I stood and I told his three companions to clear his body from the place and I told Rodolfo Fierro to line them up outside and shoot them.

I watched those three, and as they took the body of their companion and I heard Fierro's shouting outside for more rifles and I heard the gunshots that cut those men down, and as I heard all of this, I kept my eyes on the telegrapher, where he remained curled in the chair. I felt a heat behind my eyeballs, something white rising in my chest until my tongue caught in my throat to see this fear. What memory was I living again?

I turned to the washbasin. There I took the pitcher of water and filled the metal basin and then took it from the vanity and placed it next to the operator's feet. From my pocket I took a handkerchief and snapped it open and I knelt. I took the leg of the telegrapher in my hand, and I untied the laces of that man's shoe. I took off his socks. I rolled up the hem of his pants and I dipped the kerchief in the water and in that place did I wash the telegrapher's feet. One, and then the other. As I did so the man began to cry.

Once finished I replaced his socks, tied again his shoes, took the basin and stood and walked outside where I pitched the water in the dirt not ten yards from the bodies of the men who had assaulted him.

I walked back into the room and stepped over the bloodstain on the floor and I said to the telegrapher, "We are at war. I have come from Chihuahua, and tonight I will take La Junta and I will put its leaders to the wall. There is no hope for them. I care not for those who have overseen the rape of this country for a generation. But the people of La Junta are my people. I know them. I know the style of their clothes. I know the way the women wear their hair. I know what they hold dear and I know what they despise and I know their thoughts and their hopes and I will not kill them. I will not kill a single one."

I leaned forward and placed again my hand on the shoulder of the telegrapher. "My entire force must enter the center of town without knowledge of our approach," I told him. "My enemies must not make a single preparation. Not a single rifle may be loaded in expectation of our arrival." I removed my hand and I stood again. "You know," I said, "how this is to be done."

The operator's eyes moved from the me to the train and back.

"From the train station to the federal office of La Junta," I said, "is not a hundred yards. The train arrives at sunset. The shadows of the monuments," I said, "will be long on the square. The proprietors of the cantinas are walking about in the dusk with matches to give fire to the lights of their shops and the train will pull in slowly." I moved my open palm across the air before us. "The cargo doors will roll back. And I won't have to fire a shot, and I won't have to kill a man. This," I said, "is your charge."

The operator raised his battered head, and he sat back in his chair.

166

I said to him, "I am the engineer of this coal train, out of Hermosillo and bound for Chihuahua. Between here and Chihuahua a bridge has been burned by rebels, and I have found it impossible to continue. The countryside is full of mounted men. I require that Colonel Castro, Commissioner of La Junta, advise me how to proceed."

The telegrapher did not speak, nor did his eyes waver from me as I stood. What he did was that he relaxed into his chair, and he regarded me as his own time allowed and I permitted it. Then he bent to the key before him, and he tapped out the message.

The answer from La Junta was not long in coming.

Return immediately with the train and be prepared to report.

I turned from this patriot and I left him to his day, to his work.

CHAPTER XVI

The True Enemy of Mexico. On Suffering. González's Lawyers. The Lobby of the Banco Minero. A Pickaxe.

We took La Junta and scattered its troops and shot Colonel Castro against the wall of the commissary. We appointed authorities to avoid both riot and plunder, and with this the people were pleased, as was I, but I knew what was only now within our grasp. Taking 150 men I rode north to Ciudad Guerrero and overran the town, the federals having abandoned the place once they heard we had taken La Junta. We rode down the main boulevard and into a silent city, and without delay I made for the bank.

Our enemy in this time was not the rurales, nor is it now. Not the rurales nor the federals and not even their commanding officers and not perhaps even the politicians nor even Díaz. The true enemies of Mexico are those who would hold and wield their power with no concern or interest for anyone save themselves and those of their blood, and in their minds their blood is not of Mexico but is a blood independent to this place or perhaps any other; such is the totality of their greed and self-possession. These are the great families. Creel. Terrazas. It is they who would have the politicians elected at all. Of all the great families of the North these two are the principals.

As to why I had taken my men into Ciudad Guerrero without orders or direction, the answer is simple: I yearned to bring a bounty to Señora González. For in this hamlet lived the banker Luis Terrazas, one of the richest men in all of Chihuahua, and in the Banco Minero de Ciudad Guerrero did he house his fortune.

And yet as I kicked in the wide and sculpted doors of the bank the long lobby lay empty. The drawers were all pulled from their cabinets, the papers scattered about the marble floors as though a storm had blown down the room. And at the far end of the place the doors of the empty vault hung open like the mouth of a skull.

A revolution, before it may exercise its ideals or alleviate the oppression it was even sparked to oppose, must first gain power. This may seem obvious, and in conversation it is so, but in the rush of events as they unfold across a landscape that burns with the fires you have yourself ignited, the question of power becomes fraught. One is easily swayed by the suffering one sees, or even causes, in the interest of those ideals. And yet that suffering is not so much a means as a constitutive element to the revolution itself. In the revolution there will be suffering. It is born of suffering and so must pass through it in order to achieve the peace which is not the revolution itself but its product, its aim. And so first must come the suffering that leads to power. Power is, in truth, rather simple. It is a question of violence and will and numbers. But power is only a step in the long road to the complete and total control necessary for the blossoming of peace. And so if I were to crush Luis Terrazas as a simple desert warlord might do, if I were to storm his house and rape his women and take his head—this would have been inadvisable. It would have been rash, and ignorant, and I was beginning to realize that I must be neither if I were to survive the maelstrom which the revolution was, and always in truth is.

I had with me on that morning as I went to Terrazas's house rough boys from the country, boys who had seen hardship such as myself and had within them both the hatred and the will to violence that is a necessary component of our struggle, but I also had lawyers. González, once hearing of my plans, had dispatched them to me in haste, even as she warned me in telegraphs to call it all off, to return to the trail and the recruitment, and I understand why she did so. She feared for my safety. She imagined me a peon and a buffoon. And so she had sent the lawyers as my protection because she knew what Terrazas was. Indeed, was she not so herself?

And so as I had found it impossible to lay my hands upon and take the gold of the families and use it for our ongoing adventure, I had with me instead the ten roly-poly men in brown suits riding alongside me who would subdue Terrazas with their logic. They would speak to him of monies he would lose, monies he could gain. They would persuade him that the best course of action would be to contribute his fortune to the revolution. A loan, in other words—a loan that would be repaid with our ultimate and glorious victory. But first we needed to help him find his checkbook.

We rode into the courtyard of Terrazas's house at nine in the blue morning and were met there by his wife who stood tall at the foot of the long steps in blue skirts finely made. We were unannounced, and yet she acted the proper hostess, calm and arrogant in her immaculate dress for I have no doubt she knew the nature of our visit, had in fact awaited our arrival. "Good morning, Señor Villa," she said, her face disdainful as I turned my horse about in the courtyard.

We followed her down a narrow hallway and into a library where the banker Luis Terrazas sat crosslegged by a great window. He held a saucer at his chest, sipping coffee. The room was indeed beautiful, high ceilings and molded plaster, thick drapes held back from the windows by woven ropes. Books reached up to the ceiling and a wheeled ladder made of brass provided access to the higher shelves. The glassed-in bookcase to the banker's side suggested a rare and prized selection.

"Señor Terrazas," I said. He remained seated at my approach.

"Villa," he replied. He placed his cup on his saucer, then laid both at the table by his side.

All pulled up chairs around Terrazas and the lawyers unfolded their satchels and then they began to speak. They produced papers outlining the state of affairs in the town and the state: these papers detailed what the state of affairs had been, what they currently were, what they could become. The lawyers were sure and they were able and they carried themselves with confidence.

Under their patient assault Terrazas said nothing. He sipped from his cup and blinked at them periodically over his thin glasses. At times he nodded at particular statements, adding nothing. The lawyers took Terrazas's silence for passivity, for a lack of concern regarding their position and so the arguments began to grow impassioned: the railroads, you see, are damaged; the herds are dwindling; the crops are burning in unmanaged fields. If this continues there will be no food, no transportation, no hope for stability in the state.

At length Terrazas pulled from his vest a gold pocketwatch, consulted it, snapped it closed. A gesture with which I was familiar. After doing so Terrazas, for the first time of that morning, turned to me. "I am compelled to ask," he said to me, "how things have come to this."

I had said nothing since providing introductions and at this I said nothing still. I pulled on the front of my coat. I resettled myself in the chair.

"You see, Señor," said the youngest lawyer to Terrazas, "without your intervention, the state will starve to death."

Terrazas then said "I am under the impression that there are precious few in the state left to feed." Here he turned his eyes again to me. "I am under the impression that everyone has run out into the hills. Perhaps waiting to claim the plot of land promised him by the savages that have stolen it from its rightful owners. And besides," Terrazas turned to the others, "why do you come to me with this news? Don Sebastian or Don Manuel or twenty other such men could do a great deal more good than I in the procurement of funds." The lawyers only looked to one another. "That is what you are here for, yes?" asked Terrazas. "For an infusion of capital?"

"These men you speak of," said one of my lawyers, "have left the district."

Terrazas laughed. His laughing continued longer than appropriate and he seemed to take great joy in it, in the laughter and in its effect until at length he was able to say "They have left more than the district, my friend. They have left this earth, and unwillingly if I am to believe reports I hear." He calmed himself, and he picked up his coffee cup and said "but this is only natural, as they have committed the crime of personal advancement and sensible finance. And now—if I understand what you are trying so desperately to explain to me—now you have neither the knowledge nor the wherewithal to properly manage the finances of a state, caught up as you are in the process of murdering, or of driving out all those who do."

"And yet you have stayed," I said.

Terrazas now turned to me fully. He regarded me and there was in his face no fear nor apprehension, and he said "I have stayed, Señor Villa. And allow me to tell you why. I have stayed because this town is precious to me. I was born here and have watched it rise and have again watched it be stripped bare in the span of a year by hateful bandits such as yourself. And yet I still will not leave it. For it is my home."

For many moments in the room we both sat still, facing one another. And I know what I saw there, and I wonder if Terrazas saw what was indeed there, or if he saw only what he believed, what he desperately wished to see. Finally Terrazas again produced his watch, opened it, consulted it, snapped it shut, put it away.

"I can burn your house down," I said.

"You have that power, yes."

"I may have your wife raped in the street and send your daughter to the brothels to be raised a whore whose single goal in life is to provide the most perfect satisfaction to my troops."

"I do understand that the living and the dying of things now falls under your discretion."

"I have taken the town. As such I have taken your bank. In this bank was the gold you made from the blood of the peasants of this district, and I will have it, and I will return it to them. I will have the money that you put there. You are going to tell me where you've hidden the money."

"I have no money, Villa."

"You ran the bank."

"The bank is empty, and there is no gold in this house. Now I would ask you and your men to do me the utmost courtesy and take your leave of it."

I ran my palm across my mouth, and as I did so Terrazas remained as he was. Then I stood, and my men stood with me and I began to walk toward the door and then I turned. I walked instead to the great window and yanked from the wall the rope that held back the long curtains and I pulled this rope straight, doubling it in my hands. I walked back to Terrazas who took off his glasses and demanded an explanation that was caught in his throat as I threw the rope around his neck.

Slipping the two ends through the doubled loop I then with this noose threw the banker down upon the carpet. The lawyers cried out in surprise as I did so and I then began to drag Terrazas around the floor of his own library. His kicking feet knocked over the sidetable and the chairs and I smiled at the idiot tinkling of the coffecup and the saucer under his feet. He even in his panic kicked in the glass of his own bookcase, the shards falling loosely in his lap. Two of the lawyers forgot themselves entirely and screamed for me to continue, to rip his head from his body and I wondered as to the bloodthirstiness of this particular class of men, and if perhaps I had confused my judgment as to the most vicious under my command. At length Terrazas lost consciousness.

When the banker awoke I was kneeling before him, the same length of rope hanging loosely from the neck of his eight-year-old son. The boy looked at his father sullenly, bored by this game of adults. And still Terrazas said nothing.

When I returned to my quarters I summoned Rodolfo Fierro, and gave him orders to retrieve what I could not.

The lobby of the Banco Minero measured a full forty yards wide, sixty yards long. Running the length of the marble room (and all this white and pink and shot through with red and doubtless imported at great expense from Spain) stood eight massive pillars, their trunks the circumference of ancient trees. Each rose some 30 feet to the iron-worked ceiling, itself overlain with panels of cut glass.

The morning sunshine streamed through this glass and down onto the lobby floor, and the double doors were opened onto the street and the rising day. My irregulars climbed the steps behind me and walked with me into the lobby, their boot heels echoing across the marble floor. In their hands they carried rough wooden planks, nails, hammers, and saws.

At the far column the men began to construct a rickety scaffold, and in the course of a few hours a weak and tottering cage rose up and around the marble column. To a stranger the men would have appeared indeed to be some renegade breed of doctors, for around their necks hung the small and delicate instruments of that trade. From the belt of one man swung a tiny hammer, and he grabbed it from time to time to tap the column as though sounding the chest of a consumptive, his ear pressed close to the stone.

Outside the bank the soldiers drank coffee and ate tortillas from a cookfire they had built in the empty street. They sat on the steps which had served the most bloodsoaked barons of northern Mexico, and they ate their breakfast in their tattered sombreros and muddy boots. And the square below them which had seen the lives of men reduced to numbers in a book sat silent and empty and birds alone sounded in the trees. Why this square? Why this street and this building among all the others in that country or world? Who is to say when a place takes upon itself the designation of one which would decide the value of men, weigh them in games of speculation and chance, of bluff and confidence? Does the place become these things or do they arise from the place itself, indicting that place as the confluence of the evil that would there manifest?

Shouts came from inside the bank. The soldiers turned as one and rushed up the steps, tortillas in hand. And once they gained the lobby they saw, up on the scaffold some twenty feet from the ground, a workman bent deep at the knees, the hammer dangling from his belt as he drilled a tiny hole in the top of the column.

I stood at the base of the thing in full military attire: a midnight blue jacket with high jackboots and officer's cap (taken from the body of Colonel Castro not one week before), and all eyes were turned to the man atop the scaffold as the nose of the drill slipped through the stone in a jump, vanishing into some unplumbed interior space. The man raised one hand high, and a cheer erupted from the crowd.

I called for a pickaxe. I handed my hat to Rodolfo Fierro and took aim at the base of the column. With a wide swing the pick stung and bounced away. Silence again, and I eyed the tool narrowly. Again the windup, and the man above began to scamper down the scaffolding. And again the ping of the pickaxe.

I rubbed my hand over the dent I had chipped in the base of the column and I reared back once more and, turning my hips with the force of the swing I plunged the face of the tool some six inches into the marble facade. I seesawed the wooden handle, and as I withdrew the pick the coins began to spill out, to ring out on the floor and turn and twist, catching the light that fell through the glass above us. Once more I slammed the pick home and this time the hole opened wide and broke with an avalanche of specie pouring from the gash in the column like the sacred blood of a tree, rushing onto the floor and piling up around my glistening boots. I raised my arms to the cheering of my men.

Handing the axe to the crowd I walked over to Fierro where he stood against the long and empty marble changing counter. He held out to me my hat. I clapped Fierro on the shoulder and turned to the spectacle of hundreds of thousands of pesos spilling from the marble column into the lobby of the Banco Minero.

"Don't kill him," I said.

To this Fierro said nothing.

"His family is very old, Rodolfo."

"Yes."

"He was trying to escape, I suspect."

"Of course," he said.

The soldiers were wading through the mounds of gold as it piled up upon the floor, dipping their sombreros into it and pouring it over one another's heads and howling with joy. Even now the self-proclaimed engineers were beating at the base of another column, calling for more axes and drills.

"Tell them to take only what their conscience demands and no more," I said, "as would any good soldier."

"Yes."

"And if any man leaves with more than 400 pesos shoot him as a traitor."

"Of course."

Chapter XVII

Horatio Benton. So Many Marbles. A Hole in the Desert. The Widow and Her Daughter. The Plan of San Luis Potosí. A Man of Learning.

The Englishman Horatio Benton had arrived in Mexico with an honorable name and exhausted accounts. A deposed aristocrat, Benton's father had frittered away the family fortune on gambling and women and drink, a truth Benton had only come to realize after his father's somewhat untimely death. I imagine that first winter alone for young Benton in England, the young man sitting sick with rage in a large and empty house, huddling with his dog around the only fireplace there was money enough to feed. I see Benton there, watching the firelight pulsing in the logs, nursing a growing and unquenchable fury inside his soul.

In the spring Benton left for Mexico. With his remaining pittance he bought a small ranch outside of Chihuahua and within five years he had built it up into an expansive hacienda. He married a Mexican of a good family and with her had five children and three sons and yet none of this luck or success diluted his anger. He berated his help, whipped his hired hands. He was disagreeable and cruel and suffered neither accidents nor mistakes.

Horatio Benton was, therefore, displeased when I claimed

178

his lands as property of the rebel forces. He was displeased that his cattle began to disappear (commandeered by my men, of course), but Benton was principally displeased because I was common. Indeed in the past Díaz had taken from the Englishman's hacienda whatever the government required for its own troops, and so I exercised no rights other than those which were natural to power. Benton could not, however, submit himself to a Mexican of my background. After abandoning who he had been and traveling across the ocean and building up his life from the dirt the Englishman now found himself at the mercy of a man whom he believed to be an uneducated thief. This is, at least, what I imagine he believed, because in the spring of 1910 Benton, in a towering rage, packed up his family and drove them all into San Andrés. He placed them at the Hotel McGregor and he put on his best suit and jacket and he went in search of me. He did not in truth have to look far, as I had recently installed myself in the house of the governor. I was the law of that place in that time, and as such I knew of Benton and his desires—for his made no effort to hide them, indeed he would trumpet them for any who asked and for many who did not—and I knew his location and the mood of his mind. And because of this I know that, before confronting me in my own offices, Benton went to the bar.

He came in from the sun and the street in his dove-gray suit, and he walked to the bar and pushed back his hat and kicked a tooled boot onto the rail, and there he called for a whiskey and it was brought.

"Ah," murmured the man next to him. "Civilization."

"Beg your pardon," said Benton. He downed his liquor.

"It's good to see a white man walking on two legs in this country," said the other.

Benton placed his empty glass on the bar and turned. The stranger was as tall as he. Quite thin in a black and dilapidated suit. American. Burning blues eyes, whispy moustache. Benton waved for the bartender.

"You should watch what you say in a place like this," Benton said to the American. "The savages will kill you for less."

"They'll kill you for anything," said the American.

Whiskey was brought and poured and the American waved his long hand over Benton's drink and asked for the same and paid for both.

Benton downed the drink in a gulp. "Thank you," he said, "but you must excuse me. I have business."

The American turned his back to the bar and rested his elbows behind him. "A man can have no business here," he said, "unless your business is with Him."

"You know Villa," Benton said.

The American smiled. "Who else is worth knowing?"

Benton waved the bartender over again and ordered more whiskeys.

"What is your experience?" Benton asked.

The American ran the back of his hand over his mouth. He steadied himself. He stretched out his arms and opened his hands.

"Imagine if you would a blanket," he said. "Hands pull it taut in every direction. On it there is no variance or difference. All here is the same. Now." The American held up one long finger. "Drop on it a single marble," he said. "It will roll for a moment, then it come to rest. It is nothing. A tiny divot. But then drop another. Is it not true that the second marble will search out and find the first? Come to rest with a click by its side? And a third: the same. Fourth, fifth and so on, until there is a large and deepening collection. Every marble now dropped will group together with the first. The entire field is now bent around it, funneled toward it, and a space that had been without difference or designation is suddenly nothing more than a court for the exercise of a singular fate."

Benton eyed the American closely. He was a man without bearing. A lost soul in this dusty town. Benton waved for two more whiskeys. "What can be done about it?" he asked.

The American took a quick drink and leaned in close. "First, ask yourself how is this to end for *him?* The time has long passed for killing him in the open. No. A big house, land, his own peons working his fields: this is how it ends. Of course. This is where the time is going, back toward where it began." He took another gulp from the whiskey. "So. What we have to do is, we have to make a little hole in the sheet. It won't take much. Just a little nick and the first marble will slip through. Then the second, the third. Quickly the nick will stretch, will rip with the weight of the collective, and then the bottom will tear out altogether, and send everything clattering to the floor."

The American placed both his hands on the bar, his face bent upward in a distant smile.

"How the nick?" Benton said, waving again for the bartender.

"It will come from elsewhere," said the American. "We cannot engineer it from within."

"Within what?"

The American smiled and downed his shot. "Ask yourself how it came to this," he said. "Ask yourself which of the marbles are you, and which one I?"

It is agreed upon by all interested parties that the two strode to the governor's mansion and demanded an audience with myself, that is, the desert outlaw Pancho Villa. Hollering drunken oaths at the armed guards, the two men were accommodated admirably, were led to the hallway outside my office and placed on the benches beside the garden. There they were told to wait. But Benton would not wait.

It is further agreed upon that the Englishman stood and

walked across the hallway and barged without warning or introduction into my office. Once there Benton stated his business and had barely paused for breath before he accused me where I sat of outright thievery. Of banditry. Then, drunk and wild and reckless, Benton reached for his pistol. I stood quickly and, drawing my own sidearm, shot the Englishman in the leg. Rodolfo Fierro promptly placed Benton on a train to Ciudad Juarez, and from there Benton was carried out into the desert a half-hour from town. He stood by, bound and gagged, while Fierro argued with two gravediggers about the best place for a shallow hole. With nightfall the hole was dug and Benton was shot before it and deposited within it and the gravediggers covered him over. This is what is known. But this is not the truth.

In truth it was the American who was led out into the desert outside of Juarez. It was the American who stood bound and gagged and watched the gravediggers argue with Fierro, and it was the American who stood silent for the executioners who chatted amongst themselves and smoked cigarettes, waiting for my arrival on the day's last train.

It was the American who watched me drive through the dusk from Ciudad Juarez in a Ford motorcar, the American who watched as I spoke with Fierro, who watched as the riflemen lined up without a signal even as Fierro and I continued our conversation. It was the American, finally, who's body convulsed with riflefire and pitched backward into the pit. The gravediggers filled it back with loose dirt, stamped it even, and then left for their favorite cantina.

And yet it was indeed Benton who stormed into my room in the heat of that afternoon. Here we see the Englishman as he was on that day: tall and lean, impertinent and sure, his bearing every inch that of the lord he had been.

I was seated behind my desk, speaking quietly with a widow

and her twelve-year-old daughter, preparing to hand them a monthly pension of one thousand dollars for their dead husband and father, killed not three weeks before in the mountains west of San Ignacio. The woman's head was covered in black crepe, her hands open and outstretched to receive that which was her sacred right as a widow to the sacred cause. Into this moment blundered an Englishman, demanding that which he believed to be his, quoting treaties and agreements and obscure international pacts.

And now came the accusations. Benton shouting himself hoarse with them. Thief. Bandit. Fatherless bastard. What we then see is this. We see Rodolfo Fierro emerge silent from a side room. He has been awoken from sleep, and he is shirtless. His suspenders swing down at his thighs. His knees bend low, his face a grimace and in his fist a short and thick blade which he drives without an instant of hesitation and with the full force of his stride into the kidneys of the Englishman.

The widow screamed. She fainted away and fell from her chair and the girl turned, her eyes wide, her body shaking unconsciously as she watched Fierro (his belly slick with the Englishman's blood) pull out the blade and sink it again to the hilt into Benton's back. As the Englishmen fell, Fierro opened his arms and caught him there, and he put his hand at the thin man's face, draping his arm around Benton's hips. And in this way did Fierro hold Horatio Benton for not a few moments, and in those moments all was still in the room. Then Fierro dragged the moaning, bleeding man back through the door from which he had emerged, the dying man's feet bumping feebly on the carpet.

After a time a revolver was produced, its hammer found to be cocked on the single bullet in its cylinder. This was obviously Benton's weapon, his plan of assassination fortuitously thwarted through the efforts of the heroic Rodolfo Fierro. I was well pleased, and the body of the Englishman was wrapped in the rug on which he had been stabbed and was taken behind the house, and there it was set on fire.

Even as the body was still burning, Fierro and I, dressed and washed, walked back through the hallway of the house, and there we passed the American where he still sat upon the marble bench. This man stood, straightened his jackets, and he then enquired as to the location of William Benton, Englishman and owner of the Los Remedios Ranch. I responded that no such Benton had arrived that day.

"That," the American said to me, "is a lie."

Fierro stepped forward, took the American by the arm, and led him gently to the train.

But William Benton was not to be so easily forgotten. Before leaving for Chihuahua he had made appeals to the American State Department, to the British Chancellery, to the government in Mexico City. Before the week was out my office was flooded with requests from consulates and newspapers. Benton's wife, Benton's now widow, remained with her now fatherless children in their rooms at the McGregor Hotel. All were told that Benton—rash, furious and drunk—had threatened the life of the most powerful warlord in northern Mexico. As an inevitable and imminently sensible result, Benton had been executed in Juarez.

Now came the requests for the Englishman's body to be exhumed and transported back Los Remedios Ranch. Of course, impossible. After learning that Benton's widow was a full-blooded Mexican I agreed to a one-time lump payment. I addressed all further inquiries by stating that while other cultures are free to do as is their custom in their own land, Mexicans do not disturb the sleep of the dead. After a time, attention began to turn elsewhere, and most of the interested parties were satisfied.

Rodolfo Fierro, however, was not satisfied. He began with the riflemen, imprisoning them each on separate and floridly imagined charges. Each man was shot on the same day, their families provided more than ample compensation.

For the gravediggers, Fierro waited with some six other assassins outside the men's cantina of choice with long knives, and as the two fat and simple souls without family or holdings stumbled down the steps in the early morning Fierro set upon them. And then finally to the widow, and her girl.

Fierro began to make enquires. He learned that the shock the widow had experienced by witnessing the violent death of the Englishman had nearly incapacitated her. That she had taken a cab to the house of her sister across town and there she had stayed. This house was situated on the plaza near the School of Agriculture.

Fierro arrived in a dove-gray suit, his boots shining at a high gloss, the chain of his pocket watch glinting in the sun. Holding his wide hat in one hand he was received by the sister whom he knifed even as she stood in the doorway. Walking through the house he threw his hat on a chair in the main hall and he climbed the stairs, eventually finding the widow where she lay in her convalescence in a rear bedroom. At her side sat the child, her hair down and about her shoulders in her supposed privacy. Her face was taut and tired and exquisite for a child of such an age. Rodolfo Fierro entered the room, and he closed the door behind him.

"Peoples in their constant efforts for the triumph of the ideal of liberty and justice, are forced, at precise historical moments, to make their greatest sacrifices."

Señora González sat at my elbow as I struggled to sound out the sentence. The paper on the table between us lay curled from travel and her thin hands smoothed out the top of the document as I continued.

"*Our beloved country has reached one of those moments,*" I read. "*A force of tyranny which we Mexicans were not accustomed to suffer after we won our independence oppresses us in such a manner that it has become intolerable. In exchange for that tyranny we are offered peace, but peace full of shame....*"

I sat back from the table, breathing heavily, near tears from my effort. Señora González's face remained bent to the paper, her eyes following where I had broken off. Her eyes remained on the words as I rubbed my sleeve across my face like a child.

After a moment she pulled herself out of the text with reluctance and turned to me, smiling. "We will work further, Francisco. It is something you will learn. You have no choice."

I cleared my throat. "I will do so," I said. Her eyes were gentle, and I put my finger on the papers before us and I said "I will read it until it is imprinted into my very soul," and in truth I did.

She had come to me after we had ridden out of San Andrés and down into the plain, come by car from the train station with this document in her hands that we now studied in the middling light of my nighttime tent.

Her eyes were back on the document.

"Things are moving, Francisco," she told me. "It is no longer simply you in the deserts and mountains alone or I in Chihuahua gathering monies and influence. We have a champion," she said. "We have a hero." I watched her eyes as she said these things. She nodded at the paper as she read it aloud:

"*In Mexico the public power can have no other origin nor other basis than the will of the people ... they have recognized within me the virility of a patriot determined to sacrifice himself to obtain liberty and to help the people free themselves from the odious tyranny that oppresses them.*"

She pursed her lips. "I have met him," she said. "I have met him and when I did I suspected there was something of greatness. He is quiet," she said, "but a man of intensity. Of seriousness. He is a man of education, Francisco. A man of discernment, a man who understands history and who is ready to step into it fully and without fear." She smiled as she said these things. "He is tall," she said, "and true and he is right, Francisco. He speaks with the power of rightness. And this," she said, nodding again at to the paper, "is precisely what we have been waiting for. This is the declaration of the revolution."

His name was Francisco Madero. The wealthy son of a landowner, he had run against Díaz for the Presidency of Mexico and had, of course, lost. But upon this defeat the young Madero had retreated to San Antonio and gathered around him those loyal to him and his cause and had there in that safety penned the document between us, "The Plan of San Luis Potosí." For us in that time who ran in the deserts and mountains fighting and dying it was a grand thing. He called out Díaz by name. He called him a lapdog to the dons. He called him a tyrant and a butcher and a fool. And he said Díaz must be brought down.

At this moment however, on this night, I was more pleased with the attentions of Señora González. In those long days and nights with only my men and my command, only her letters to me kept me tied to her vision and, I will admit, to her approval. I believe that in this time I did this all for her first, and for Mexico second.

"Your man sees the problem clearly," I said to her, "and yet this is nothing you yourself have not told me, nor nothing I have not heard around campfires or have thought through in my own private moments."

"Of course we think it," she said, her hand on my arm. "But we do not proclaim it. We do not have the safety, the reputation or the gall. And we do not have the money."

"I have given you a fortune," I said quietly. "Ciudad Guerrero is a fortune."

"Madero is an important man, Francisco. His family is excellent. He has support in the highest reaches of the country."

"He is a landowner."

"He is a landowner who knows the people and can speak for them. This," she said, her finger again down on the paper between us, "is the bond of our action. Without him we are fated to the inconsequential operations as we have executed thus far."

"Inconsequential," I said. I shook my head in disbelief. "You have the spine of the sierra. We have over a thousand men."

"Would you ride into Mexico City with a thousand men, Francisco? They would butcher you in the suburbs." She sat back and looked at the sides of the tent. She opened her arms to them. "They would crush us," she said, "if we left the mountains. Even the towns you take for us are only taken back by federals days after your departure."

"It's not true."

"It is. They are on your tracks, Francisco. They're killing your men. They're killing anyone you leave. You can't see what's happening a week behind you. And Francisco Madero is building an army of ten thousand as we speak."

I was incredulous. "Ten thousand?"

"This is what I am saying. They are gathering even now in El Paso for the invasion. This is the revolution, Francisco. It is happening. He had galvanized the country."

"With this," I pointed at the paper.

"He has become our leader."

"An invasion?"

"A battle proper. Not incursions. Not raids. A march into Ciudad Juarez."

Even as she spoke I began to see it. Columns moving down blasted streets. Cavalry and cannon. Bayonets in the afternoon sun.

"He is impressed with your successes in recruitment," she said. "He is impressed with your ambition and your victories."

"Temporary victories."

"You need more men. More supplies and ammunition and weapons and horses."

"More money."

"Of course."

"Does he want to give me these things or does he want to judge me?"

"He wants to make you a captain," she said.

These were strange moments for me, for they sounded at once upon the bottom of things. I admit freely that in these early days of the fight I feigned a conviction that only came upon me at intervals, and never quite the whole. As the leader of men I could in truth look upon them and see in their faces that which they wanted and needed their leader to be, and I leapt to be that man and take them where they would allow themselves to be taken. But alone. Alone and without assurance I still found myself in the intermittent and sudden grip of doubt. I found myself at times uncertain. I had seen enough of the world to know for myself that there existed within it no way of untrammeled justice, and yet I wanted with each and every fiber of my being to find just such a way. I wanted that way to be. And so was I then to surrender all that I had earned, all that I had driven myself to become, to an aristocrat simply because others agreed with him? Or was I to enfold myself into his command, legitimizing my own command, my successes and violence and will? Did I need that legitimation? Or what would come in its place without it? There was no answer then; nor is there now, for the decision has been made as it must have been, for there is no other world save this, and those decisions we wonder at in our advancing age are mere illusions to prevent us from facing the thing that is. No answer then, only the decision.

I looked at the far wall of the tent and I spoke to it. "I will accept this charge," I said, "and I will execute it to the best of my ability for the glory of Mexico and its people."

Señora González was adjusting her scarves. "We must also discuss other concerns," she said.

"Such as."

"The banker. Luis Terrazas."

"He was trying to escape."

Her chin was raised to me. "His entire family was trying to escape?"

"I don't understand."

"His wife, his daughter and his young son were attempting to escape?"

"Yes," I said.

"And they were all knifed to death for this attempt?"

I said nothing.

"Bloody handprints on the walls of the bedrooms. The hallways looked like a slaughterhouse, Francisco."

"How would you know what a slaughterhouse looks like?"

Señora González pulled at her dress. "Tell me," she said. "Who is Rodolfo Fierro."

"He is a soldier of the revolution," I said. "He has acquitted himself admirably in any of a number of directed actions in the service of the people."

"I would like to meet him."

"He is not with us currently," I said in a quick and unexamined lie.

Señora González said nothing for a time, and in that time I could not meet her eyes. When she spoke she did so quietly. "There is a danger, Francisco," she said. "A danger in this desert and these mountains. I would even say that it lives here like a spirit and moves from man to man who lives and who would do their work in these places. I would like you to remember something," she said, "and I would like you to remember it for me. This work that we do is work that we must do, and we must do it for the good of Mexico."

"I don't understand you."

"You know very well what this work is, Francisco," she said evenly. "It is necessary work. It should not be inhabited, or encouraged, or above all enjoyed. When we are through of it, it should be cast aside. Promise me that you will do this."

"Do what?"

"Cast it aside. Once it has served its purpose."

"It is the wise thing to do," I said.

She uncrossed her arms and she put her hand on my knee. She said nothing but looked into my eyes as she stood, and I stood with her. "It is a joy for me to see you," she said. "You are becoming who you were born to be." She placed her scarf over her hair and held it with both hands. "I return to Chihuahua tonight. I leave this here for you," she said, her eyes back to the papers on my desk. "I would like you to practice."

"Of course, Señora González." As I spoke I felt tears once more at my eyes and I looked about the emptiness of the tent once more.

"I love you," I said to her.

"You are a hope to me, Francisco. Goodnight."

CHAPTER XVIII
Odd Shapes. The Bargain in the Jailhouse. The Indian at Caborca. Another Face.

I did not lead the detachment that ran back out toward Santa Isabel the next day, but Fierro asked if he could ride with them and I agreed. He needed to move, he told me. To place himself in relation to things. He had begun to feel restless.

"My hands itch," he said to me in the halflight of the tent. "Odd shapes form in the corners of my eyes."

He rode out the following predawn with my blessing in what was indeed a ragged and vagabond white linen suit, a straw hat tilted on his head. He was quiet on the ride up into the mountains, saying little other than what was necessary, and the ride into Santa Isabel was simple and plain.

In the glare of a high midday the men arrived in town and stopped to rest the horses and take on water. Fierro took a brace of pistols from his saddlebags and slipped them into the front of his gunbelt, the holsters of which already held two sidearms. As he did this a string of schoolchildren passed him by, small and chattering and holding one another's hands in a long and undulating line. Fierro watched them pass, and then immediately fell in behind them. Crouching down so as to be closer to their height he took the hand of the last boy in the line, who turned to him, first smiling, then confused. But then. Here was such a nice and gentle and well-dressed man. Perhaps this man is a friend of my father's. Surely he knows him. A sweet and decent uncle. Yes, of course I know him. I know him well.

"Are you going to school?" Fierro asked the boy, and the boy nodded vigorously. The line walked on through the square, the children speaking naturally amongst themselves, Fierro trailing behind.

"There are a great many things to learn at school," Fierro told the boy. "Would you like to learn something new?" The boy looked to the line as it proceeded on before him and looked back at the sweet man, and he nodded once more with great energy.

Fierro pulled himself up to his full height. The boy dropped the hands of his companions who trundled along, oblivious and away. Fierro smiled down at the boy. He turned to the building at their left and they, holding one another's hands like a father and son, walked into the town jail.

Fierro approached the desk of the jailer and there made known his name and rank and his affiliation to myself. All of this was heard and given the proper respect. He had come, Fierro told them, with strict orders to address all the prisoners. He had come, he told them, with a bargain offered one time only to those who would otherwise live out their days as outcasts to their people.

"I come," said Fierro, "with a reprieve."

The boy watched all of this with awe, and he held Fierro's hand as they were led back through the hallways of the jail and into the courtyard at the rear—a long and narrow yard surrounded with high and whitewashed walls. There they stood with only the blue patch of the sky above them. A sky empty of cloud or tree or any defining feature. It opened up depth upon depth of a blue that doubtless deepened in its intensity until even this too was lost in the beyond. Across it flew a crow.

Ten prisoners were led out into the yard by the jailer and stood before Fierro and boy. The prisoners were old and young, dressed in plain cotton shirts and pants. They were shoeless, their hair matted, their faces unshaven. For what had they been detained? For the pilfering of bread, for the refusal to pay a tax, for the stealing of a horse. The boy held his ground before them as he felt the confidence of the tall man beside him.

Fierro took off his jacket and hat and he called for a table and was told that none in the jail would fit out the door. Fierro looked to these prisoners who stood before him and he handed his hat and jacket to the jailer. He then took the two pistols out of his waistband and he knelt down before the boy.

"Listen to me," said Rodolfo Fierro. "There are times when the imbecility of others would occlude even the most patient of designs. Do you understand?"

The boy nodded.

"I need your help," said Fierro. "I need you to help me. Will you help me?"

"Yes."

"I need you to hold my pistols." Fierro held those two pistols out to the boy who took them by the barrels and held them with splayed fingers against his chest. Fierro stood and then remembered the two in his holsters. He bent back down, the knee of his suit now yellowed by the dirt.

"And this," he said, handing the boy a third. The boy reached out with his fingers and hugged this as well to his chest. Fierro ruffled the boy's hair. Then he stood.

Fierro took the remaining pistol from his holster and he told the prisoners that they would today be given the chance to atone for their misdeeds. That they would be given reprieve by the benevolent hand of Pancho Villa and for this they should be grateful. The prisoners stood as they were.

Fierro flipped opened the cylinder of the gun in his hand and, ensuring the chambers were full, he told the prisoners that he would give them each an opportunity to test their fate against the hand of God. A murmur ran through the group of men. Fierro told them that he had at his disposal twenty-four bullets. He told them that the distance from where they stood to the far wall of the prison yard was roughly thirty yards. He told them that, at his signal, they had the opportunity to run for the wall.

"Any man who makes it over the wall," Fierro told them, "may go free. As such he may consider himself absolved. His debt is paid, and his crime forgiven. You have until the count of three." Fierro snapped shut the cylinder and raised his weapon. "Young man," he said to the boy, "Hand me a revolver when I ask you for it." He did not look to the boy, and as such did not see him nod with great seriousness.

"Now," Rodolfo Fierro said, settling his shoulders, raising his arm and siting down the barrel of the gun. "One, two, three."

Ten bodies lay in the midday yard. Some looked as though they were sleeping. Some were stretched out like wakening cats, clawing for something just outside of their reach. Some had taken on comical positions, elbows and knees bent up at ridiculous angles. The blood was only beginning to pool in the dirt from the bodies and the jailer himself stood cowering in the doorway. Fierro called for his hat and his coat and these were brought to him and he put them on with deliberation and he bent down again to his knee in order to address the boy.

The boy still held one pistol at his chest. His eyes were wide, his mouth shut tight. He shook just so slightly where he stood, the one pistol held in his arms as though it were precious to him, a favorite doll or toy the removal of which would loosen the dam of his fear. Indeed the boy clutched at the thing as though it provided succor and assistance, and Fierro watched the boy as he vibrated in the day like the string of a guitar. He searched out the boy's eyes until he held them. When Fierro spoke it was quiet, gentle, and full of concern.

"This is not school," said Fierro. "In the world are lessons that school could never hope to convey. Now," said Fierro, "I would like you to tell me what you have just learned."

The boy said nothing. Fierro took the pistol from the boy's hands. He slid it into the holster at his hip, and then he reached up and gripped the boy's shoulder with force. Fierro then shook the boy violently. Had he not held the child tightly the boy would've fallen over and into the dirt.

"Tell me."

I asked Fierro to join me the next night in my tent, where I prepared to accuse him of treachery and betrayal of the people. I sat at my small table with a bottle of mescal and my pistol in my belt. After Fierro had entered the two men who had accompanied him took up positions as guards at its entrance.

I offered Fierro a drink and he refused. This surprised me, remembering as I did his attitude from years before at our first meeting at that desolate campfire. But in truth his entire demeanor had changed completely from that time. It was a slow evolution but on this night it could be seen in total by the light of the lamp. In his face and his posture and his presence. Fierro sat in complete stillness, his eyes wide, his hands folded in his lap. He sat as though an anchor in an otherwise listing world.

"The time was when you drank a great deal," I said to Fierro.

"I drank what I was able."

"And now you do not."

Fierro smiled. "I have all the intoxication I need," he said.

I watched him as his smile faded, and his face once more

resumed the appearance that I have described. I sat back in my chair. I felt the weight of the pistol on my hip and I heard the boots of the men move in the dirt outside of my tent.

"Why did you first come to us?" I asked Fierro. "In that dank and desolate time when we were bandits in the mountains. What made you search us out?"

"I heard that you were a commander of talent and violence," he said. "That the coming insurrection would be prosecuted by your hands."

"What did you know then of insurrection? You are a railroad man."

"I was at Tomochi," he said.

The name of the town froze me. The story of its rebellion and ultimate destruction at the hands of the federals was well known in Chihuahua at that time and may still be so known, even as our own accomplishments have eclipsed the struggle of so many others for identical aims and goals. Tomochi had bucked at the reins of Díaz's despotism, been subsequently burnt to ash by Díaz's soldiers. Whole families put to the wall. It was illustrative of Díaz's savagery, often invoked as demonstration and cause of any violence against him and his despotic regime. The name of the town was a sacrament in circles that would rise up against Díaz. As if to say one was present at Golgotha. I narrowed my eyes at Fierro, waiting for a tic that would brand him a liar. I pulled the pistol from my hip and I laid it on the table between us. Fierro remained as he was.

"Tomochi was burnt to the ground," I said.

"It was."

I fingered the trigger and watched my hand as I did so. "What did you see there?"

Rodolfo Fierro had not looked at the pistol. I could sense that it was beside his concern. He smiled once more. "I worked for a company driving goods to the town."

"You were a delivery man."

"I was."

"And as you made your deliveries what did you find there?"

"What I found there were simple people under persecution from their government. After I had fulfilled my debt to the company I lingered in the town, drunk in the gutters, working off my wages with the labor of my addiction. At length I saw the federals come, and I saw them demand their tribute for their distant king, and I also saw the men of Tomochi kill those emissaries and take their rifles. At this I arose from my own stink and, wretch that I was, I followed the men of Tomochi up into the mountains. Federal reinforcements came close behind.

"The men of Tomochi took me in and told me they travelled to take the counsel of the Saint of Cabora, a child in the mountains who healed the sick and spoke of a flood that would drown the country and the evils of it. The people of Tomochi had great faith in the powers of this girl, and they said we would speak with her in Cabora and she would tell us what was to be done. When we arrived, however, we came to understand that she had already fled. Had heard of our resistance, and in fear of the federals had left her chapel and went down the back of the mountains. And so we barricaded ourselves in her empty church. We shuttered ourselves in, and there the federals with their superior numbers and weapons surrounded us. The first day they could have killed us to a man, but the federals were afraid of the power of the girl, and they did not know she was gone. And they were afraid of the mountains as well, for Cabora is a silent place without trees or water or birds. For a day we huddled in that church, whispering among ourselves."

I placed my thumb on the hammer of the pistol and cocked it back. I watched Fierro again as he breathed. He watched the pistol and when his eyes met mine they were as benevolent as before.

"At nightfall," he said, "a man walked up to the front of that church. He was unremarkable. Small, stout, with the hair of a full-blood Indian. A flat face. A bulbous nose. He moved with conviction to the dark and abandoned pulpit, and once there he began to speak about God.

"This man spoke about a God that he knew and that I had always suspected but about which I could not myself speak. And as this man spoke about Him I came to recognize this man's God as my own. The Indian said to us that there are those who would question the wisdom of violence. Those who would condemn us for our actions against the federals, regardless of provocation. Those who would say that a drop of blood spilt is a sin against God. And it did not surprise me when he said that those who say these things say them because they are weak and they are afraid. But then the Indian said something that did surprise me. He said that doubt and weakness and fear is essential, and necessary.

"The man said that the doubt of those who would doubt must be embraced by all of the people, amplified so that it feeds on itself, be worked up into anxiety, the embers of its rising fear sparking up into a fire of ambiguity and simmering terror. A terror which as it grows blots out all thought, feeling and sight. And it is in the midst of that terror, a terror so self-evident and certain, a terror that is in truth inversion of the doubt from which it has sprung—only in the midst of that undeniable terror may we begin to understand certitude, the one thing of which we can be certain in a world so otherwise contingent and the only certitude in the world is the truth that we will die. This is the truth from which our doubt and terror spring, said the Indian. And it is horrible. And only in knowing this, he said, may we begin to understand God.

"The Indian said that his will was a degenerate thing, sinful and base. He told us that he was a violent man. That he beat his woman and his child. That he had killed men whom he had considered his friends, and he went on to say that he had even strangled his own infant brother in the crib when he was but five years old. He had considered indeed turning this violence upon himself because he doubted the rectitude of his violence, as natural to him as it was breathing, as walking. That doubt grew within him until it consumed him, until he began to see himself as a curse and a scourge and a vessel of evil and an outcast and he went about each day in terror at his own bloody thoughts and in that terror, a terror the only answer to which was his own violent hand, did he come to an understanding of the nature of that terror, the nature of that violence, the origin of that hand. The Indian came to understand that only God could have made him as he was. As such, the Indian began to see that he was but an organ of his creator's will, and that it was a murderous will indeed. He was but a tool of God's natural hate. The God of death and fury and pain. God, if God He be, loves, without question. This is what we are told but we are not told the whole for God hates as well. And His hate is a great hate indeed.

"God, the Indian told us, sanctions our violence. In His malignance He gives meaning to our sin. And it is because of this and this alone that the Indian urged us to reject the power of a despot who would tell us otherwise. We would instead resist that despot. We would resist him and his federals with our anger and our hate, and we would do so because this is how our God has made us, as the bloody hammer of His murderous hand.

"We crept from the chapel that night," said Fierro, "and we walked in silence through the goatpaths and we killed each federal where he crouched fearful among the stones. And we came down out of the mountains knowing who we were to a man, and we killed the next wave of federals, and the next. We resisted for nearly a year."

"Until the federals captured your Indian," I said. "Tortured him to death in the square, and razed the town."

"This they did."

"Yet you escaped."

"I did."

"And was that God's will as well?"

"It was."

"Is everything you have done the will of God?"

"There are those living who should die," Fierro said. "There are those who should kill them. I count myself lucky that I am born into this time of," he looked up, searching for the proper word. "Strife," he said. "I am lucky that I can make something hard and real from my wretchedness. I am fortunate that my hate can become the expression of a greater will, through which moves the very essence of the coming and immutable war. You ask me why I have come to you and I tell you this," Fierro said, opening his hands before me in the air in something I could only call gratitude. "I have come to you because I suspect that you harbor within you the truth of this God which I know and it is this: that against the slow and grinding and dehumanizing war that Díaz has waged against his own country for two generations you may bring another war, swift and nimble and terrible. For only war may counter war, and death is the only answer to the death that it brings. All that flows outward from it cannot transcend the wisdom of the first murder that brought us into time. And if allowed to bloom, the beauty of war in each and every incarnation turns rancid toward excess unimaginable, burning all which does burn, until finally and completely burning itself."

"As did Tomochi," I said.

"As did Tomochi."

"Who am I to you?"

"You are this fire."

"*We* are," I leaned forward. "We are but a means, Rodolfo," I said to him. "We are in the service of an end."

"There is no end greater than what we are in ourselves," he said. "We are not a means, but are expressions of the God of war and His war is not a lesson, it is a location. When its violence has come to know itself and the arc of its performance inscribed, so closes the space of its presence. Another face, then. That of history. And commerce."

At this Rodolfo Fierro stood. He buttoned his jacket.

"But not yet." he said. "Not yet."

He turned from me, and he walked out of the tent.

I watched him go. And I said nothing to him as he left and I said nothing to the men who stood waiting at the door. I looked down at the pistol. It still lay cocked on the table, its barrel aimed at an empty chair. I pushed the grip with my finger, spinning the gun around on its cylinder. The barrel rotated to me, to the empty chair, and back again. I took the bottle and pulled the cork and poured my cup full. I drank it down. I spun the pistol again.

CHAPTER XIX

Esmerelda Torres. On the Present of the Past. The Evils of Marco Torres. Villa's Mother Dies Again. Children Here and Gone.

Esmerelda Torres came across the morning square of Gomez Palacio with her children in either hand. Her jaw was set and she wore a dress of black without a veil because she wanted the monster who had taken her husband to see her face free of adornment and her hair disordered and coarse. Her children, a girl of four and a boy of seven, cried softly as she dragged them through the garden past old men at checkers and drunks awakening in the flowerbeds.

One way alone did she know to save her husband. He was not a great man, but a good man, surely, and though he had but found her in the winter of his years she had at that point become herself a woman who had abandoned hope until him, and she would not therefore abandon it now again.

I have come to believe that the past revisits itself in ways strange and impossible to predict, as though history lives in a place alongside this time in which we move, and at moments ordained by a hand unseen these dimensions may indeed intersect, the past rushing in upon the present. In that past a younger and a forsaken and a desperate Esmeralda Torres lay in the bed of her parents' house in the spring of her twenty-fifth year. Such moments from her past rose up ceaselessly. Lost moments with men when her life could have taken any other route than the one in which she lived, old and passed over and alone. *Here,* she would say to herself in her bed, was the instant when the possibility of love elided my path. *Here,* when a choice had been made each time with this man or that, a choice unrecognized in the instant. *There* was when his eyes looked away, when his hips turned and his smile became merely solicitous. A single gesture and single word; Esmeralda lived them all again each night as the flower of her youth faded and fell, and even as she in the daytime had begun to believe that each moment had been lived through in its essential elements, and that there be no other time than this, each night the past came alive for her once more.

And did she welcome this past in the nighttime as a beauty alive and arrogant as she had been, or did she refuse it and embrace the day that edged her with each sunrise closer into death? Then came Marco Torres.

A retired gentleman from Durango, a man who had known power and influence and even some wealth. Quiet and serious, tall and still strong in his advancing age with eyes that flashed such a furious blue that Esmeralda had shuddered to think what he had been. Indeed Torres had been a difficult man, a lord over territory, and he wielded this power with such intensity that he had foregone in his youth all comforts, even that of family. But as he entered the late autumn of his life and his influence waned and as his shoulders began to hunch around his neck with age and his beard turned strand by strand to a snowy white did Marcos Torres come to realize that yes, even he was going to die.

Moving to a town in which his name and deeds were unknown, Torres began to search for a wife. None would have him. Near 70, the young girls laughed quietly at his suit. After a handful of seasons Marco Torres was left on the edge of things. And it is there that he sat in 1901 at the summer's last festival, a warm night of dancing when the square through which Esmeralda now walked dragging her children was ringed instead with lights and vendors and music. The laughter of children. A younger Esmeralda sat in the twilight alone, watching them pipe and scream and run about.

She watched them as another day of sanity seeped away into the night which would threaten to tear that sanity away once more, and she looked as well to the elder gentleman where he sat. She saw him and his white beard against his chest and his profile: the large thin nose, the brows relaxed and steady. There, Esmeralda in the oncoming night saw for an instant the dark thing that had escaped her, slipped away at forks of a path unseen each time fleeting and quick. Here it was now, in an unforeseen iteration, paused, and resting. And so she had risen, and she had gone to him. And he was a gentleman.

Marco Torres gave her two children and with them in her hands she strode to the large and yellow house at the western edge of the square wherein the foreign bandit had installed himself in his arrogance and his cruelty. Who is to say how many the monster had put to the wall in the two days since he and his marauders had rode in looting and raping?

She approached the house. Two guards stood by the door, young men both in mismatched jackets and the ridiculous sombreros of peons. They stepped in front of the entrance and forbade her passage. Esmeralda Torres stopped. She stepped back, her children now silent, as though they sensed as well the imposition of another force. Esmeralda Torres then dropped their hands, and she flung herself at the guards.

From inside of the great house the men heard the wailing of a woman and of children and the cursing of soldiers and

I, smoking nervously in a large damask chair, stood at the clamor and walked to the large window. There I stood for some moments, looking out at the low streets as the racket behind me only increased in intensity: a madwoman at the gates, wild children. This last sound concerned me, as the front of the house was open to the square. I gave orders to let the woman inside.

She came dressed in mourning, disheveled and unkempt and her children twisting in her hands. I crossed my arms at her approach and I looked at her eyes and I ordered her children be taken from her and held at a remove.

As this was done, the panic of the woman redoubled. She turned on the guards who clapped her back down onto the tiles of the sitting room floor until I said "Enough." I walked down to where she was held, and I stood above her.

"Your children are here," I said, and I gestured toward them where guards held them not ten feet behind. "They are yours, and we will not take them. You have come with them and will leave with them. Before you do, tell me what it is that you want."

Esmeralda Torres looked back to her son and daughter and she looked to the man before her and told him that her husband had been falsely arrested this morning by thugs unlicensed and brought here to this house. This house which was further occupied under pretenses invented and false and further, she told me that I was myself a brute and a bully and a peasant, and that I should ride my men back out of this town and into the desert from whence we had come.

"You husband was arrested this morning?" I asked.

"Yes," said Esmeralda Torres. "Without warrant or cause."

"Your husband," I said. "He is an old man?"

"He is."

"And tall, and strong with blue eyes and fierce and a long and snowy beard."

"That is he."

I nodded and called for the prisoner to be brought forth and he was.

"I have not touched a hair upon his head," I told her, and indeed the man in a long blue coat was as described but silent. His eyes moved to his wife and the look she saw there told her in no uncertain terms that her husband knew very well why he had been taken.

"I have not touched him," I said, "because I have not decided how I want him to suffer."

"He has done nothing," said Esmeralda Torres.

I looked from the man to his wife. "How well do you know your husband, Señora Torres? Do you know of what he is capable? Here stands before me," I said, "my mother's murderer."

Marco Torres with his head held high looked not to his wife nor his children but to the hallway from where they had come, to the doorway behind it and the town behind this, and Esmeralda Torres knew then that it was true. And then I told her this story.

"In San Juan del Rio, my eldest brother provided for our family as my mother had been laid low by a sickness brought forth by mourning for my dead father. My brother would load our only donkey with wool and travel down from the sierra to sell such wares in the plaza of the town. This man before us was the boss of this town, serving the interests of that doddering tyrant Díaz.

"One day, without cause, my brother was arrested as he took the wool to market. We waited one day, two days, until finally on the fifth day we raised my mother from her bed and dressed, and down the mountain I walked with her and my sisters. I was at this time six years of age.

"My brother had been placed in less than a jail. He sat in a wooden shack some ten by ten feet along with eight other men whose crimes were unclear. To the town hall we all walked, my sisters and I supporting my mother, whose faulty steps frightened me as we climbed the great stairs to beg for an audience with the boss, but no audience was to be had.

"What had happened was that the government of Díaz needed soldiers. Needed men from the mountains, for strong men they were and hard with discipline, and yet Díaz knew that none would volunteer. He knew rightly that none would agree to fight and to die for a tyrant such as he. His jefe knew it as well. And so this jefe had taken to imprisoning young men from the country, shipping them down to the capital at his leisure. So there we sat, my sisters, my mother, and myself on the steps of the town hall, and around us began to gather other women in similar states, for my brother was not the only young man treated so unjustly. Out there in the heat of the sun we sat, my mother growing weaker by the hour. We begged her to take shelter but she would not budge. We put over her shawls to shield her from the sun and still she sagged as the hours stretched on until toward sunset the doors finally opened. Out ran the bailiffs in dark blue uniforms and foolish hats and stood on either side of the stairs at attention. And from the doors of the courthouse came this man.

"He walked to the street and the carriage that awaited him there and my mother, withered and sick, brought herself to her feet. She cried out there for the man who did not stop nor turn, and then my mother did this thing. She threw herself in total at his feet, and she did this because my brother was good and was gentle, and further he gave us all that we could have in this world, for we lived hand to mouth out in the mountains, and my mother could not work, and my sisters took care of the house such as it was, and I was just a boy. A boy.

"And the jefe. This man. He looked down at my mother as though she were an animal. A sneer passed over his lips. He pulled back his riding whip and he commenced to beat her, there, on the steps. Beat her like a mule. The silence around us all was terrific. The world itself felt as though it had began to open, and that which rushed upon me from the other place was black and dark and it pushed into my ears, and it crushed my heart where it beat in my chest. The jefe then kicked my mother away. She rolled off and on to the cobblestones of the street, her face pale and eyes wide in shock, her mouth full of her own bright blood.

"The following day my brother was sent to the front and there he died of consumption and my mother met her end not long after. And no matter what I said to her, no matter how I tried to assuage her fear and her mounting despair in those final days and tell her that I would soon be a man, and that I may unburden her and provide for the family, and that I would grow to be that which was required, she still slipped away. And so I have come here," I said, "with my horses and my arms to this putrid little town in order to find this man and to deliver upon him that which he has earned."

The eyes of Esmeralda Torres at this tale were full of tears, and she asked her husband if what was said were true. The old man nodded his head, and he said that it was. And I then said, "Take your children, Señora Torres, and take them home and let them see no more of this man whom they would call father. Let them forget his name. Forget that he ever lived, for my plans involve expunging him from the history of this place. He is not with us," I said, "even now."

And Esmeralda Torres stood before me, tall and still in the silence of that room and her tears fell freely down her face that was hard and set. Then she lunged forward and she threw herself around my black-booted legs, and there did she beg for the life of her husband. In instinct I drew back my hand to strike at the woman where she lay and at this moment did the room slip before me. I staggered as the ringing in my ears reached up as though to overwhelm all sound and I looked to my feet at the heaving shoulders of the pleading Esmeralda Torres, and as my eyes rolled around the place I met where he stood the plain and open eyes of the seven-year-old boy.

It is true that Marco Torres was released that day into the care of his family. And it is true that on that night the town of Gomez Palacio was abandoned by the revolutionary forces. It is furthermore accurate, always and inevitably so and documented as all facts of the revolution are and have been, spread far and wide by the people who would allow themselves to be so touched by it, by the people who would find some point of intersection with it and the multitudinous experience of their own myriad lives that I then moved westward, into the mountains of Coahuila, toward the city of Monterrey.

CHAPTER XX

Soldiers and Prisoners. A True Villista. An Experiment. Shoes. The Warmth of Stones. A Hole in the Sky. Into the Canyon.

Eight men rode out on a white day into the vine cactus. Four wore blindfolds, and three rode behind them cradling rifles in their arms. It had been two days of riding out deeper into the desert, and it had as well been two days since the prisoners had been chained to the floor of a courthouse jail in Ciudad Jiménez.

Rodolfo Fierro sat at the head of the column in his broken white suit. He wore spats on his shoes. From his vest winked a silver watch chain.

Wisteria and creosote. The dim mountains jagged on the horizon. At the bottom of a dried ravine Fierro halted them, and the prisoners sat gaping on their mounts tied one to each. Behind them the soldiers dismounted.

They pulled the prisoners from the horses and watered the animals from their canteens, and they situated the blindfolded men on the dirt and tied their hands as one. The prisoners sat in silence, each one turned out from the other. The soldiers gave the prisoners water and then gagged them, then gathered wood for a fire and unrolled their bedthings and tied up their horses as the sun fell behind the mountains to the west. They dug a shallow hole and ringed it with stones, and one man took a knee beside a bristling pile of shavings and struck his flint, blowing gently into the sparks that fell on the whiskers of wood until at last they began to smoke. He cupped his blackened hands around the embers, held them to his face with tenderness. He blew upon them as though whispering to a child.

Rodolfo Fierro lay on the dirt in his full suit, staring at the pulsing logs.

"Commander," a soldier said to him. "We have been riding now for some days. The nature of our journey remains unknown to us."

Fierro said nothing.

"We are to kill the prisoners, yes?"

At this Fierro sighed, and his eyes moved to the soldier who had spoken, the man whom I had embedded in this strange and obscure journey named Jose Calderon, a vicious and trusted renegade and without question a man of the people. Fierro turned his eyes back to the fire.

"If we are to kill them," said Calderon, "then let us kill them soon and return in haste."

Fierro heard this, and when he turned his head he looked to the shapes of the prisoners where they sat silent in the dark. He looked up to the blackness of the ridge and the blue of the night behind it.

"Soldier," Fierro finally said, "how many men have you killed?"

Jose Calderon blinked at the suited man who lay in the dirt by the fire.

"I have done what Villa has demanded of me," he said.

"You are a disciple of Pancho Villa, are you not?"

"Without question."

"You are an excellent soldier."

"I am Villista, Commander."

"Pancho Villa demands of you to march," said Fierro, "you march. Camp, you camp. Kill, you kill. Pancho Villa demands of you to shit, you shit," he said. "You burn a house, you kill a man, and you rape his woman, and you ride into the desert because this is the task that has been assigned to you."

"Sir," replied Calderon.

"Tell me," Fierro said, running his finger in the dust, "and please be honest. Tell me what else you are, other than, this Villista? If Pancho Villa cut you loose, what would you do?"

"I would go home, sir. I would return to Saucillo."

"And what would you do in Saucillo?"

"I would plant crops, sir. Corn and tomatoes." This is what Calderon said to Fierro. And he also said this: "I would go to the house of my woman and I would see my son."

"You have a son."

"Yessir."

"Delightful."

Calderon looked at Fierro in silence.

"You are," Fierro said, standing, "without question, a man of the revolution. A representative of all that is good and strong of the soil of Chihuahua." Fierro took his hat from his head and beat it against his leg. "Tell me," he said, "how have you killed the men Pancho Villa has demanded of you? Your rifle?"

"My rifle, sir."

"You are an able shot?"

"He is a marksman, sir," said another of the soldiers.

"Now listen to me." Fierro drew from the holster at his hip his revolver and cocked it and pointed it at the face of the seated Jose Calderon. "I want you to take out your knife."

"Sir?"

"If you call me *sir* one more time I'm going to blow your fucking head off. Now please," Fierro said, "take out your knife." As he looked to the faces of the soldiers Fierro added soothingly,

"I'm going to answer all of your questions. Now take out your knife."

"I will not," said Calderon.

Fierro turned to the soldier closest. "Get his knife out of his belt."

"Sir," this man responded.

The pistol in Fierro's hand jumped with the shot and the soldier fell back as though kicked in the chest, his arm falling oddly across his face. His breath went shallow for many otherwise silent moments and his legs kicked in the dirt and then they were still. The soldier next to him turned on his palm and stood and ran out into the dark.

Fierro turned back to Jose Calderon. "Get your knife out of your belt." This Calderon did.

"Now. What I want you to do," Fierro drew in his breath sharply, "is cut off your little finger."

Jose Calderon kept his eyes firmly on Fierro. He blew fiercely out his nostrils.

"You will do it," Fierro said, and began to advance upon Calderon, speaking as he walked. Rodolfo Fierro crouched, the gun rising until it found the very center of the forehead of Jose Calderon. "If you want to return to your fetid little town and plant your corn and tell your little boy what a worthless murdering gonorrhea-infested soldier you were in the great army of Pancho Villa," he said, "you will cut off your little finger, and you will do it now."

"You are a madman," said Jose Calderon.

"I am the only sane man among us," Fierro replied. His eyes were wide. "If you could only see it in all its aspects," he whispered, "you would understand it as a single thing."

Jose Calderon placed his splayed hand on the dirt before him.

"Good," Fierro said quietly. He stood, and he kept the barrel of the pistol on the head of Calderon, who brought the blade of the knife down on the first joint.

"Lower," said Fierro. "Good," he said. "A gun," Fierro said, "is either a threat or a conclusion. There is no advancement. Don't saw it. One straight chop through. Good," he said. "Good man. Well done. Now don't move." Fierro turned and placed the barrel of his own pistol straight into the flames of the lapping fire. He kept it there for some moments as Jose Calderon gripped his mutilated hand at the wrist and the blood ran blackly down his sleeve. Fierro waited until the gunbarrel had heated to a dull orange, and then he applied it directly to the pulsing stump of Jose Calderon.

Calderon bit his lip and pushed air out heavily through his nostrils.

"Good," said Fierro. "You're a quiet one." He picked up the curled finger from where it lay oozing in the dust.

Fierro stood and looked at the corpse of the murdered soldier, sprawled on his side like a drunk. Fierro holstered his revolver and opened his suit jacket, dropping the finger into the inside pocket.

"Now," he said. "If you don't understand what I've just told you," he said to Calderon, "I advise you to apply a blindfold and have a seat with the others."

Out in the dark, the prisoners chewed on their gags.

The prisoners awoke in the morning to find themselves shoeless. They murmured through their bindings and, finding themselves unguarded, they hurriedly began to untie one another. None left the circle until the work was complete, each for each, and as they pulled off their blindfolds the sun stunned their blinking eyes. A broken landscape, dark vegetation. A smoldering firepit. The body of the murdered soldier lay precisely where it fell. The prisoners saw one another. They saw the desolation of the place.

They saw the arrangement before them.

Three objects lay on the desert floor: one pistol, one canteen, one pair of shoes. Before these sat a small rock pinning to the dirt a fluttering paper. A note, written in a brown ink that was—although how could they have known?—in fact blood.

There are but two ways out of the desert. One path lies through accretion, the other through denial.

High on a ridge some half mile away sat Fierro, field-glasses to his face. He watched in the valley below him the reading of the note, the shaking of the canteen. He watched as they checked the cylinder of the weapon. One poured the three shells into his hand. This man was neither the oldest nor the youngest. He put the bullets in the pocket of his pants and handed the gun to another. After some discussion, they gave the oldest the shoes.

By the third day this is what Fierro has seen. First, a disagreement over the shoes, since on the first day the youngest had stepped on the spines of an opuntia and punctured his foot. This foot has become infected and the youth carries it gingerly. The man with the bullets has established himself as leader and attempted to mediate the disagreement over the shoes to no avail. Some time after midnight, the youth killed the oldest man in his sleep with a large rock. Fierro was impressed at the ferocity of the murder, willing as the young man was to drive the stone home not once but several times.

Fierro had picked them all himself, supervised their arrests and their jailing. The old man so recently passed had been a baker in life, a father to two boys now grown, a native of Sonora, his wife long dead. The youth who killed him, the son of a merchant, home after an expulsion from his university in Spain. The next, a retired soldier on a pension. Lastly a tailor. This tailor was the leader, although Fierro sensed this to be a strain on the soldier, who was himself a broken man incapable of leadership. Fierro knew this from the first when the soldier said nothing at the dividing of the supplies, eyeing no one until spoken to. He also imagined this soldier would be the first to murder his comrades and Fierro was, admittedly, disappointed. The cruelty of the youth was some consolation.

Outside the ring of their nighttime campfire Fierro crouched in the darkness divested of his clothes and watched them where they sat. His smooth chest scraped the ground and his fingers gripped the rocks, his genitals swaying under him before he dropped himself once more on the stone, still warm from the heat of the day.

The youth went no further the night of the murder. He sat by the low fire as it died into embers, his legs crossed. The breeze moved his hair. The night was starless, the clouds low, and Fierro lay not fifty feet from the boy for nearly half an hour. Only once did the boy wheel and peer out into the black.

By morning Rodolfo Fierro had regained the ridge, and he sat by the cookfire contentedly scrambling an egg in his pan. Jose Calderon sat apart from his commander with his arms around his knees and avoided his eyes. With the awakening of the prisoners below Fierro listened to the shouts as they discovered the body of the old man. He hummed to himself as he chopped at the bubbling eggs.

Forking his food into his mouth Fierro watched through his glasses as they argued over the corpse. To murder the murderer, they decide, deprives them of the hands necessary for the foraging and hunting and firemaking. To keep him tied up presents the same problem. They take his shoes. They place them back on the feet of the dead man. They move on.

"Excellent!" said Rodolfo Fierro, and moved to saddle his horse.

Animated at the next night's fire, Fierro spoke with Jose

Calderon. "Don't you see? It's better than I could have imagined. So much more." Calderon remained silent, looking intently at the coals. "There are things that we can plan," Fierro said. "Things we can gauge in isolation, but to have the opportunity to put such speculation to the test. To observe the true pattern with complete impartiality," he said. "Just excellent," Rodolfo Fierro said, and he stood. And when Jose Calderon raised his eyes, of course Fierro was gone.

The ex-soldier held the pistol and the tailor held the cartridges. They had taken to hog-tying the youth at night and the two men sat together at the fire and Fierro sat in the darkness behind them in a reflection of their own attitude and position. The conversation of the men was halting, uncertain. They discussed the contents of the canteen. They discussed the decision to leave behind the shoes. The punctured foot of the youth is gangrenous, the soldier said, and the boy should be either left behind or put down. The tailor wouldn't have it, nor would he have any discussion of uniting the pistol with the bullets.

"The twain shall never meet," said the tailor, and Fierro stifled a yawn.

After the fire had died down and the men gone to sleep the youth remained awake and he remained afraid. Looking out into the flat and the impenetrable dark, the youth's imagination was fired with series after series of bloody images. He imagined a wolf. Wolves. Around this his feverish brain began to coalesce. The youth imagined principally his own death by wolves. The worst thing about wolves, he believed, is that they would first eat his stomach, shriveled and empty as it was. Five gnashing mouths at his stomach and he, helpless, tied and gagged. In the long and sleepless night this became his obsession. Teeth at his belly, ripping the skin, his blood running hot down his own sides. He wondered if he could feel the mouths on his entrails, if ripping his intestines would actually cause pain. These thoughts, along with the mortal stench from his leaking foot, were his only companions.

And so the slender figure of a man emerging from the dark, tall and perfectly nude, seemed to the youth little more than a dream. The youth's head lay sideways on the dirt and so the man approached from an impossible angle, a phantom in the waste. The man bent down to take in the face of the youth: high cheekbones, skin pockmarked with acne. The eyes of the phantom searched the eyes of the youth. Yellow teeth smiled from under a ragged mustache. The youth could not comprehend, indeed was incapable of imagining, what the phantom found so pleasing.

"Yes," Rodolfo Fierro said quietly.

The youth felt a bare foot on his shoulder. He was pushed flat on his back, staring up only at the faceless black of the clouded-over sky. Then the phantom's face above, its previous joy abated. The youth noted that the man was aroused. And then the great rock descended, swiftly, and with force.

The prisoners awoke into the gray predawn. They looked about for whatever had awoken them and they saw only the pale earth and the pale sky and the broken stones. Near them lay the youth, prone on his back, his face a concave mass of teeth and meat and bone. Rifling his clothes, the solider and tailor came to understand that the youth had been violated. The men did not speak. They took what they could and moved on into the north.

No tracks of men did they see, nor tracks of animals, for the ground was untouched by the evidence of living things. The sky maintained its own hushed absence until it too dimmed, like a light going out around the corner of the world. After a time the men began to search for wood. Their faces hollow around the low fire. The soldier and the tailor, no break for untold miles.

"I can understand," said the tailor to the soldier, "why you would kill the boy. I understand this. But then this I do not understand. I do not understand why you would abuse him."

The soldier said nothing.

"And also what concerns me," the tailor went on, "is whether the boy was lain with before his murder, or after."

"You are a fool," said the soldier.

"It matters," replied the tailor. "It matters because I must know with whom I am lost in this place. I must know if I can allow myself to sleep. I do not think I can allow myself to sleep."

"I don't care if you fucked him before or after," said the soldier. "I'm not sleeping."

"You think I killed him?"

"Let's not talk," the solider said, and looked at the ground. "Let's not."

The tailor was silent for a time, squinting at the soldier, whose eyes remained on the dirt between his knees. The low fire glowed in the coals and would soon be gone.

"What do you think you're doing to me?" said the soldier.

"Anything that could've been done to you," replied the tailor, "was done long ago."

And so they sat throughout the approaching night, the small and dying fire the only light in the endless abyss, the only focus in the enclosing dark.

Morning. Sleepless, the men staggered to their feet and moved forward once more, and the day as before, and the earth and the sky as before. Through it they moved, senseless with hunger and exhaustion, two figures with blackened faces and hands and bruised feet shuffling across the dust of the floor of the world and on this world there before them as though placed stood a dead and dried stump. The only disruption in the white forever. And on it sat a man.

The man was nude. He was dark. He wore a ragged straw hat and he squatted on his haunches on the flat top of the stump some three feet above the ground, his scrotum resting simply on the jagged wood. He watched the two men walk across the distance toward him, his dark hands loose around his knees. At their approach he doffed his hat, not without some ceremony.

The tailor and the soldier stood before him. The tailor sank to his knees.

And above them the wide blanket of sky opened as though it were an aperture into the depthless blue of the beyond that may indeed peer down upon just such a scene and all of those like it. Tendrils of cloud peeled across the face of that blue, wandering forever eastward, forever shredding themselves, forever coalescing once more into shapes impossible absent the design of even yet another high and removed and unfathomable mind.

Jose Calderon sat his horse on the ridge above. He watched this and he watched Rodolfo Fierro rise from the stump and place his hand on the tailor's head. He watched Fierro place his hand on the soldier's arm. He watched still as Fierro reached for the soldier's hand and he watched it be freely given. The tailor rose and then the three turned. They walked west, unhurried, hand-in-hand like children. The sky above them all closed. Calderon rode on.

For half a day the clouds above moved as though pulled like a sheet, the canyon into which the three men walked becoming increasingly narrow, forcing Calderon to retreat from its lip in order to remain unseen. The three below walked on as before, and Calderon could see that Fierro was speaking to them both, constant, incessant, unstoppered.

The day dimmed as the sun sank below the horizon, and as the dusk settled the odor of a campfire came to Calderon's nose. The smell of fire and more. The smell of meat. And he smelled horses, and he heard voices from a place unseen, down below him or around a bend in the canyon he had not yet reached. Riding back up to the lip of the rock, Calderon could no longer find the three, their tracks disappeared as though snatched up into the walls of stone. Calderon stopped his horse. The wind shifted, and the scent of all that was before was gone to him, and the voices gone as well. An echo of them perhaps. A camp somewhere. A collection of who can say, lost back in the canyons.

The bone shaft of the arrow burrowed through Jose Calderon's side like a dagger. Calderon looked down to see the stone tip of the thing protruding from the front his shirt. The small twine that held the arrowhead to the shaft seemed impossible, the pattern intricate, alive.

Another arrow flickered by his head. He watched it spiraling past him and through that further air and then falling down, down into the air of the canyon, and still not a sound. Calderon leapt at the reins and kicked the horse beneath him and turned. As he did so more arrows came, the air suddenly heavy, suddenly buzzing with them. One found his shinbone and the impact vaguely registered in Calderon's escalating horror as he kicked the animal again and another shaft stuck with finality behind him into the leather of the saddle. Calderon ran his horse for both their lives back out into the desert and its gathering dark, and the whispering arrows ran behind.

PART IV
IN THE MANNER I SEE FIT

Chapter XXI

Madero at Bustillos. Patriots. The Hotel Sheldon. Garabaldi.

I expected a serious man. Madero was without question a man of intellect, who at great disadvantage to himself had thrown his influence behind the emancipation of the people. He had debased himself for an idea. This was a great man. And so I expected a great man.

At the end of the summer of 1910 I had been engaged with federals in the mountains. They had come down the Chihuahua Road, and we had met them on the high plain of La Piedra, and there we had ridden them down. We took their artillery and their horses, and we left their bodies to dry in the wind. I would wager their mummies still lay where we left them in that high place, like hollow gourds in their tattered clothes.

I left my wounded at the Rancho de Almagre, and we rode back into San Andrés, where we were received with cheers by the people who lined the streets and threw flowers before our horses. It was in this time, while we rested under the care of those villagers, that I was summoned by the Provisional President, Francisco I. Madero, to his quarters in Bustillos. I left on the train that night.

I was taken from the station to the Hacienda de Bustillos, a prominent estate on the edge of Bustillos Lake. The hacienda was heavily fortified—armed men were everywhere, snipers crouched on the rooftops, mounted patrols circled the grounds and reconnoitered the surrounding hills. With all of this I was pleased.

Walking into the main room of the house I saw empty couches spread about under a great high ceiling, the timbers crossing above me holding an immense wrought-iron lamp suspended over the floor. Beyond lay the dining room. Its large doors opened on a vista of the lake that lay not a quarter mile down.

As I stood there two soldiers entered from a side hallway. They came with rifles and took positions at either exit and did so without a sound, their eyes boring holes into the opposite walls. We three stood for some moments in silence.

At length, reverberations of talk echoed down a far hallway and more soldiers entered, followed by two suited men who spoke with great animation to a figure who trailed behind and nodded along with their speech. The two walked past me without acknowledgement, so absorbed were they in their argument, and crossed the room, turning their conversation upon one another as they exited. The guards followed them to the doorway, then turned and faced back in.

"Señor Villa," said a voice behind me. I turned to see the third man. He was small and well-groomed, a broad face, elegant mustaches. "I cannot tell you how pleased I am," he said, "to finally meet you."

"President Madero," I said. "I am your humble servant."

We were able to exchange little more than cordialities at this time as his staff continually demanded his attention. Indeed for the rest of the afternoon and through dinner I was plied with mescal by his servants (which I did not drink) while Madero was engaged in deep conversation with his retinue of attachés. We ate a sumptuous dinner of braised beef and I spoke little to the men on either side of me, keeping my eye on the principal, on his manner and mode of expression until, after pouring all members of the party a serving of brandy, Madero rose, came to my chair, and asked me join him alone outside.

Only the stars hung over the lake, and the lights of the house shone on our backs as we took our seats and lit the cigars he most graciously provided. It was then at last that we engaged in honest and open talk. Madero told me that Señora González had told him much about me. That she praised me and had great faith in my continued success.

"She believes that you are a just and able man," Madero said in a voice as if he were reading from a letter, as though quoting or mocking. He looked at the cigar that he held before him. "She believes that you will bring this country into its destiny." Madero said. And then he turned to me with a gentle smile. "Here is what I believe," he said. "I believe the destiny of this country is sitting with me now," he said. "I believe that you, Señor Villa, represent all that is good in Mexico, and all that she can be."

I detected no falseness in this statement. His smile was the smile of a man who was convinced of what he said. I thanked him, and I told him that I was anxious to begin that very labor of which he spoke. I told him that I would be the first and foremost expert to him in all matters of warmaking and siege.

"The coming war will be prosecuted on many fronts, Señor Villa," Madero said. "We must take care to retain all that is good and decent, and not allow it to slide into the storm."

This talk excited me. "What fronts do you envision?"

"Fronts across the north. From east to west along the mountains," he said, moving the hand that held the brandy across the body of the lake.

"What do you think," I asked him, "of a march on Chihuahua?"

He pulled on the cigar and blew the smoke and watched as that smoke rose up into the dark and away. "That would be a great battle," he said.

"Would you have us attack it first?"

He shook his head. "I think it would be dangerous."

"War is dangerous," I replied.

"Perhaps Juarez is a better choice."

"I have considered Juarez," I sat forward, anxious to finally discuss plans, large plans that would strike serious blows to the enemy. "I think if we keep ourselves stationed in El Paso that you can use your influence in America to build up the necessary supplies in relative safety."

Madero said nothing. He pulled on his cigar and blew his smoke as he had before and I struggled to understand his attitude. I was afraid I had overstepped myself. I sat back in my chair, and attempted to adopt his position.

"America," Madero said. He sipped at his brandy.

"Yes," I said slowly. "We make our foothold in El Paso. From there we plunge in the knife into Juarez."

"But then," he said. "Chihuahua would be so much more glorious."

"Chihuahua would be dangerous," I reminded him.

"Of course." He sipped the brandy again. "The danger with Juarez comes with America."

"What danger could there be to America?"

"She foresees danger everywhere."

"If all is dangerous to her then why not proceed with Juarez?"

Madero turned to me again with that same smile as before. "My friend, you are not the only, nor the first, to suggest it. I will take your counsel into account."

I pulled on the cigar, barely able to control myself. If he were not to discuss further plans at this point I had a veritable list of concerns. "President Madero," I said, "I have to an important issue to bring before you."

"Señor Villa. Anything."

"At my command I have some 700 men, poorly armed and underpaid."

"Yes."

"What can we do to compensate these men for the hardships they have endured?"

"Are your men patriots?" he asked me.

"I don't understand you."

"Do they believe in the future of Mexico and in the rewards that will come to them with our victory?"

"Without question," I said. "For nearly a year they have sacrificed their lives for those ideals. With your ample support we can surely—"

"When we are victorious they will receive compensation beyond their wildest dreams."

"They have modest dreams, my President."

"Then this is what we must first undo!" said Madero, speaking with intensity for the first time. "What is the freedom of the people without first the freedom of the mind? If they be but slaves in their hearts, how can they know freedom when it comes to them from our hands?" He sat back, and he brought the brandy again to his lips. "This," he said, "is perhaps where we should have begun." He shook his head. "There is so much work that should have been done."

"Should have been done by whom, Mr. President?"

"But please," Madero sat forward and gripped my knee. "I do know that we have both vitality, as well as truth, on our side. With your addition I feel that keenly. Bringing you into our ranks revitalizes our purpose. We are revived by you, Señor

Villa, and with you I am sure we cannot but succeed." He stood.
"I will send you my decision in one week's time."

"What decision, my President?"

"Whether we be for Chihuahua, or Juarez, or whether we
be at all."

"Be in what way?"

"Thank you so much for coming to see me, *Captain* Villa,"
he said, and he gripped my shoulder. "We are indebted to you
already, and I sense that your drive, your energy, and your belief
will lift us on to victory. Goodnight."

I stayed in the hacienda that night and I did not sleep nor
did I sleep on the train ride back to my troops where they
convalesced, but when I spoke to them I did so with passion
and conviction, with the spirit of a man sure of both himself
and his charge. And I was none of these things. Nor would I be
for some time.

The barroom of the Hotel Sheldon in El Paso sits today as it did
then: wide, spacious, airy under tall ceilings crowned by a large
dome of multi-colored glass. The midday light still scatters as it
did then about the leather chairs and the patterned carpet and
the tall ferns that stand in brass canisters about the floor. Today
it remains beautiful, but perhaps it is beautiful only, lacking in
the spirit that manifested itself there in the days before freedom
broke. For in that time this bar was full of elegant women and
serious men and smoke, talking and talking at all hours of the
day and night. It never closed for it could never afford to do so
and men from all parts of the world met here, young and old,
and easily half of them feigning to be something other than that
which they were. Sitting with practiced ease at the bar so many
claimed to be masters of self and place, seeking to cajole and
convince, to lure the unsuspecting into the fog of their schemes.
How things are lost to us now, even as the rooms remain and

the stories change with each telling. For whomsoever would make the story would make the world with it, and if that story be supple and good, so goes a world that would last a hundred years.

Madero called me to El Paso not one week after our meeting, and I rode north with my command. We crossed the river into America under the protections afforded by Madero's military contacts and we then camped outside the city and waited for Madero to conclude his deliberations with the Díaz regime, for Madero had, before anything else, chosen to deliberate. This was a foolish step, but for Madero, the most logical. He was a man of thought, of consideration, and he believed all others to be the same. Díaz was not the same, and I knew the despot was manipulating the younger man, buying from him more and more time to mount against him an attack. The hours stretched into days. The days into weeks. We all grew increasingly restless.

Señora González had taken the trains north to be with us even as my men were falling to drink and to women, while federal reinforcements poured across the river into Ciudad Juarez by the day. El Paso itself swelled with volunteers and profiteers, confidence men and managers, and they all seemed to take refreshment at the Hotel Sheldon bar.

So it was that Señora González called me there to meet Menotti Garibaldi, son of the famed revolutionary and a potential recruit to the cause. I was anxious to meet him, as the reputation of his father as a man of action and high ideals was known at that time around the world. And I was told expressly by Señora González how essential it would be to add him to our numbers, not only for his potential expertise, but for the positive coverage it would gain the revolution, painting us not merely as a faction of dissatisfied peasants but instead as a righteous and legitimate rebellion; such was the aura of this man's father at that time. As I entered the Sheldon I saw them seated together, reclining in wide leather chairs. González waved me over and I lowered myself into a seat directly across from Garibaldi. His eyes were closed, his head back as though resting. His long legs were crossed, and his hands hung over the armrests.

"We are pleased to have you with us, Señor Garibaldi," I said. "The reputation and experience of your father precedes you."

Garibaldi's chin fell to his chest and he opened his eyes. "I am unconcerned," he said to me, "with the legacy of my father as it applies to Mexico. Or to its people."

"We are pleased," I continued, "to elicit the assistance of a European aristocrat against the criminal presidency of Porfirio Díaz."

"A criminal," he said, "whom you have tolerated for decades."

"Díaz has been in power for generations, yes," said Señora González.

"A man who bleeds Mexico dry," Garibaldi said.

"Yes," said Señora González.

"Who sends its silver and its copper and every ounce of surplus he does not keep for himself to the United States for little more than a handshake and a promise."

"This is true," she said.

"I have come to end it," said Garibaldi.

I sat back in my chair. I smoothed my mustaches. "You have come to end it?"

"I have. I have come to give Mexico back to its people."

I ran my hand full over my mouth. I looked around the room, and I saw those men whom I despised speaking in ways that made my blood rise into my ears and I said "What is it that you believe is happening here, Señor Garibaldi?"

"I believe that we are on the cusp of revolution," he said. "I stand as witness to it. As do we all."

"Who is we?"

"The people."

"You mean the people of Mexico."

"I mean you. Me. Everyone. It is happening to us right now."

"Are you prepared for war, Senor Garibaldi?" González asked. "Do you understand what it will be?"

Garibaldi reached for his glass where it sat on the table between us. "Always this question," he said. "What is war?" He took a sip. "In time of war, we would do better to ask ourselves, *What is peace?*"

I folded my hands in my lap. "What is peace, Mr. Garibaldi?"

"Peace," he said. "is nothing more than the unchecked perpetuation of the power which has dared to practice war."

Señora González's face was trained on Garibaldi's, her brows knitted in a concentration that I could not place.

I said, "No one is shot in peace, Señor Garibaldi. Nothing is burnt, nothing blown down. The towns stay as they are. The cities are full. The crops are grown and the families go on and sons are not led out to slaughter. There is joy in peace."

"Ask the Mexicans if they are joyful."

"Have you ever asked a Mexican anything, Señor Garibaldi?"

"I believe," he said evenly, "that I know what the Mexican knows."

I leaned forward. "Then who do you believe is the Mexican's enemy?"

Garibaldi placed his glass back on the table and he said, "The enemy of the Mexican is he who offers only smug condescension out of nothing save an abhorrence of the excitement brought about by masculine violence."

And I knew that González had brought me to a public place so that I would not kill this man.

I bit the insides of my cheeks until they near bled, and I said, "You are familiar with our General, Francisco Madero."

"I am familiar with the one Mexican who has demonstrated courage. Madero has fascinated me. His work indicates a man of greatness. I have written to him and presented my credentials and have applied for the rank of Captain in his revolutionary army."

"You have," I said.

"And I have attained it."

González's face was tight and smiling.

"I have enlisted the forces of some thousand men from America, from Europe and from Canada," Garibaldi went on. "I have taken those cast off even by your own command, Señor Villa, and I have crafted them into a potent fighting force. I will be leading my own troops under the direct command of General Madero. And I am pleased to make your acquaintance."

At this he rose and he straightened his jacket. "Good day," he said to me. He nodded to González, and then he strode out of the bar.

I turned to her. I opened my hands.

"Welcome to the revolution," she said.

CHAPTER XXII

The Prevarications of Madero. Journalism. A Nighttime Raid. Madero Furious. A Woman in the Water.

Garibaldi: but one face of many, and all of these changing by the day. Some would arrive in El Paso—soldiers, politicians, financiers—and then leave, then arrive again expecting from us all unwavering consideration and care. Commanders and captains were anointed and ignored, secret meetings were called of which nothing came. Madero remained in his rooms above us at the Sheldon, while González shuttled from one group to the next and counseling all sides.

Here then was Blanco, and that hateful traitor Orozco, even then silent as a wolf, waiting and watching and biding his time. González was thinner then that I had ever seen her but she was tireless. She came to my camp nearly every day to converse on the state of things. And regardless of how long deliberations stretched on with Díaz she defended Madero. Indeed she could find no fault in him, and provided explanations of his behavior that would fill a book such as one so cultured as he may write. I questioned whether Madero himself was capable of such nuanced and layered thought.

"He is insubstantial," I told her.

"He is the way, Francisco," she said.

Regardless of my impatience, the money still flowed freely: money for troops and housing and horses and food. With it I went into town each week to buy supplies for my men. Americans swarmed from all over the country into El Paso and, disappointed not to find it a playground of dirty Mexican rebels, they took guided tours out to the encampments. With my own eyes I had seen my soldiers fraternize with American women who would walk up to them in the light of day as though they were approaching not men at all but some beasts in a zoo. Still Madero deliberated, uncertain as to when to attack Juarez or even if to attack at all.

He prayed. He wrote. He consulted maps and stars. In truth I believe that Francisco Madero could not imagine war. In truth I believe he longed for peace. Uncomfortable with this longing after all the machinery he had brought to bear, Madero's command began to falter. His comments to his aides became fragmentary and unclear. Madero spent his nights eyes wide at the plaster ceiling, while in the daytime, tourists descended into the camps for Wild West posing and beer with my soldiers.

And as I walked down the swollen streets of El Paso each week I was pursued by an ever-growing mob of journalists. None of them were from this place, few if any from Mexico, but all of them were hungry for whatever I may say, seemingly excited by the simple nearness of me, by my presence alone. They shouted out the names of places about which they had read. They called out the names of men they believed I had killed, or befriended, or both, names of people who would've buried them where they stood. In the dry goods store as I navigated the aisles looking for rice—looking for nothing more than rice, and I cannot find it, and down every aisle is another pack of these little men—one man with papers and pencils in his hands stood precisely in my path, small and arrogant and certain I would do him no harm, and he said:

"Pancho Villa!"

The cries of the others behind me for unknown reasons quieted. "Pancho," this man shouted, with a look on his face of confidence and anonymity and security. "Mayor Ahumada of Ciudad Juarez has stated publicly that, and I'm quoting here, *A collection of filthy bandits could never hope to occupy Ciudad Juarez.* Do you have a response? Pancho? What do you have to say?"

I moved in on the man, close so that he could smell me. Close enough for him to give him his fill of whatever this was that he truly and in his heart desired.

"I'm going to murder Ahumada with my two hands," I said. "I will cut his ears from his head and I will kill his women and burn down his house and drive his people into the desert to die."

As I said these things he grinned.

I was not sleeping. I was pacing continually. Walking the lines, checking the shoes of the horses, the cleanliness of the rifles, trusting no one, speaking little, drawing odd shapes into the dust with sticks.

"Any man we find drunk," I said to my commanders, "shoot him on the spot."

And we did.

To one unfamiliar with the land it would seem as though a single city were but cut through by a wide and peaceful river. But if one were to walk the streets of both Juarez and El Paso one would find in the north a city of lights and broad promenades and culture and food and to the south but a village. Ciudad Juarez was a town of serfs, save the thoroughfare itself, and there you had little save the cantinas and brothels and dead-eyed mariachi. It was there the Americans came to drink and to whore. And yet as Madero's forces gathered in El Paso even this street had closed. Its lights were as dim as the rest of the low city, the bottles taken down from the shelves and the women spirited across the river to the north, where people were clamoring for that service which they were uniquely able to provide. The city of Juarez in the days before the battle lay empty, silent, waiting to be filled.

The river itself is not deep. Sometime near midnight the twelve men entered the water, holding their rifles above their heads. As they waded out into the deeper channel they lifted their boots off the bottom and let the river take them. The water lapped at their faces and they kicked with the push of the current and the stars winked ten thousand miles above them in the dark. At length, the lights of El Paso began to smear up white against the otherwise dark of the sky. The speed of the water increased as the river channeled between the embankment walls that rose up around the men and they continued on. As the river pushed past the city centers, the walls fell away and the banks widened and the water calmed and slowed once more. The men turned and kicked for the shore.

On the riverbank walked the sentry. Ten young men, shipped north not two weeks ago to defend a city unknown to them. They walked across the sand and stones of the riverbank and as they did so they watched the water and they watched the shore and they watched the lights of El Paso. They listened to the laughing of the women therein and the singing and the shouts from the gambling tables that had caught in the wind and carried them to the young men's ears as though all of this be but around a corner, just over the hill, close enough to touch with their hands.

The hands that clapped across their faces were wet and cold and calloused, and the slim blades that slid across their upturned necks felt like little more than edges of paper. Slight.

Inconsequential. In stunned surprise at their own blood—at its warmth at their necks, at its seemingly limitless supply—the sentry were of a sudden forgotten to themselves.

But there was no panic. Even before panic could rise up around them those same cold hands dragged them down the stony bank and toward the water, and the coolness of it expanded upon them, filled up their shirts and pants and boots. The knives drove home again into their bellies, thin and quick and rude. The water seeped into every crevice and pore until the men were not in the water but of it. Held like children in the black of the river, the sentrymen bled out quickly and the night, already dark, went darker. And then it was gone.

The assassins pulled themselves back onto the shore. They went to their rifles and they shouldered them and they began to lay down fire at the sandbag fortifications some forty yards up the bank.

The federal guard shuddered awake. Two, then three and then fifteen, twenty young men went staggering in their half-sleep and shouting that the invasion had begun. Running down the makeshift trench lines that riddled the riverbank and stumbling into pillbox turrets and screwing closed bayonet collars with the thumbnails of stunned and sleepy hands the federals loaded and aligned and fired their cannons out into the dark. And as Juarez exploded above them with the terrific belch of cannon and of gunfire, the assassins slipped back into the water, rifles held high. They lifted off from the floor of the river in slow strides, leaping eastward down the belly of the Rio Grande.

Or so I was told.

Madero was furious. In the gray morning he called us all into his rooms and there he commenced to demonstrate that fury, putting on a magnificent show, slapping the table, mustaches shaking with emotion, demanding to know how such a breach of decorum could have been allowed to occur, what with he still waiting, perhaps today, for terms of further negotiations from President Díaz.

At that long table we sat: doddering Blanco, vicious Orozco, Garibaldi, myself, Señora González.

"My President," I explained, "the men are undisciplined. These are, you must remember, rough men. Men from the plains. Men unused to being controlled."

But Garibaldi disagreed. Garibaldi believed the soldiers were each professional fighters capable of remarkable restraint, and he let it be known to the room that he suspected another motive. He let it be known that he suspected a select cadre of men were in fact loosed upon Ciudad Juarez in a coordinated attack.

"By whom?" Madero demanded.

"By their commanding officer, of course," said Garibaldi.

"Captain Garibaldi," I said, turning to the Italian. "Could it be said that you suspect a covert chain of command?"

"I would suggest, Captain Villa, that it is less covert to some than to others."

Orozco sat forward, his voice flat and without emotion. "I think Captain Garibaldi would like to discuss only the organization, communication and timing of an attack," he said. "As it was an attack which was, at any rate, inevitable."

"Señor Orozco," said Garibaldi, "I think that I would like to discuss the possibility of a coup d'état within our own ranks."

"As I understand it," I said, "an Italian would like to suggest to five Mexicans that there is one of the group who is suspicious and untrustworthy. General Madero," I continued, "the men are nervous and excited with war. It is impossible to hold such men so close to a battlefield and not expect even some of them to antagonize the enemy."

Madero was hysterical. Jabbing the air he told us that we had failed to appreciate the difficulty of his position. That we were simple and rough and untutored in diplomacy, and that we could not possibly grasp the demands these negotiations had put upon him.

"What if," Madero asked us, he voice nearly breaking with the strain, "what if America is to feel as though she has been attacked? How are we to make sense of it? What are we to say?"

For a moment the room was silent. Even Garibaldi himself said nothing as he began to understand the true focus of Madero's attentions. Satisfied, I chose to break the silence.

"It is," I said, "a shameful day indeed for all Mexicans when we bring the benign forces of our sister to the north into such danger as would arise out of our own adolescent quarrels."

Madero's face was pale. "What if it happens again?" he asked.

"I will see to the matter myself," I said.

Outside, the streets of El Paso were packed to overflowing. Gawkers arrived in the traincars hourly. Carriages and car rides through the city became impossible. Riotous drunks fell out of the bars and fought amongst themselves in the streets. Boxing matches in the intersections drew mobs of bettors, and the lines for the brothels stretched out into the steaming streets to mix with the lines for the dress shops, the restaurants, the saloons. Shop owners charged fees for roof access and up on the rooftops called cotton-candy salesmen and popcorn vendors. The crowd jostled with balloons and lollipops while pickpockets weaved in and out.

In these days did El Paso teeter on the edge of control. Waiting for the mad war of the brown hordes to the south, America herself redoubled any such imagined obscenity in the mud of her own streets, while the moneyed stood at the edge of the country with opera glasses to their nose, viewing Juarez as it shook in the heat like an empty stage.

And on this day, on that far riverbank, they see a woman. She is young. She must be young. She walks by the water in the white cotton dress of a peasant. Her hair is unkempt, and it moves about her shoulders in the wind so faint it would feel to the gathered crowd that it may even be an illusion of their packed-in desire. This woman reaches down, and she lifts her skirts. And then she steps, with naked feet, into the Rio Grande. The crowd entire has hushed itself into silence and this silence as the woman moves into the river begins to expand. It grows, as though it be passing from the city against which she moves, through her own body and then across the moving water and out into the streets of El Paso itself, covering and quieting the jostling crowd entire. The woman walks deeper into the river. The water rises up her calves. She gathers higher her skirts. The buildings of Juarez freeze into place behind her and she moves before them as though altogether outside of the register in which they lay. A separate being from the scene presented. As though a figure single and alone and overlaid onto this day. A thousand years ago a woman walks into a river. The water is now around her thighs. Her skin glows in the light of the sun and it is slick with the water of the river that bubbles and breaks about her. The empty morning, the unlived day. Only the challenge of her limbs and her hair in the wind. She moves further into the river, and further into the rising roar from the rooftops of El Paso as the rebels now gather on the shore behind her. Their wide hats spread out to the east are doubled again into the south: bristling rifles and stepping ponies, the cannons unnoticed until the moment they are noticed and at this a moment the cannons erupt.

The twin prongs of the revolutionary force streamed like rivers themselves into Ciudad Juarez, breaking and turning up streets and alleyways, sliding into the city with the rupture of cannon and the pop of riflefire as the smoke crowded into the sky. And below this the river itself unfurled eastward. Flat, gentle, and unoccupied.

CHAPTER XXIII

Into Ciudad Juarez.
González at Camp.
Calle del Chamisal. The
Amulet. A Conversation
at the Customhouse.
Fierro Returns.

The federal cannons were posted at Calle del Porvenir and Calle del Comercio with a third placed on the southern end of the Avenida Juarez in order to meet us with a crossfire of some magnitude. The soldiers knelt to either side of the larger guns, rifles raised, and their captains unsheathed their swords and squinted through the smoke, bracing for the moment to give the order to fire. There would be no such moment.

Each rebel carried on his person a shotgun, a collection of crude grenades, and a crowbar used to demolish the adobe walls of the buildings. In this way did we move through the town, avoiding the thoroughfares entirely. Working four to a wall, we struck with the bars in double-handed arcs until the walls were fully punctured through. Another rebel then knelt and inserted the barrel of his shotgun into the hole and fired without warning or discrimination. Following this came no less than three hand-fashioned grenades, stuffed with lead filings and dynamite that fizzed and clapped inside each little room, sending the residents of Ciudad Juarez screaming into the smoky streets, peppered with gunshot and lead that stuck upon

244

them like deep-seated ticks. There they were in turn shot by the federals who positioned themselves in the squares and squinted into the gloom for rebel movement.

As the first day passed the city echoed in gunfire and explosions. One by one the federals began to abandon their posts, running through the smoke to seek close combat with an enemy unseen. Soon great masses of uniformed men, wild and hatless in the haze, swarmed up and down avenues and streets that were to them unfamiliar. Unable to hear the calls of their officers they flailed in the whiteness and fired indiscriminately and did no small damage to their own ranks. Around this our rebel forces moved forward, taking what we needed, commanding the highest rooftops, gradually locking and holding the city entire.

Back at camp those who had been at the front came to rest as those who were to cycle back in prepared their materials, their weapons and their minds. Pots of beans and pork and coffee simmered over the fires as my men ate and spoke among themselves, sketching with their fingers in the dust the positions of the enemy. Through this walked Señora González, wrapped in simple garments, ministering to the wounded and tending the fires and fetching the water, and she did so unrecognized, moving quietly about the men that slept about her on the bare ground. As the night came on the city behind us sat clouded in smoke, popping, globular, illuminated.

Dawn on the third day found some twenty federals blockaded into the church on Calle del Chamisal. Rebel lieutenant Leon Yescas sat his horse not twenty feet from the steps of that church, studying the iron-banded doors. His hand lay on the horn of the saddle, and a cigarette burned between his fingers. His night had been long and not without torment, and this most recent development vexed him.

Yescas turned to take the measure of the boulevard, its damaged buildings and its street choked with dead animals. The bodies of the men that lay about the city like drunks had begun to stink. Standing in the midst of this were some thirty revolutionaries, gray from the ordnance and the dust of the preceding days. Sepulchered in the church of this quarter before them lay the last remnants of some two hundred federals, originally stationed in the northeastern neighborhood, and they were well dug in.

Yescas turned his horse and looked at the men, and he told them that they were indeed admirable fighters of natural ability. He told them that their performance of the last days left no doubt in his own heart, nor should it leave doubt in any of their own, that they were the finest fighting force this country had ever seen. At this the men, as though of a mind unified and natural and unspoken, formed a line as though for review, and Leon Yescas moved the horse down them, dutifully surveying each face.

Once finished, Yescas turned back to the tall and ridiculous church and dismounted. Its narrow windows and broad doors were limned in an orange plaster, and in its tower hung four dirty copper bells. Framed above the door, some eight feet in height and crowned by a signature in Latin proclaiming nothing of sense to Leon Yescas (himself illiterate in even his own tongue), stood a brass replica of the Virgin.

Months ago Leon Yescas's own daughter had been baptized in a church not far from this one, a whitewashed single-room building. Fussy and impatient she was in the arms of the priest, but as the water was poured over her head she became quiet, and her arms waved about in the air of the place. Yescas's wife had her now, as she had his two sons, and she would keep them even after Leon Yescas fell some six months later at the Battle of Tierra Blanca.

The wood was procured quickly, and the men began to stack it round the church even as the townspeople filtered out of their ruined homes and into the street. These people were haggard and wild, wandering from their hovels into the haze of the day. Shuffling, dazed, their hair awkward or absent in chunks and their clothes torn, faces white with dust or dried black and matted with blood. Their eyes struggled in the daylight to focus. And as the rebels raised broken doors and furniture and abandoned carts up to the flanks of the church walls, those residents who were still capable of it began to shout. Others who lacked the breath were reduced to mouthing their alarm, and in truth some did in fact scream but could not hear themselves, their eardrums blasted in the clamor of the preceding nights.

The first one to reach Leon Yescas: an old woman in torn skirts. She had found, somewhere in the ruins of her house, a black shawl, and pulled this around her head so as not to go unadorned in the street on this of all days. She reached out and touched Yescas on the elbow, and he—startled, instinctual—turned at once, and he pulled from his holster his revolver, and he shot her. The body of the old woman crumpled, folding in upon itself like paper. The men at the church turned from their labor to see Yescas standing in the street, pistol in hand, and before him little more than a black pile of clothes.

But the old woman was not dead. In fact she was writhing in the street, twisting in her shawl, her skirts whispering about her in the dust. There she made no sound, and Leon Yescas walked up close and aimed his pistol and shot her again and she was still. He ordered two men to drag the body into the closest house and this was done, the heels of the corpse digging twinned ruts in the dust. Leon Yescas holstered his pistol and turned to the church once more and directed the laying of the wood in ways most advantageous to the bonfire. A rebel boy, thin in his clothes, held the torch, its flame invisible and shaking in the daylight. The boy walked toward the pile and awaited the order.

But now a woman. Young as she must be. Breaking through her own people, breaking through the soldiers, running across the dirt in bare feet. She is without name or place and as she came on the church and even the town itself became with each footfall worn away, the instant flattening out with each step into an amulet free of dimension.

Into this transubstantiation flowed Leon Yescas, alive here forever and forever cruel and omnipotent in the square before the church. The cries of the woman before him were disjointed, her reasoning unclear, her face caught in a spasm of righteousness, and this she said to Leon Yescas: May you leave the church and leave the town and take with it your machinery of death for if such forces were to be delivered into my hands as lie now within yours I would drive you out to the plain from which you have ridden with your malice and your fear.

He did not shoot her. Even as she reached out her bare arms and beat Yescas about the face and bloodied his mouth his hands remained at his sides even as behind him did the wooden doors of the church catch flame.

The federals that huddled in the gloom of the apse which had always stood to be only their tomb leapt from behind their pews at the smell of the smoke. Some dove blind through the thick stained glass as the rebel grenades shattered over their heads and into the floor of the nave. Others ran for the far end and gained the great door, hot and immobile under their shoulders and their stomping, kicking feet. Other men wandered aimlessly about the church, searching for egress where none would be had as the smoke filled the place entire, and as the fire rode higher up through the wooden skeleton of the church, the roof overhead (and this, remarkable) lit with the flames that ran down its high spine in the gathering smoke black and billowing, and to the men trapped inside it was as though the very sky above them had begun to glow out of the smoke like the ribs of a breathing animal.

Outside, the bodies hung shot in the gaping mouths of the broken windows. Rifle fire popped intermittently from the soldiers in the street. Leon Yescas squinted into the smoke that rolled before him and out and into the blue sky, this smoke mixing then with the smoke of five hundred fires across the city which burnt on this day as a testament to the strength of men who willingly do force man to build again that which has been destroyed by its passage through the hands of power.

Across town, in the customshouse on Calle del Comercio, lay the remnants of the federal forces, some five hundred men. The lights were dead and the water lines cut. Feces stood on the floor, and bodies lay in the feces, and rats ran through it and into the dark. The men crouched in the hallways to get out of the heat and otherwise stared at the walls. Some of the men prayed, and some spoke softly to people who were not there. Their eyes were rimmed in red, their faces pale in the oncoming heat.

I was led through the hallways of the place by the surviving lieutenant, one Ramon Santos, a clean-shaven young man who played poorly at experience. I had approached the customshouse in the high midday with the white flag of truce in my hands, and it was he who called from an upstairs window to state my business and I did so.

"In the end," I told Santos, "we are all Mexicans. Would it not be better to meet one another as men in the daylight and discuss the conditions of surrender? With so many men under your command, would it not be better to see them home again, safe and alive?"

The two main doors opened for me and I entered alone, walking through the wide yard and following the haggard Santos past the wreckage of oxcarts and bodies of dead men and dead horses. We walked back through the corridors and up the stairs until at length we arrived at a low room overlooking the yard.

He was perhaps thirty, his attitude uncertain. He veered from confidence to suspicion to fear and then back. He confessed to me his failures of leadership, and I listened patiently as he did so. He believed the misjudgments of his captains over the last few nights to be his alone. He believed his abandonment at the hands of Díaz to be warranted and just. Such was the degree of his guilt and his self-possession.

He took a seat behind the desk of the chief agent of the Ciudad Juarez Customhouse, stacks of papers before him. Orders of feed and tallies of silver and other such business now useless and gone. Santos bade me sit and I did.

"How long have you been here?" I asked him.

"Three days."

"Is there food?"

"Some."

"Water?"

"We are low on water," he said, shifting in the chair. "This is why I'm entertaining your offer."

"You do not know my offer."

"I am waiting for it."

I turned to look out of the wide windows behind me that opened on the yard, yellow in the blue of the day. It was empty save the dead, all the soldiers hidden about the place like rats, hiding from the sun.

"Who is your commanding officer?" I asked.

"Captain Vasquez."

"Is he still alive?"

"I haven't seen him since we entered the customshouse."

"Perhaps he left you here."

"You're saying he's a coward."

"I'm saying that you are alone."

"I know that I am alone."

"What does that feel like?" I asked him.

"What is your offer?"

"Did you," I said, "enter the army with high ideals? Did you believe you were serving your country?"

"You would have me surrender," he replied. "You would have me a coward as well."

"I would have you be a leader of those under your command."

His eyes moved around the room. He scratched at his chin. "What has become of the Mayor?" he asked me.

I said nothing.

"I have heard Mayor Ahumada is dead," said Santos. "I have heard he was found behind the billiard hall with his hands tied behind his back. I have heard his ears were removed."

I put my hands into the pockets of my jacket. I produced two ears and threw them on the table before him.

"His hands were not tied," I said.

Santos chewed on his fingernail as he looked at the ears.

"Your men are dying," I told him. "There are those in my battalion that thirst for the blood of the weak and I am holding these wolves at bay. I do so because I believe that Mexicans should not spill one another's blood."

"You are a leader of a faction of rebels."

"I am at war for the heart of our country. You are a man on assignment."

The young man looked at the ceiling and he took in a tremendous breath. Then he let out a long howl like a wounded dog. I sat and I watched him and I waited until he was finished. At length he looked at the floor and he laughed. "How does this end?" he asked.

"You tell your men to gather in the yard," I said. "They pile their weapons and they strip off their clothes. They place their hands on their heads. I open the door, and I lead them out safely."

As I said these things Santos fixed me with an expression of great intensity. I watched him envision this conclusion and watched him experience the relief of it. And then, as though all of this passed and was gone, his face tightened once more.

"I mean how does your war end," he said. He eyes moved up past me, out the window and into the yard. "What does it look like?"

"It will be marvelous," I said.

"You would kill us, and by doing so you would kill the families of my men that depend on them."

"There need not be any killing today."

"But after today," said Santos. "In another battle, another town. In the coming years."

"We will be in Mexico City by winter," I said.

"I am going to die," Santos said to me, "and soon. And I will die at the hand of another Mexican. This is the nature of this thing. I will be killed by a brother. A man of my age." And then he stood. "I imagine my death," he said, and he walked past me to the window. "Here is what I imagine," said Santos. "I imagine the man who kills me to go on to live a life as I might live. I imagine this man would do that which I have not. He would ride horses. He would love," said Santos. "Would wed, would produce children that would care for him in his advancing age," said Santos. "Would his children look so different from my own?" Santos looked down at me in the chair.

"No one need die today," I told him.

"Why not today?" said Ramon Santos. He walked past me and out the door and onto the porch overlooking the yard. There he cried out to his men to gather in the yard if they be men at all. He called on his men to face the enemy with their rifles in their hands.

At first only a few soldiers walked out from their shade

to discover the cause of the disturbance. As Santos became more agitated in his speaking more men steadily emerged. They stood in the heat with their hands shading their eyes and they watched him rave there until at length, some members of the crowd became infected by Santos's unhinged enthusiasm. They shouted to their comrades. They seconded Santos and then others seconded these. Within minutes the soldiers were pumping their rifles in the air and cursing the rebels and singing the songs of their state.

I stood from my chair and I walked over next to Santos and I pulled my Mauser from its holster and I fired three times into the air.

Such was the pitch of the yard that the soldiers barely noticed my presence. At the firing of the pistol they pointed their own weapons in the air and began to fire madly, and even with the rising sound of the gunfire I could detect, low and heavy and beneath my ears and in my gut, in the center of me in which the sun had not reached nor would ever the shaking of the thing that I knew was waiting for us. Madness had brought the madness on. Perhaps a further madness had even brought on Santos's own and though I had tried to assuage it, though I had tried reason and argument and sense, the thrumming at the base of things had already begun. And once begun could not be stopped.

Santos reached for the pistol in my fist, his face twisted up in hate. I pointed the barrel at him and I fired into his shoulder.

"This cannot be undone," I said, "but I would keep you alive as witness."

That which I felt in my own gut could now be felt generally. A deep and a continuous thrumming just on the edge of sound. A drum, a series of drums and each wide and stretched with skin the origin of which indeterminate but it continued in its pressure within each of the men where they stood in the yard, and slowly the men began to quiet themselves. They dropped their rifles and in that silence the vibration within them slowly and inexorably coalesced into sound, and that a pagan sound, twilit and strange. The soldiers turned, one by one, to the great doors of the customhouse. Together they listened to the hollow booming of the drums that must be located somewhere on the other side of it. Ramon Santos held his bleeding arm and screamed for each man to take up again his weapon and to wait for his order.

Now joining the low chorus of the drums came from the other side of the great doors the pounding of hands and of other things unseen, slapping and kicking and ticking like the legs of a great and senseless insect and up above this, moving in and out of the rolling rhythms, came a short and persistent phrase, the refrain odd, its tones sliding and high and alien to the ears of the men, its words shaped by the progress of an unknown tongue. And then, as though something caught in a glimpse out the corner of an eye, a whisper of white fletching.

One man in the yard was shot through the thigh with an arrow. He fell heavily, clutching at the thin bone shaft that pierced straight down his leg like a spit. The soldiers turned from the doors, and they gathered around him where he lay, their eyes wide with a dim comprehension of the meaning or the implication of just such a wound. The soldier gripped his leg with both hands, as though any second it would of its own accord fly away from his hip.

The arrows rose up from behind the walls like a venomous flock of birds, blackening in an instant the otherwise blue of the sky. It was a dark tide that rose in the song of the drums that then crested at its natural peak and fell down with vengeance on the men in the courtyard. The drums increased and the pounding on the great doors rose to a clamor—I could in fact see them shudder on their hinges—and the screaming in the yard became general. Arrows stuck into men as though they were dolls in the hands of heedless girls and the soldiers crawled under the toppled carts and the dead animals and the corpses of their own comrades to shelter. I watched those men scatter about the yard like anything other than men.

And then the doors gave way, burst in by those clamorous incantations, and as they did so, as those great and iron-banded things broke as though beaten apart by a surging tide did the pagan horde arrive like galloping death. Shirtless torsos dotted with white greasepaint, headdresses of red and green, yellows like electric sunsets, eyes round in delight with long skirts of grass whispering between their thighs and at their head Rodolfo Fierro himself, nude and plastered in rancid paintings of archaic design and at his back ran the sons and the grandsons of the Apache rim-roamers, exiled and forgotten in the rocks of the sierra and now forgotten no more as they swarmed in ecstasy upon the soldiers of the Federal Republic of Mexico. Here, at the end of the beginning of our revolution came the past into the present as though a hole had been torn in the skin of the day. Here, in the courtyard of the Juarez customhouse: a massacre in the old style.

CHAPTER XXIV
In Madero's Rooms.
A Mexican Youth.
Garibaldi in Retreat.
Remaining in Texas.

The next morning dawned clean and clear as General of the Federalist Forces Alfonso Navarro moved with effort up the stairs of the Hotel Sheldon. Shot twice the day previous, General Navarro's wounds had been bound in secret, and at this time the severity of his condition was uncertain. With effort Navarro gained the second floor, and standing at the stairwell there, the General saw, fidgeting in his doorway, the rebel leader.

Upon seeing Navarro, Madero stepped forward, eager and smiling. He apologized for the previous days of battle. He apologized for his appearance and for the inconvenience of rousting the General at so early an hour. Navarro walked in silence with Madero through the young man's rooms and he noted principally the opulence of the furnishings. They sat themselves at opposite sides of a long and narrow table, and Navarro listened there as Madero spoke too quickly about things that were outside the realm of importance. He watched Madero cross and re-cross his legs as he spoke. He watched him wave his hands before him in his attempts to illustrate the argument he described and he watched the younger man laugh with his nervousness. As the morning progressed Navarro became secure in the knowledge that this man before him could never lead Mexico.

Across the river oxcarts circled through the streets of Juarez collecting the dead. The bodies were taken to an open field on the southeastern edge of the city where some twenty-five laborers dug yawning pits. Men with scarves tied over their faces tipped back the carts and the limp bodies slid down the dirt sides of the mass graves. Quicklime was thrown over their clothes, catching in their hair.

Past this and through the cool morning I rode with twenty of my men, each armed with rifle and pistols and their shoulders draped with bandoliers. I sauntered my horse at the head, the reins loose in my hand.

The night before a young soldier had approached me in my tent, for he said that his situation demanded my attention. He was a youth from Durango and he had been confronted and assaulted by Texans operating under Garibaldi's command. This youth had been beaten, and further he had been vilely shamed by those who had accosted him, by larger and older men. Americans had the advantage of him, and they took it without mercy. And what reason did they have to denigrate this soldier, their own comrade, except that he was young, and small? And was Mexican. Garibaldi disputed these events vehemently. He disputed them in the lobby of the Hotel Sheldon not two weeks later, and he disputed them from the observation deck of a steamer out of Veracruz in another month's time. I am certain that he would continue to dispute them from the balcony overlooking his father's estate.

But on the morning in question Captain Garibaldi had risen early to survey the medical units, to take a count of the wounded and to speak with his lieutenants about the previous day's maneuvers. Alerted to my entrance, Garibaldi excused himself and he walked through his men to me where I sat my horse at the head of his camp. Garibaldi stood before me, thin and arrogant, squinting up at me with his hands on his hips.

"Of what service may I be to you, Captain Villa?"

"I have nothing but contempt for your entire troop, Señor," I told him. "I have brought only thirty of my men and these are enough to commandeer every last rifle and bullet in your entire miserable battalion."

Garibaldi crossed his arms. "I have heard of your raid on the customshouse yesterday," he said. "Very theatrical. Do you think these tricks will work when the enemies know us for who we are?" His eyes moved from me to my men and back.

I stepped my mount around Garibaldi and pulled my revolver free from its holster and cracked the Italian over the head with its grip. Garibaldi fell to one knee, clutching at his scalp. Blood began to pour through his fingers, and I dismounted. I bent close to the ground and advanced toward Garibaldi where the Italian knelt in the dirt.

Grasping Garibaldi by the hair, I leaned in close to the man. There I asked him, simply, if he knew, even yet, who we were.

Garibaldi swung a fist awkwardly, striking me on the shoulder. I raised up a boot and brought it down heavily on the back of Garibaldi's knee and the Italian cried out in pain. With the revolver in my hand I began to strike Garibaldi repeatedly on the top of the head, still holding the man's heavy black hair in my fist.

Reaching out for my leg, Garibaldi received a knee to his nose that broke it flat against his cheeks. I threw the pistol behind me and moved around him and kicked him in the ribs with the toe of my boot, two of his bones giving cleanly away. I then threw the Italian into the dirt and pulled up one boot and stomped down on his head. The force of the blow bounced my leg back up to my own chest, and I stomped down again, and then Garibaldi was still. At this I raised my eyes to the crowd. I looked at the shocked and silent men of Garibaldi's command as my soldiers' rifles pointed out and over my shoulders in a black sunburst behind me.

"If there were a single Mexican among you," I shouted, "he would've already shot me."

I pointed at the body beneath me. "If I ever see you leading a battalion in this country again, you'll wish I had killed you."

Later that day I went to the bakery of José Muñiz and ordered that proprietor to assemble his men and to bake as much bread as possible. Returning at four the next morning, I took the bread to the jail and distributed it among the captured federals, along with several barrels of water. That evening, I met and spoke with a much-improved General Navarro, and we all took cars across the river into El Paso for a dinner of steak and twice-baked potatoes.

We sat around a sumptuous table in the private room of the Hotel Sheldon. Bread and wine were distributed and the mood became jovial as orders were taken and my lieutenants laughed along with the General's own in the haze of the smoke. There the General spoke to me openly, praising my graciousness. He said that such a display of magnanimity would not be soon forgotten.

"General," I replied, gesturing around the table, "allow me to say that the greatness or weakness of men is undiminished by the outcome of battle. I have found it to be true that great men should be justly celebrated for their greatness, for any slight may be forged, within the mind of a great man, into a suitably great calamity." All true Mexicans hurrahed at the toast.

Tremendous plates of beef soon arrived and we turned to our food with vigor. As the conversation rose at the table the General leaned in to me and spoke privately.

"I can tell you," said the General, "that President Díaz will be grateful for the respect you've demonstrated here this evening, Captain Villa."

"Of course," I said, cutting into my steak. "We must remember that, regardless of this terrible war, no single Mexican is the better of another. We are every one of us equals, and every deprivation does little more than aggravate the bitterness of defeat."

General Navarro responded that he too believed that this was so.

"And of course," I added, smiling through my food, "defeat is the most bitter thing of all."

It was agreed upon generally that I was no less a gentleman than any at the table, and after several glasses of wine one of Navarro's men joked about his desire to remain in Texas with such estimable company rather than return to a Mexico ruled by unlearned peasants. This man was later escorted from the room by Rodolfo Fierro, and did not return. Later that evening, as I rode back into Ciudad Juarez with the General and two of his men, a question was put to me regarding the location of the third.

"It was my impression," I replied, "that he had a strong desire to remain in Texas."

Chapter XXV

Return to Chihuahua. Villa's Opines on the Fitness of Madero. Salsa and Water. Ten Thousand Strong.

Señora González called me to her not three days after our liberation of Ciudad Juarez, and I left for her house in Chihuahua immediately. It was only a day later that I stood with her in her kitchen, that same kitchen in which I had stood little more than a year before. She and I were alone on this afternoon as I watched her cut the tomatoes, onions, and cilantro for a small bowl of salsa. A plate of tostadas lay at her elbow. We spoke softly to one another. We spoke of the battle we had won, and we spoke of the El Paso camp.

"These men," she said, "men who would bring about the future with little more than their faith and their blood ..." So overwhelmed was she that she could not continue her thoughts in this vein, and yet she returned to it, indeed incapable of thinking or speaking of anything else. "Illiterate farmers," she said. "Cowboys. Many had children whom they had left behind at home."

"Most," I said.

"I knelt down with one man," she said, her knife moving through the work before her. "I knelt down with him in the dirt

261

as he spoke of his young boy, not even two years of age, who stood in the doorway of his house and who waved goodbye to his father as he left for this war." She slipped the blade underneath the pieces and slid them off into the bowl. "And that man knew what could happen, and he had made such peace with it as one may make. I do not know what in truth that peace would be. What it must demand. And he did so because he believed in us," she said. She stopped for a moment. Then she said, "He believed in our *acts*. He believed in our desire to make the future better than the present. He believed we could do what we said we would. He believed in you, Francisco. And in Madero. In what we have planned to do. This is for whom the war is waged," she said. "Not for this one man, but for this man's boy."

"Do you know if he survived?" I asked.

"I do not. And I wonder if his family will know and when such information will reach them. Are they to wait for a month? A year? When our men and the enemy's men fall on the field we have no way to tell one from the other. Tell me," she said, "how is a wife to know if her husband still lives? How is a child to understand such a father?"

We walked out to her courtyard and sat at a table underneath the portico. There we reflected on what had been said in the heat of the battle when the outcome of our endeavor was uncertain, when all was wonderment and fear. In reflection, each decision made by each of us seemed now destined, proper and correct. At length I stood and walked to the low table beside the doorway where a tray sat with water and glasses. I took from inside my pocket the metal case and it was cool in my hand, slender in my fingers. I brought two glasses of water to the table.

"Juarez," she said, "is behind us. Now. Tell me your honest opinion of Madero." The shadows from the colonnade hung across the courtyard. The water whispered in the small fountain that lay in its center. I weighed the question in my mind and I questioned the reason behind it, if there be reason at all.

"Madero," I said finally, "was afraid to attack."

"I know."

"He could have ruined it all."

"Yes."

"How can we trust this man going forward?"

"We would not have Juarez without him."

"He was not the only one at Juarez," I said.

"Francisco, there is much left to do."

"He is not the man to do it."

Her eyes narrowed at me. "You dined with General Navarro after the battle," she said. "Madero knows this." She sipped her water. "You cannot afford to be reckless, Francisco."

"I am confident I can detect any treachery from Madero," I said, "or from those loyal to him."

She spooned the salsa onto her tostada. "What did Navarro say to you?"

"We spoke about the battle," I said. "We agreed to operate from henceforth with mutual respect."

"Navarro has no respect for Madero."

"No."

"Madero knows that too," said Señora González. "Francisco, you are not listening to me." Her eyes turned up to me and they were urgent. "Madero suspects you. I fully expect him to move against you soon, and in secret."

"Me alone?" I asked.

She leaned forward. "You are too open with your attitude," she said. "You must conceal your desires. Make obscure your intent." She sat back and looked at the table. "You have not touched the salsa. Please, Francisco."

"What would you have me do?"

"I ask only that we are able here to speak as friends, and that we may speak in this way from this point forward." She looked me closely. "Things are going to change, from now on," she said to me. "Things will become strange. Enemies will approach you, feigning friendship. Old friends will prove treacherous. There is real money in play now, Francisco. Real power. People will change."

"Of course."

"But you and I must remain as we have always been. There must be one whom we can trust completely. This will keep us sane, and allow us both to survive. To see this through to the end."

"I agree."

She took another sip from the water. "What ever happened to your man," she asked. "Rodolfo Fierro?"

"He is still with us," I said.

"He is not good for you."

"You are not the only one to think so."

"Do you understand why?"

"Of course."

She eyed me. I looked back out to the courtyard and listened to the water, and the birds.

"Please," she said. "Eat. I am beginning to take offense."

"Forgive me," I said. "I ate just before coming. I beg you do not wait for me."

Her eyes cut to the bowl of salsa and to me. "Whatever became of Garibaldi?" she said.

"He was compelled to leave his command."

"Compelled by you," she said.

"Garibaldi's men assaulted a young man under my care. As such I deemed him unsuitable to lead."

"This is not your decision to make."

"I make decisions about command as I see fit," I said. "In any event I can only make decisions for myself. It was Garibaldi's decision to abandon his men."

"Where is he now?

"His men have been reassigned under trustworthy commanders," I said. And I said "Your questions regarding the incident unsettle me. If I am to prosecute the war in the necessary manner, I must be given complete autonomy. I must be able to follow the battle as it moves, and not be constrained by the insecurities of Madero. Or by your allegiance to him."

Something passed over her face. Only for an instant, then it was gone. Señora González sat back. She took a deep breath, and settled herself. She squared her shoulders to me.

"You have not touched your water," she said.

"In fact," I said, "it has become increasingly clear to me that the leadership as it currently stands is inadequate. That neither you nor he understand the people you profess to serve. That neither you nor he grasp their truth."

"Why have you not touched your water?"

"You have not eaten, Señora González." At this she smiled. Her mouth opened as though she were to speak, but she did not. She nodded. She looked at the salsa and at the water and at me, and she nodded again. She looked at me across the table and she searched for my eyes and she found them and she held them. And then the moment was gone, had never taken place, a moment from another time surfaced for an instant and interrupted by our own and vanished back from where it had come.

González's eyes ran about the table all over again, fast and uneven. Her face turned as though a hand had gripped it in panic.

"This?" she said. "This is what it is?" She reached for the bowl of salsa and held it up in her hand. Her eyes were on fire. She grabbed the tostada on her plate and shoved it in her mouth, shouting through the bread even as she chewed.

"You would suspect me, Francisco? Even me?"

She stood and she picked up the glass of water and she threw it into the courtyard and it broke there upon the stones. And she looked about the place and she spit out the food and she called for her servants and they did not come. She ran shouting over to the other side of the yard and she called for her guards and they did not arrive. Señora González looked up at the clear sky above her and she looked into the shadows of the portico.

I sat where I was and I watched her do these things, and at length I watched as she quieted herself. She pulled her arms about her, holding each elbow in her palms. She walked back to the table, and she took her seat again.

"I know you, Francisco," she said. "I know who you are. I know who you are and I know who you have been."

Even as she spoke, her throat had begun to close around her words but still she kept on. She kept on trying to speak to me even as the color rose up around her neck. Her head began to shake but she willed it still, and regained her composure.

Señora González opened her mouth to say more, but now the air was gone. Her eyes grew wide. They rotated around that courtyard as though the place was suddenly unfamiliar, as though not only the courtyard but the world entire was composed of something unique and without precedent.

She tried to turn her eyes back to me, tried valiantly, but the poison had her now. Her head could no longer move at her bidding, and it stuck there, as though in mid-thought. She fell from the chair.

I stood, and I and buttoned my jacket as her body began to tremor on the stones, her skull and shoes tapping out an unconscious tattoo.

I walked into the kitchen and back through it, past the servants where they stood in the hallway and at my passing they lowered their heads. I walked past the guards, who saluted me and fell in behind me and followed me outside to my horses and my men. Rodolfo Fierro sat on a black mare before the rest of them, and he looked for my eyes as I came into the sun.

I mounted, and we rode back out of that town and into the plain where my men had made camp, now some ten thousand strong. And there we lay, on into the night, the light from a thousand campfires like the pricks of a pin into the darkness that we would soon but tear away from the face of the world.

But by God, there is so much more to say. Our further and our greater victories on the plain. The taking of Chihuahua, of Durango, of Monterrey. And even as I now speak, every day I hear more of Zapata to the south. I yearn to meet with him in the one and great City that lies between us and on that day we will unite our Mexico with his own, south and north in that one and singular moment when she may touch her own fingers one to each and come to know herself for the first time. I yearn to tell her who she is.

By God, how much to tell even as our time runs short. Even as our time runs on to the river, which runs through the country, which runs to the sea, which I have never yet seen.

Acknowledgements

My sources for this novel have principally been *The Memoirs of Pancho Villa*, by Martín Luis Guzmán and translated by Virginia H. Taylor, *Twenty Episodes in the Life of Pancho Villa*, by Elías Torres and translated by Shelia M. Ohlendorf, *The Wind That Swept Mexico: The History of the Mexican Revolution 1910–1942*, by Anita Brenner and George R. Leighton, and *The Life and Times of Pancho Villa*, by Friedrich Katz. The title of this novel is based on a phrase from Guzmán's *Memoirs*.

About the Author

CAMERON MACKENZIE was born in Virginia and has worked as a dry cleaner, doorman, house painter, farm hand, contractor, editor and teacher, residing in Santa Barbara, London, Tokyo, Philadelphia, San Francisco, and now Virginia once again, where he lives with his wife and child.